INSPECTOR HADLEY

THE GOLD BULLION MURDERS

by

PETER CHILD

Benbow Publications

© Copyright 2007 by Peter Child

Peter Child has asserted his right under the Copyright, Designs and Patents Act, 1988 to be identified as the author of this work.

All rights reserved. No part of this publication may be reproduced, stored in a retrieval system, or transmitted in any form or by any means, electronic, mechanical photocopying, recording or otherwise without the prior permission of the copyright owner.

Published in 2007 by Benbow Publications

British Library
Cataloguing in Publication Data.

ISBN: 978-0-9540910-9-5

Printed by Lightning Source UK Limited,
6 Precedent Drive, Rooksley,
Milton Keynes, MK13 8PR

First Edition

OTHER TITLES BY THE AUTHOR

MARSEILLE TAXI
AUGUST IN GRAMBOIS
CHRISTMAS IN MARSEILLE
CATASTROPHE IN LE TOUQUET

ERIC THE ROMANTIC

INSPECTOR HADLEY-
THE TAVISTOCK SQUARE MURDERS

NON FICTION

VEHICLE PAINTER'S NOTES

VEHICLE FINE FINISHING

VEHICLE FABRICATIONS IN G.R.P.

NOTES FOR GOOD DRIVERS

NOTES FOR COMPANY DRIVERS

ACKNOWLEDGEMENTS

Once again, I wish to gratefully acknowledge the help and assistance given to me by Sue Gresham, who edited and set out the book, and Wendy Tobitt for the splendid cover presentation. Without these talented and patient ladies this book would not have been possible.

Peter Child

INTRODUCTION

Since the beginning of recorded history, gold has been the supreme material that has driven mankind mad with lust to own this precious metal. Before Egyptian Pharaoh's had their jewellery, ornaments and death masks made from the material, the civilisations that swept through the Sumerian lands, used gold for every purpose that they could devise. Gold is synonymous with wealth and high social standing as well as jealousy and death. From the early civilisations, through medieval times to Victorian England, the desire for this precious material has remained paramount in the lives of men. However, when murder is involved in its acquisition it falls upon Inspector Hadley and Sergeant Cooper to bring the murderer to justice.

Characters and events portrayed in this book are fictional.

CHAPTER 1

It was a grey, cold November morning in 1880 when Inspector James Hadley left his home in Camden and made his way to New Scotland Yard. As the rain began to fall, the Hansom cab rattled down to Marylebone High before turning into Regents Street. Hadley looked out gloomily at the busy horse drawn traffic that surrounded the Hansom and was sure that if London's population grew any more then the whole city would become locked up in one enormous traffic jam. He sighed and hoped today would be a quiet day at the office. Sergeant Cooper, his right hand man, had taken some of the tedious work off his shoulders, but even so, Hadley was becoming overwhelmed by the new cases allocated to him by his Chief.

Hadley eventually arrived in his office and the first thing he did was to ask George, his clerk, to make a pot of tea to revive him after his cold, damp journey to work.

"Right away, sir" smiled George.

"Thank you, no sign of Sergeant Cooper yet?"

"Oh, yes, sir, he's been into the office but has just gone down to custody" replied George.

"Right" murmured Hadley as he settled behind his desk and began to look at the latest file that had arrived from the office of Chief Inspector Howard Bell. He had started to make notes on the case when Cooper arrived back in the office in time to share the pot of tea with his superior.

"Morning, sir" smiled the young Sergeant as George poured the reviver into two cups.

"Morning, Sergeant, how are you this miserable morning?"

"Fine, thank you, sir, and you?" he asked as he sat down opposite Hadley.

"Cold, damp and overworked" replied Hadley as he closed the file that he had been reading.

"Yes, we are a little pressed at the moment" said Cooper.

"The latest urgent investigation is this theft from Hudson, the banker" said Hadley as he tapped the file.

"Indeed, sir."

"God knows how we recover a diamond necklace and matching ear rings in time for Mrs Hudson's Christmas party" said Hadley.

"Very difficult, sir."

"According to the file, the whole of London society will be unable to celebrate Christmas unless we do."

"Good heavens, sir, is it that serious?" asked Cooper with a grin before he sipped at his tea. Hadley laughed and said "I sometimes think that certain wealthy members of our society don't know that they are born."

"Quite so, sir."

"Still, never mind, we'll start as usual at the beginning and call at the Hudson's to verify what actually happened on the night of the robbery."

"Then we'll make our discreet enquiries in Whitechapel?"

"Quite so, Cooper."

"Well with one thing and another, it looks as if we are in for a busy time up until Christmas, sir" said Cooper.

"Indeed" nodded Hadley before he sipped his tea. He just put his cup down when the office door opened and Jenkins, the Chief Inspector's clerk, entered.

"Good morning, sir, the Chief Inspector would like to see you straight away" said Jenkins.

"This very moment?" queried Hadley.

"Apparently so, sir."

"Right, Mr Jenkins, lead on" said Hadley as he stood and raised his eyes to heaven and murmured 'no peace...' and Cooper smiled.

Chief Inspector Bell studied the report in front of him once again and he became increasingly concerned. This was another investigation for Hadley if Scotland Yard wanted quick action that was discreet, and the Commissioner would want answers before the Press got hold of the story and printed a fanciful account of titillating, macabre, gory detail.

Hadley knocked and entered the spacious office overlooking the Thames and sat as Bell waved him to a seat in front of his desk.

"Morning, sir."

"Morning, Hadley. Now, I know you've got a lot on your plate with one thing and another..."

"Indeed, sir."

"By the way, any movement on the Hudson case yet?"

"Getting started today, sir."

"So, the answer is 'no'?"

"I've just received the file, sir."

"Right, well before you start that, I want you to follow up this" and the Chief tapped the file.

"Right, sir."

"Late yesterday a man's body was found entangled in the pier supports just up river from Charlton wharf, he was examined at the scene and it was assumed that he had drowned, but subsequent examination showed that he had suffered a heavy blow to the head before he entered the river."

"Why am I being assigned this investigation, sir?"

"Because, Hadley, my suspicions are aroused that this misadventure has serious undertones, and I need your quick and incisive mind on this, I can't afford our usual slow, plodding methods." Hadley smiled at the compliment.

"Do go on, sir."

"The dead man is almost certainly French…"

"He had identification on him?" interrupted Hadley.

"No, nothing in his pockets, but his torso was heavily tattooed with various dragon designs with slogans in French."

"I see."

"Then a Captain Marcel Lefevre, master of a French brig, the 'Arabesque', reported his mate, Pascal Dalmas, was missing."

"When did he make his report, sir?"

"This morning."

"Has he seen the body?"

"No, not yet, I want you to talk to Doctor Evans at the Marylebone first."

"Right, sir."

"The 'Arabesque' is moored at Charlton wharf, apparently, she's unloading a cargo of wine and spirits from Marseille."

"I'll get on to it straight away, sir."

"Good, time is of the essence because the Captain will want to leave London as soon as he's unloaded, but if you uncover anything that gives me an excuse to hold the vessel, I will."

"Right, sir."

"Well done, Hadley" replied the Chief as he handed the file to his over worked Inspector.

Cooper had a look of anticipation when Hadley returned to the office.

"Something exciting, sir?"

"Yes, Cooper, exciting and immediate, get your coat, we're off to the morgue at Marylebone!"

"I'm sure that Doctor Evans will be pleased to see us again, sir" smiled the Sergeant.

"I'm not so confident about that, go on down and call a Hansom, please."

When they arrived at the hospital, the rain had eased to a fine, grey drizzle and Hadley was not in the best mood when he entered the Doctor's office.

"I'm glad your Chief sent you, Hadley" said the Doctor as he looked up from his paper strewn desk.

"Why is that, may I ask?"

"This case is unusual, I am somewhat overworked and I really would prefer to explain to you rather than one of your less enlightened colleagues" replied Doctor Evans and Hadley smiled again at the compliment. The day was improving.

"Make a mental note of that, Sergeant" said Hadley and Cooper grinned as the Doctor arose from his desk. They followed him out into the examination room where the corpse was laid out on a marble slab. The man was aged about forty, dark skinned and with a mop of black hair, some of which had been cut away from the top of his battered skull. The torso was covered in elaborate tattoos of dragons with the French Tricolour emblazoned by the head of two of them. Hadley and Cooper studied the naked body for a few moments.

"It's not often I get a body with illustrations" said the Doctor.

"Indeed" replied Hadley.

"If you look closely at the two dragons with the flag you can just read liberty, equality and fraternity, in the body of each, but it's all faded somewhat" said the Doctor.

"So, he's French, how did he die?" asked Hadley.

"By a massive blow to the head."

"He didn't drown then?"

"No, there was only a very little amount of water in the lungs, so he was dead when he went into the river."

"What makes this such an unusual murder case?" asked Hadley.

"When I examined the skull I was certain that he had been struck on the top of his head by a house brick…"

"A house brick?" interrupted Hadley.

"Yes, look for yourself" and Hadley peered down at the indentation in the skull.

"You can see definite corners in the wound and if you look carefully where the brain has leaked through, it is quite sharp" said the Doctor.

"I'm glad I didn't have porridge for breakfast" murmured Hadley.

"The interesting thing is that I was wrong about the house brick" said the Doctor.

"You were wrong, Doctor? I find that hard to believe" smiled Hadley.

"I think our friend here was struck by a solid gold bar…"

"What?" interrupted Hadley.

"I found a flake of gold embedded in the fracture of the skull, I removed it and it is over there on my table" the Doctor pointed at his instrument table "it's in the kidney dish, look for yourself."

Hadley and Cooper went over and peered down at the flake of bright gold laying in a solution in the dish.

"Good heavens" said Hadley.

"So, in my opinion, Inspector, someone has committed murder with a gold bullion bar!"

"He might have had the flake of gold in his hair and then it was driven into the skull by your house brick" said Hadley.

"Possible, but doubtful, in any event, it will be an interesting investigation" replied the Doctor and Hadley nodded.

"We believe that he's a mate on a ship called the 'Arabesque' moored where the body was found, the Captain reported him missing" said Hadley.

"So get him to identify the body so I can complete my report" said Doctor Evans.

"We'll go and see him now and make arrangements" replied Hadley and the Doctor nodded.

The drizzle turned into a heavy downpour as the Hansom arrived at the Charlton wharf and Hadley eased forward in his seat as he looked for the 'Arabesque'.

"There she is, sir" said Cooper pointing forward past one other vessel.

"Indeed, Sergeant, she looks a little shabby in the rain... cabbie, you can stop here!" The Hansom stopped and Hadley stepped down onto the cobbled road, standing in the rain whilst Cooper paid the driver. The 'Arabesque' looked forlorn and Hadley watched as some of the crew busied themselves on the deck. He was very intrigued by the murder of Pascal Dalmas and he knew that the Chief was right, the incident had very serious undertones.

"Let's get aboard and see what Captain Lefevre has to say for himself, Sergeant."

"Right, sir." Hadley stepped on the slippery walkway up to the ship and Cooper was surprised by the agility of the Inspector, although a heavy built man he stepped quickly up to the ships side.

"Hello there, do you speak English?" Hadley called to a sour faced man close by.

"Oui, monsieur, what do you want?"

"To speak to your captain, if you please."

"Who are you, monsieur?"

"Police, Inspector Hadley and Sergeant Cooper" replied Hadley firmly.

"Wait here, monsieur, I will tell the Captain" with that the man disappeared through a door by the rear upper deck.

"I fear this is going to be a difficult case, Sergeant."

"I would not be surprised, sir."

As they stood in the rain, Hadley used the time to study the crew and his hard, blue eyes watched every move they made as they worked unloading wooden crates marked up 'vin' and 'London, Angleterre'. The sailor arrived back and asked them to follow him to the captain's cabin. The interior of the ship smelled of tobacco, spirits and fish, an unpleasant mixture but Hadley was pleased to get in out of the persistent rain. Captain Lefevre stood as the two policemen entered his spacious cabin. Introductions were made and the captain waved them to seats by his desk.

"I expect this is about my Mate, Pascal Dalmas" said the Captain as Hadley fixed the Frenchman with his steely gaze. Lefevre was about fifty, weather beaten, with a mop of grey hair and shifting black eyes. Hadley guessed he was from the south of France as the man had what Hadley called a 'Mediterranean look about him'.

"Yes, Captain, a body of a man was recovered from the river and we have reason to believe that it is your missing man" replied Hadley.

"A tragedy" mumbled the Captain.

"Indeed, we will require you to give a formal identification of the body."

"Impossible, Monsieur Inspector, I have to sail with the tide today, as soon as I have finished unloading my cargo" replied the Captain.

"Captain, there are certain investigations that we have to carry out and I would be much obliged if you would co-operate fully, I assure you that it will make things easy for us all if you do."

"Monsieur Inspector, I regret the death of Pascal, he sailed with me for many years and I regarded him as a friend as well as a good sailor, but, I have my orders, and I must sail today for Rotterdam before returning to Marseille."

"Captain Lefevre, you are in the Port of London under British law and I assure you that you are not leaving until our investigations are complete…"

"This is monstrous! This is a French ship and you have no right…" interrupted the Captain angrily.

"Oh yes, Captain, I have every right to hold the ship, so let us remain calm and proceed as quickly as possible" Hadley smiled and Lefevre relaxed back into his chair.

"Then hurry, Monsieur Inspector."

"When did you last see Dalmas?"

"The night he disappeared."

"What time was that?"

"About eight o'clock, he said he was going ashore."

"What for?"

"The usual things sailors go for, drink and women, Monsieur" snapped the Captain.

"Did anyone see him when he returned?"

"No, he didn't return."

"I see."

"It was assumed that he'd found a woman for the night."

"Quite so, Captain, now, tell me, what cargo are you unloading?"

"French wine and spirits, Monsieur."

"Have you any other cargo on board?"

"Some tobacco and a few assorted crates of machinery, but not much else."

"Who owns the 'Arabesque'?"

"She's owned by Maritime du Provence, with the office in Marseille."

"So the ship is wholly French owned?"

"Oui, Monsieur, the business is a family concern."

"And the family name?"

"Roguefort, Monsieur, they are well respected and have five other ships."

"Good, and presumably they are all trading around the Mediterranean as well as London and Rotterdam?"

"Oui, Monsieur."

"Do any of the fleet sail to America?"

"Non, Monsieur, we stay strictly around Europe."

"Right" said Hadley and he paused for a while to gather his thoughts.

"Is there anything else, Monsieur?"

"Yes, Captain, I would like you to accompany my Sergeant to Marylebone hospital to identify the body of Dalmas whilst I remain here to question your crew." Lefevre blanched at that and seemed lost for words for the moment.

"If I must" he half whispered.

"I am afraid so" replied Hadley. Captain Lefevre stood up, went to the door and called his cabin boy. He spoke rapidly in French and the boy made off.

"I will instruct Jacques Mornay, the man you first spoke to when you came aboard, to assist you Monsieur Inspector, his English is good, and you may use my cabin to conduct your investigations" said the Captain in a resigned tone.

"Thank you Captain Lefevre, I appreciate your help" replied Hadley. As Cooper stood to leave with the Captain, Mornay arrived and Lefevre spoke to him in French. The expression on Mornay's face showed that he was a little concerned about the situation and he looked nervous.

"Let us get this over with, Monsieur Sergeant" said the Captain as he stepped out of the cabin. Cooper followed and said in passing to Hadley "we'll be as quick as we can, sir."

"No hurry, Sergeant, take your time."

As soon as Cooper had left with the Captain, Hadley turned to Mornay and said "please sit down, I have some questions for you before I talk to the others on board." Mornay nodded and sat down, pale faced with an anxious look.

"When did you last see Pascal Dalmas?"

"The night he disappeared, Monsieur."

"About what time?"

"Eight o'clock or perhaps a little later."

"Did he say where he was going?"

"Non, just ashore for a drink and perhaps some company."

"That was usual?"

"Oui, Monsieur, he liked to get drunk and find a woman."

"So when he didn't arrive back on board, you assumed he had found a lady for the night?"

"Oui, Monsieur, it was normal for him."

"Yes, I see, now then, what cargo are you carrying on board?" Hadley asked and the question seemed to make Mornay apprehensive.

"Wine and spirits, Monsieur" he stammered a little nervously.

"Nothing else?"

"Some tobacco, I think."

"What about machinery?" Hadley smiled and Mornay went pale.

"Possibly some crates, I'm not sure, Monsieur."

"What type of machinery?"

"I don't know, Monsieur, you must ask the Captain."

"Perhaps we should go and have a look."

"No, Monsieur, that will not be possible."

"Why not?"

"Some of the crates have already been unloaded and taken away" replied Mornay nervously.

"Where to?"

"I don't know, Monsieur, you'll have to ask the Captain."

"I will, be assured, but in the meantime, I would like to see the cargo hold."

"Oui, Monsieur" replied Mornay and he led the way out of the cabin down to the cargo hold where several of the crew were tying ropes around crates prior to them being winched up to the top deck. The cargo deck was slippery with rain and Hadley took his time as he made his way along the rows of crates marked 'vin' and Angleterre. He looked for any crate marked up as machinery but found none. In one corner he saw two crates marked 'tabac' and decided that the machinery had been off loaded.

"When did you start unloading your cargo?" Hadley asked.

"Yesterday morning, Monsieur."

"Will it still be on the dock?"

"Possibly, Monsieur." Hadley was very suspicious and he searched through the crates once again inspecting each one carefully as the crew eyed him with concern as they went about the business of unloading.

"Let's go out to the dockside so you can show me the crates that you've already off loaded" said Hadley to the pale faced Mornay.

"Oui, Monsieur" he nodded and Hadley followed him up to the top deck and out on to the quay side.

"This is all so far, Monsieur" he said as he waved his hand at the pile of crates.

"You say the machinery crates were taken away?"

"Oui, Monsieur."

"When?"

"Yesterday afternoon."

"Who took them?"

"Two men came and loaded them onto a wagon and drove away."

"How many crates were there?"

"Three, I think, Monsieur."

"Did the Captain speak to the men?"

"Oui, they came aboard and went to his cabin."

"Thank you, that will be all for the moment, I'll wait for the Captain to return."

"Oui, Monsieur."

CHAPTER 2

Captain Lefevre looked down at the tattooed body on the marble slab and nodded.

"Oui, Sergeant, that is Pascal Dalmas."

"You are certain, sir?"

"Oui, I am certain."

"Thank you, sir."

"What will happen to the body now?"

"Unless you wish to make arrangements to return the body to France, it will be buried here in a pauper's grave" replied Cooper.

"I think that is best in the circumstances" replied the Captain.

"Will you notify his next of kin?"

"Oui, he only has a mother, all the rest of the family are dead."

"We will leave that unpleasant duty to you then, Captain" said Cooper.

"Oui, it is a catastrophe."

"Now, I have to inform you that we are sure that Dalmas was murdered…"

"Murdered?" interrupted the Captain.

"Yes, he received a blow on the head before he fell into the river."

"He didn't drown?"

"No, Captain, he didn't."

"Mon Dieu!"

"Do you know if Dalmas had any enemies who might wish to kill him?"

"No, Sergeant, he was well liked by everyone who knew him."

"Do you have a cargo of gold on board, Captain?" At that the Captain looked anxiously at Cooper for a moment before replying "no, Sergeant, just wine and spirits, that is all, why do you ask?"

"Because the Doctor here found a flake of gold in the head wound."

"Mon Dieu" whispered the Captain.

"A little unusual, I am sure you would agree, Captain?"

"Oui, but I have no idea how any gold could have got there."

"Quite so, that will be all, Captain, I'll take you back to your ship."

"Merci, Sergeant."

The rain had stopped when Cooper and Lefevre arrived back at the wharf. Hadley watched them arrive from the top deck and smiled when he saw Cooper nod to him as he followed the Captain up the walkway.

"So you have identified the body, Captain?" asked Hadley as Lefevre stepped aboard.

"Oui, Inspector."

"You know that Dalmas was murdered?"

"Oui, I do."

"Have you any suspects amongst the crew for the crime?"

"Non."

"I see" Hadley paused for a moment before continuing "now, Captain, I understand that you had some crates of machinery on board that have been off loaded and taken away already."

"Oui, Inspector."

"Who took them and where have they gone to?"

"Shipping agents, and I understand that they have gone by goods train to Liverpool" replied the Captain.

"What exactly were these pieces of machinery?"

"Ship pumps."

"For clearing water from the bilges?"

"Oui, Inspector."

"Do you know where they were bound for when they arrive in Liverpool?"

"Non."

"Perhaps you would kindly give me the name of the shipping agent, Captain?"

"Oui, Inspector, the manifest is in my cabin, please to follow me."

Half an hour later Hadley and Cooper were in a Hansom cab on their way to an early lunch in the Kings Head public house in Whitechapel.

"Well, Sergeant, what do you make of it all?" asked Hadley as the cab rattled over the cobbled street.

"Something is very amiss, sir, and I'm sure that the Captain isn't telling everything" replied Cooper.

"Quite right, and I am very suspicious of the very attentive shipping agents who collected the machinery so promptly."

"Do you think that gold is hidden in the crates, sir?"

"Anything is possible, Sergeant, and we'll know more when we call upon the agents after lunch."

"Indeed, sir."

The Kings Head was unusually busy and the two detectives had to struggle through the crowd of dockers, wharf men and layabouts before they reached the bar that was swimming in spilt beer. The harassed bar maids recognised the two and smiled before Vera, the older, blonde one asked "what can I get you gents?"

"Two pints of stout to start, Vera" said Hadley.

"Right, sir, and any lunch today?"

"Oh, yes, two cheese and pickles" replied Hadley.

"And a slice of ham with mine, please" said Cooper. Hadley gave him a stern look at that whilst Vera nodded and began to pull at the pumps.

"A slice of ham, Sergeant?"

"Yes, sir."

"I must remind you that we are on duty and I do not wish to see you over eating, Sergeant."

"No, sir."

"Too much food might make you comatose and less effective as a police officer."

"I'll bear that in mind, sir" replied Cooper with a grin.

"Now let's try and find a table" said Hadley as Vera placed the two foaming pints on the bar. Cooper paid for the drinks and food before following Hadley through the crowd to a corner where they squeezed in around a small table.

"Busy in here today, sir."

"Yes, it must be the cold weather driving them in" replied Hadley as Agnes Cartwright entered the bar. Agnes was an attractive, well proportioned mature lady of uncertain years who gave personal relief to gentlemen for five shillings a time, two shillings and sixpence on Monday evenings to encourage business, she had known Inspector James Hadley for over twenty years.

"Hello, Jim,… Sergeant" she smiled as she saw the detectives and came over to them.

"Agnes, my dear, come and join us" smiled Hadley as Cooper nodded.

"I can't stop long, Jim, got things to do" she replied as Cooper stood up and offered his seat.

"Sergeant, get a sixpenny gin for Agnes" said Hadley.

"Right, sir, is Florrie likely to arrive soon?" asked Cooper.

"No, dear, she's still sleeping" replied Agnes.

"Busy night?" asked Hadley.

"Yes, Jim, she's been giving so many of her clients her 'special treatment' the word has got around, so, she's much in demand at the moment" replied Agnes.

"I can imagine" said Hadley with a smile.

"So just a gin for you, Agnes?" asked Cooper and she nodded.

"If things don't pick up for me I'll have to change my trade name from Fifi Toulouse to something else" said Agnes.

"No, Agnes, stay as Fifi, it's so you" replied Hadley.

"I thought something German might be better, you know, attract a client who liked a bit of domination instead of a fluffy French thing" said Agnes and Hadley laughed out loud at that.

"I never thought of you as a fluffy French thing" said Hadley and gave her a little kiss on her cheek.

"Oh, Jim, why don't you come round home so I can give you some special attention for all your kindness to Florrie and me?"

"We've been over this before, Agnes, you know that Alice would know the moment I slipped, and that would never do."

"Jim, you're too good."

"I know, but that's our secret" he smiled as Cooper arrived back with the gin, followed by Vera with their lunches.

"Can I pinch your pickles, Jim?" asked Agnes with a smile.

"Anytime." Agnes laughed at that before saying 'cheers' and sipping her gin.

"Now then, Agnes, talking about things French, we're looking into the death of a French sailor" said Hadley.

"I heard about that" she replied.

"Tell us what you know."

"Not a lot, Jim, only that he was fished out of the river down at Charlton wharf, some say he drowned and some say he was murdered" she replied.

"He was murdered" said Hadley and Agnes looked concerned.

"Dear God" she whispered.

"Anything else?" asked Hadley.

"No Jim, but I'll keep my ear close to the ground and let you know" she said.

"Thank you, Agnes." Hadley then changed the subject and talked of plans for Christmas as they enjoyed their lunch in the busy pub.

It was after two when Hadley and Cooper arrived outside number 26, Tooley Street, the address of Johnstone and Bradley, shipping agents. It began to rain heavily as they stepped down from the Hansom cab.

"I hope someone here can give us some answers, Sergeant."

"Yes, sir."

"Pay the cabbie will you?"

"Yes, sir" replied Cooper as Hadley entered the building. It was dark and smelled musty in the corridor. Hadley opened the first door on the left which had a sign on it that read 'Tooley Insurance Company'. Cooper joined him as he stepped through the door. A bespectacled clerk looked up from his desk.

"Can I help you, gentlemen?" he asked.

"We're looking for Johnstone and Bradley, shipping agents" said Hadley.

"They're upstairs" replied the clerk, pointing upwards with his pen.

"Thank you" said Hadley.

"But nobody seems to be there today" added the clerk helpfully. Hadley nodded and swiftly left the office, he ran up the dark stairs to the landing where the first door he came to had a sign 'Johnstone and Bradley'. He opened the door and strode into a dark, damp, musty, empty office. There was no sign of any activity and a forlorn, heavily stained desk with a chair beside it was all the furniture in the room.

"Good God, Sergeant, this case is getting deeper by the minute!"

"Indeed, sir."

"Let's get back to the 'Arabesque' and talk to Lefevre and see what he has to say for himself."

"Right, sir."

The persistent rain did nothing to improve the Inspector's humour and he was aggressive in his questioning of Lefevre.

"We've been on a wild goose chase, Captain, and I want to know everything about Johnstone and Bradley!"

"Monsieur Inspector, I have the names of them on my manifest and I was given written instructions that they would collect three crates of machinery as soon as they were unloaded and that they would take care of all the arrangements to ship them by rail to Liverpool which, as far as I am concerned, is the final destination, as I told you, these crates contained bilge pumps for ships, and is not Liverpool a grand dock that handles ships?"

"Yes it is!"

"Well then" the Captain shrugged his shoulders.

"Did you see these men?" asked Hadley in a calmer tone.

"Oui, Monsieur, they came on board, made themselves known to me, they had paper work that tied up with my manifest, they signed for the crates and left, what more could I do when everything is in order?" Lefevre smiled.

"Please describe these men to me, and Sergeant, take careful notes" said Hadley. The Captain's description was vague and Hadley was not a happy man as he climbed into a Hansom cab en route to 12, Cavendish Square, the London home of Mr and Mrs Anthony Hudson, merchant banker of London.

"We've got this unsolved murder to cope with and we have to divert our attention to a diamond theft from a silly woman" grumbled Hadley as the Hansom rattled on through the rain. Cooper remained silent, not wishing to say anything that might upset the Inspector.

"Tomorrow I'll ask Bell to take us off this theft case and give it to someone else" said Hadley.

"Right, sir."

"So just take the salient points down, Sergeant, for the time being."

"Yes, sir."

Hadley announced himself to the butler at the Hudson's home and the policemen were immediately shown into the study to await the arrival of Mrs Hudson. The room was both elegant and tasteful with a proud woman's touch everywhere to be seen. It appeared to

Hadley that the mistress of the house was probably in full command of everything and it was likely that her wealthy husband was subordinate to her will.

"Everything is a touch too tidy, don't you think, Sergeant?" asked Hadley as he surveyed the room once again.

"Possibly, sir."

"It appears more of a woman's study than a man's" said Hadley as the door opened and Mrs Hudson swept in with an angry look on her elegant face.

"Good afternoon, Madam" smiled Hadley.

"You are the police?" she demanded.

"Yes, Madam, I'm Inspector Hadley and this is…"

"You should have been here hours ago" she interrupted.

"I'm sorry, but we have been…"

"Why have I had to wait?"

"Madam…"

"My husband is a very important man in the city…"

"I know, Madam…"

"And he was late for a very important meeting at the Bank of England!"

"I am sorry…"

"He remained here awaiting your arrival, and heaven knows what might have gone wrong at the Bank if he'd waited any longer!"

"I am sure that…"

"My husband pays his taxes and he expects prompt service from the police when his household is in danger" she said forcefully before she sat behind the desk and waved the two of them to seats before her.

"Very good, Mrs Hudson, I note your complaint and it will be passed up to our superiors, now, may we get on with the investigation please?" asked Hadley in a stern tone. She acquiesced and sat back in her chair.

"Very well, Inspector."

"It has been reported that a theft of your diamonds has taken place."

"Yes, some low miscreant forced his way in through the scullery door, ransacked my bedroom and stole a priceless diamond necklace and matching pendulum ear rings" she wailed.

"Would you please describe the jewellery, Madam, and Sergeant, take careful notes."

"Yes, sir" replied Cooper as he opened his pad and licked the tip of his pencil.

"The diamonds were bought for me by my husband from Asprey's as a Christmas present three years ago, the pieces are known in fashionable society as the 'Hudson diamonds', and every Christmas we hold a very select party and I wear them as a tradition" she beamed.

"I see" murmured Hadley and he nodded as if he were suitably impressed.

"Tradition is so important, don't you agree, Inspector?"

"I do, Madam."

"It's what our empire is founded on" she smiled.

"Indeed, now when did the actual robbery take place?" asked Hadley.

"Two nights ago, when my husband and I were at the opera, we returned to find my room in disarray and the necklace missing."

"Were there no servants in the household?"

"Only Woods, the under groom, the others were enjoying a night off, an un-necessary and foolish practice to my mind but my husband insists that the servants have a night off, once a week" she replied in a resigned tone.

"And why didn't Mr Woods apprehend the thief?"

"He had left the house to see to the horses in the mews stables and that was when the break in took place."

"I see, you said the scullery door was forced open?"

"Yes, when Woods returned he found it open and he assures us that he locked the door behind him before attending to the horses."

"You only discovered the theft when you returned from the opera?"

"I have already told you that, Inspector."

"Why didn't Mr Woods search the house?"

"Good heavens, Inspector, Woods is an under groom, he would not have dared venture around the house and especially not upstairs!"

"I see, Madam."

"And you informed the police that night?"

"A constable was summoned immediately and he took notes

before sending for his Sergeant who then handed the matter over to your Chief Inspector for his personal attention" she replied.

"Very good, Madam."

"My husband and I were assured that special detectives would be assigned to the case so that my diamonds would be recovered in time for my Christmas party."

"Yes, indeed, Madam."

"And we've had to wait for two days for your arrival!"

"I am sorry…"

"Not a very commendable start, Inspector" she interrupted.

"We make progress slowly but surely, Madam."

"I hope that is so, the whole of London society will be shocked and disappointed if I am unable to wear the 'Hudson diamonds' at Christmas!"

"I'm sure, Madam."

"So, Inspector, on your head be it, everyone of any importance will know if you fail in your duty."

"That thought will spur me on to undoubted success, Madam" replied Hadley in a resigned tone.

"My husband and I will wish to be kept fully informed of all developments" she said forcefully.

"Of, course, Madam, now may we please see the scullery and then have words with Mr Woods?" She nodded and led the way down to the scullery where a small girl was struggling to wash a pile of dirty dishes in the enormous sink. The girl bobbed a curtsy to her mistress as Hadley and Cooper went to the back door and studied the damage around the lock. Hadley made a few observations which Cooper noted and they then returned to the study whilst Woods was summoned. The young man was nervous but answered all the questions that Hadley put to him and the groom was relieved at the end of the interview when Hadley told him that he had been very helpful.

The detectives returned to Scotland Yard where Hadley ordered a pot of tea from George as he sat disconsolate behind his desk.

"I really can't be too bothered about Mrs Hudson and her diamonds" he said to Cooper.

"I can understand that, sir."

"I'll see the Chief tomorrow and let him know that she expects 'special detectives' to recover her priceless pieces, so that excuses us, Sergeant." Cooper laughed at that as George appeared with the tea.

"You are a life saver, George" smiled Hadley.

"Glad to hear it, sir" replied the clerk with a grin.

"After tea, we'll get down to a case review of the murder and make some notes, Sergeant."

"Right, sir."

Hadley arrived home at seven o'clock and was pleased to sit in front of the fire in the parlour whilst Alice, his wife, put the final touches to dinner in the kitchen. The day had been difficult, and Mrs Hudson combined with the rain, had made things worse. Hadley cleared his mind of the day's events and over a delicious dinner of lamb cutlets he engaged with his family. He asked Arthur, his son, what he had accomplished at work as a cabinet makers apprentice and was pleased to learn of his progress. Anne, his daughter, was struggling with her French lessons but her English grammar was improving, according to Miss Smithurst, the class teacher. Hadley smiled at that and caught an approving look from Alice. The Inspector's family and home in Camden were the very sanctuary of his soul and well being. He was devoted to Alice, who supported him all the time, and the children brought them both, great pride and joy. It was after ten o'clock when the Hadley's retired to bed and the Inspector cuddled his wife before falling into a deep sleep, much to the disappointment of Alice.

CHAPTER 3

The morning was brighter than yesterday and Hadley arrived at the Yard in good spirits after a restful night.

"Morning, Sergeant."

"Morning, sir, glad you're here" replied Cooper as he stood up from his desk.

"Why?"

"There's been a development in the French murder case, sir."

"Go on, Sergeant" said Hadley as he sat down behind his desk.

"Jacques Mornay who you spoke to on board the 'Arabesque' when I went with Lefevre to Marylebone, has been found stabbed to death in Whitechapel, sir."

"Good heavens!"

"Yes, sir."

"When did it happen?"

"Sometime in the early hours of this morning, sir."

"Any more details?"

"Not yet, sir, apparently the attack took place in Gypsy Lane and a constable was summoned after the disturbance, but Mornay had been fatally wounded."

"Where's the body now?"

"Taken to Marylebone, sir."

"Doctor Evans will be pleased."

"Indeed, sir."

"Any suspects?"

"None, sir, apparently one of the women looking for business in the Lane heard an argument and then a shout, but when she went to look, the assailant had vanished in the fog, she then saw Mornay in the gutter who gasped and said something, but she screamed and someone else called for a constable."

"Right, Sergeant, we'll get over to Charlton wharf and see if Captain Lefevre can shed any light on this matter before we go up to Marylebone. Call for a Hansom, and let's get underway!"

The detectives arrived at Charlton wharf, which was as busy as usual and to their great surprise, discovered that the 'Arabesque' was no longer moored by the quay.

"Good God, she's sailed with the tide!" exclaimed Hadley.

"Do you plan to stop her, sir?"

"You can be sure, Sergeant… cabbie return us to Scotland Yard as fast as you can!" The Hansom bumped and rattled at speed back to the Yard and Hadley left Cooper to pay the cabbie as he rushed into the building up to Chief Inspector Bell's office.

"Ah, Hadley, glad you've called in, I've had a complaint from Mr Hudson, he says…"

"Never mind that for the moment, sir…"

"What did you say?" interrupted the Chief Inspector quizzically.

"I've just been to Charlton wharf and have to report that the French ship 'Arabesque' has sailed and I want her stopped!"

"Why?"

"Jacques Mornay, another member of the crew has been murdered in Whitechapel, sir."

"Good God!"

"Have I your authority to hold the ship, sir?"

"Yes, Hadley, you do, I'll organise the warrant."

"I will need the cutter and several constables, sir."

"Right, take it and make sure the constables are armed just in case there's trouble."

"Yes, sir" replied Hadley as he left the office. He and Cooper rounded up four constables, drew rifles and ammunition from the armoury then hurried down to the Embankment Pier where the Metropolitan Police steam cutter was moored. The urgent mission was explained to Sergeant Butler, who was in charge of the vessel and as steam pressure was always ready for the normal days river patrol, the cutter departed within minutes of Hadley and his men arriving on board. The cutter made fast progress out into the mainstream of the Thames and Hadley briefed the constables on their mission. The sound of the steam engine thumping at full speed and the occasional blast from the fog horn gave some confidence to Hadley that they would soon overhaul the 'Arabesque'.

"Sergeant Butler."

"Yes, sir?"

"What time was high water this morning?"

"About six o'clock, sir." Hadley looked at his fob watch.

"It's now after ten, how far do you think a brig could get in four hours?"

"Well, sir, if she makes three knots an hour, she'll be downstream some twelve nautical miles, if she manages five knots, then twenty miles" replied Butler.

"Well on towards the estuary" murmured Hadley.

"Yes, sir."

"Are we at full speed, Sergeant?"

"Yes, sir, we are."

"I hope we can catch her before she reaches the Channel."

"Indeed, sir, we're making a good eight knots so we will be overhauling her."

"Is it possible that she might be able to sail faster than five knots?"

"I doubt it, sir, a brig would only make about eight knots under full sail at sea, so to clear the river safely, I think her speed would be nearer three knots."

"I hope you're right, Sergeant."

"Yes, sir."

Hadley left Sergeant Butler at the helm of the cutter and went out on the rear deck to talk to Cooper and the constables.

"I intend to board the ship and order the Captain to stop, he may well resist and a show of force will then be necessary" said Hadley and the constables nodded.

"Load your weapons and be prepared to fire warning shots if I give the word, hopefully that will be enough to concentrate the Captains mind."

"We will board the ship with you, sir?" asked Cooper.

"No, Sergeant, you will remain with the constables on the cutter until I give the word to fire a volley and then after that, you must board the ship."

"Right, sir."

"Sergeant Butler will keep the cutter close to, so that boarding can be quickly accomplished" said Hadley.

"And if the crew resist, sir?"

"Overpower and handcuff any who do, they will be under arrest at that moment."

"Right, sir."

Hadley turned away and gazed at the moored ships along the docks, wondering what mischief lurked amongst them. He then looked forward in the hope of seeing the 'Arabesque' but then realised that if she had a four hour start on the cutter it would be a while before she came into sight. He willed the steam engine to run faster and he fancied that the 'thump, thump' of the pistons obeyed his wishes. He knew that the stokers below would be hard at work shovelling the coal into the firebox as Sergeant Butler kept the cutter at full speed. The Thames broadened out and Hadley began to relax a little as he felt confident in the outcome of the chase. He sat next to Cooper on a platform seat by the stern rail and looked at the scenery slipping by.

"This is quite pleasant, Sergeant."

"Yes, sir, it certainly makes a bit of a change to our usual routine."

"Have you been on the cutter before?"

"Once or twice, sir, the last time was about a year ago, I was assisting in a case of murder in Richmond, a suspect boarded a boat and we gave chase" replied Cooper.

"Did you apprehend him?"

"Oh, yes, sir."

"Well done." They then remained silent, each man deep in thought, preparing himself for what was to come next. It was nearly midday when Hadley caught sight of the brig that he believed was the 'Arabesque'.

"I think that's her, Sergeant" he said to Cooper.

"We'll soon know, sir, we're over hauling her fast" replied Cooper as Butler waved them to join him on the bridge.

"I can just make out the name on her stern, sir, although it's a little faded" said Butler as the two detectives arrived at the helm.

"Any glasses?" asked Hadley.

"Yes, sir, over there on the hatch top" replied Butler. Hadley picked up the binoculars and steadied himself on the gently swaying deck before peering through them. He focused on the stern of the brig and could make out the first part of her name in the faded paintwork.

"Yes, sergeant, that's her alright" he said with conviction.

"I'll bring us alongside, sir, and keep station with her" replied Butler.

"Good man, now, Cooper, let the men know that we are almost upon her. Tell them to be prepared to present their rifles as we get close."

"Right, sir" said Cooper as he left the bridge to rally the constables. Hadley then turned to Butler and asked "where are we exactly, Sergeant?"

"Close to Tilbury, sir, the docks are no more than a mile or two ahead" replied the sergeant.

"Excellent, the brig can be held there if necessary" said Hadley with a smile. The cutter over hauled the 'Arabesque' quickly and as her stern became ever closer, Hadley felt the tingle of excitement. He picked up the loud hailer and positioned himself by the out rail of the bridge. He could see some of the French crew looking over the side of the brig, watching the fast approaching cutter. In minutes Sergeant Butler had brought the cutter alongside and reduced power so that it slowed to the speed of the 'Arabesque'.

"Ahoy, 'Arabesque', this a police cutter, bring the ship to a halt and prepare for me to board!" shouted Hadley through the hailer. A crewman shouted something back in French and disappeared from the rail. Hadley waited for a few moments and seeing no action aboard called again.

"This is a police cutter, I order you to stop!" Suddenly Captain Lefevre appeared at the rail and looked down at Hadley, whom he recognised.

"What do you want, Monsieur Inspector?" he shouted.

"To come aboard, Captain."

"What for?"

"To talk to you!"

"Non, Monsieur Inspector, I am behind already and we have nothing to discuss" replied Lefevre.

"Captain, I am prepared to use force to stop you, make no mistake!"

"What force do you threaten me with, Monsieur?"

"Sergeant, a volley if you please!" shouted Hadley, Cooper obliged and the constables on his word fired into the air. Lefevre looked shocked and shouted down "you have no right to threaten a French ship in such a way!"

"Come to a halt and let me board" shouted Hadley.

"You are making a big mistake, Monsieur!"

"Stop the ship, that is an order!" On hearing that Lefevre disappeared and Hadley heard orders being given followed by the sight of crew men climbing the rigging and furling the two top sails. The 'Arabesque' slowed appreciably and then began to wallow gently in the water as she came to a standstill. After a few moments, a rope ladder was flung over the side. Butler brought the cutter close to the hull of the brig and a police crew man reached out and caught the ladder.

"There you are, sir" said Butler.

"Thank you, Sergeant, well done." Hadley left the bridge and called out to Cooper "follow me, Sergeant."

"Right, sir." Hadley clambered up the swaying ladder followed by Cooper and the armed constables. When they had all arrived on the deck they were surrounded by Captain Lefevre and his crew.

"Well, Monsieur Inspector, what is the meaning of all this?" demanded the Captain angrily.

"Captain Lefevre, I am investigating the murder of Jacques Mornay…"

"Mon Dieu!" exclaimed the Captain with a shocked expression.

"I suggest that we discuss the matter in your cabin whilst Sergeant Cooper and my men remain here" said Hadley firmly.

"Oui, of course, please follow me." Once the two men were alone in the cabin Lefevre asked "you say Jacques has been murdered, when did this happen?"

"Last night, in Whitechapel."

"Mon Dieu" the Captain whispered.

"So, Captain, why did you set sail without your Mate on board?"

"Because, Monsieur Inspector, Jacques was paid off yesterday and left the ship" replied the Captain. That surprised Hadley and his thoughts raced for a moment.

"Why would he do that?"

"I don't know, he had his reasons and it is not unusual for sailors to leave a ship and stay for a while before joining another to return home" Lefevre replied.

"Can you prove that?"

"Oui, Inspector, I have written in the ships log for the day" replied the Captain as he reached for the leather bound log book on his desk and opened it.

"See here, the 25th of November, the unloading of the cargo completed, Jacques Mornay, Mate, paid off and left the ship, and then there are some other details about repairs to rigging, read it for yourself, Inspector." Hadley looked at the log.

"It's written in French, Captain, so I am at a disadvantage" replied Hadley, but he had seen the name of Jacques Mornay in the text and was satisfied.

"Oui, Inspector, it is well known that the English do not pay the French the courtesy of learning the language" smiled Lefevre.

"Quite so, now, I intend to hold your ship at Tilbury whilst I make further inquiries regarding the murder of Mornay and I want you to come with me back to London to identify the body…"

"Non, Inspector, I will not do this, I must get under way to Rotterdam, I have no knowledge of the murder and will not submit!"

"Then I shall arrest you, sir, and all your crew if necessary!"

"Mon Dieu!"

"I must remind you that a murder has been committed and you and your crew are suspects, so I advise that you come quietly, sir."

"This is outrageous, Inspector!"

"So is murder, sir." The Captain looked crestfallen but realised that he had no option. He shook his head and said "very well, Inspector, we'll put into Tilbury."

"Thank you, sir."

Two hours later the 'Arabesque' was moored at Tilbury dock under the watchful eye of the Harbour Master and Lefevre was on board the police cutter heading back to London. The Captain had left all the crew on the brig under the command of Pierre LeValet, the newly appointed First Mate.

Hadley paced the deck of the cutter with Cooper at his side.

"Do you realise it's only a month to Christmas, Sergeant?" asked Hadley as he gazed out over the meandering Thames, bathed in the weak, late autumn sunshine.

"Yes, sir, and I wonder if we'll recover the Hudson diamonds in time" he replied with a grin.

"If we don't, our names will be dragged through the mud and apparently the whole of London society will have to cancel

Christmas" Hadley replied with a sardonic smile and Cooper laughed.

"We appear to see both sides of life at the same time, sir."

"We do indeed, Sergeant" replied Hadley and he paused for a moment before he asked "tell me, what do you make of this murder case?" and he nodded in the direction of Lefevre, who was standing at the side rail of the cutter.

"All very suspicious, sir, first of all, why should Mornay suddenly decide to leave the ship? What was he doing in Whitechapel late at night and did he murder Dalmas with a gold bar?"

"And did someone kill him to keep him quiet for ever?"

"Possibly, sir."

"Or was his murder just another street robbery, a drunken fight perhaps, that ended in his death?"

"It could be a coincidence, sir"

"A very convenient one if this is as deep as I think it is, Sergeant."

"Do you think the Captain is implicated, sir?"

"Right up to his neck, Sergeant."

"Why, sir?"

"We know from Doctor Evans that Dalmas was killed with a gold bar, now, none of the low life, flotsam and jetsam that frequent Charlton wharf have ever seen a bar of gold, let alone possess one, so, I suspect that there was gold bullion aboard that ship and possibly Lefevre knows about it as well as the identity of the killer"

"Do you think the gold's been off loaded, sir?"

"Yes, and it's on its way to Liverpool, courtesy of our disappearing shipping agents, Johnstone and Bradley."

"Are we off to Liverpool again, sir?"

"Yes, Sergeant, after I've telegraphed our colleagues up there to check freight trains from London."

"Right, Sir."

"And mind you don't get shot this time" replied Hadley and Cooper smiled as he recalled the incident on the train to Liverpool when the murderer, Richard Nevers, fired his pistol at him.

"I'll try not to, sir."

"I expect we'll be called soon to give evidence when the

Nevers trial begins, Sergeant."

"Has a date been fixed yet for the hearing, sir?"

"Well, if it has, I've not been advised" replied Hadley.

"Meanwhile we've got this to keep us occupied as well as the Hudson diamond theft, sir."

"Yes, Sergeant, never a dull moment" replied Hadley.

"I hope we have a quiet Christmas, sir."

"All men live in hope, Sergeant, even policemen" Hadley smiled.

An hour later the cutter reached its station on the Embankment and moored alongside the jetty. Hadley thanked Sergeant Butler for all his assistance before disembarking with his men. The constables returned their rifles to the armoury whilst Hadley reported to Chief Inspector Bell, giving an account of the day's events. Meanwhile, Cooper took Lefevre to the office and George made a large pot of tea. Hadley joined them presently and advised the Captain that they would go immediately after tea to the morgue at Marylebone Hospital, whilst Cooper prepared a full written report for the Chief Inspector. An hour later Hadley and Lefevre arrived by Hansom cab outside the Marylebone as the daylight faded into dusk and the rain began to fall. Doctor Evans looked up from his desk as the two men entered.

"Good heavens, Inspector, I was just about to go home for the night" he said with a smile.

"Indeed, Doctor, well I am sorry to delay you, but I've brought Captain Lefevre to identify the body of the man killed in Whitechapel last night" replied Hadley.

"It seems to me, Captain, that unless you return to France soon, you'll have no crew left to sail your ship" said the Doctor.

"You may well be right, Monsieur Doctor."

"Come with me then gentlemen" said the Doctor as he stood up and led the way out into the dissection area. They looked down at the pale, naked body of Jacques Mornay laying on the marble slab.

"Captain, is that the body of Jacques Mornay?" asked Hadley.

"Oui, it is" whispered Lefevre.

"How did he die, Doctor?" asked Hadley.

"Two stab wounds to the lower chest, here" the Doctor pointed at the ugly, bruised openings.

"Did he bleed to death?"

"No, Inspector, his death was instantaneous, the knife penetrated the heart" replied the Doctor.

"Had he been drinking?"

"Yes, he'd had a fair amount of beer."

"Any food?"

"Not much to speak off" replied the Doctor.

"So was he drunk?"

"I'd say so."

"Let me have your report as soon as possible, Doctor."

"Of course, now Captain, are you taking the body back to France or are we going to do the honours as usual?" asked the Doctor.

"Please, Monsieur Doctor, make the necessary arrangements and I will notify his wife when I return to Marseille."

"Very well, Captain."

"Thank you, Doctor" said Hadley as they left the room and went to the adjoining area where the victims' belongings were laid out on a long bench. In the flickering gas light, Hadley examined the clothes and then the wallet of Jacques Mornay. It contained no money and Hadley wondered if this had been a street robbery that had gone tragically wrong as the Frenchman fought in a drunken state to save his hard earned wages. The two men left the morgue and Hadley hailed a passing Hansom to take them back to the Yard in the pouring rain. As the cab clattered over the wet cobblestones, he decided to tell Lefevre what he suspected to see if the revelation brought any response.

"You know, Captain, this is a very bad business that you are mixed up with."

"Really, Monsieur Inspector, I do not need you to tell me that with two of my crew murdered here in London" replied Lefevre.

"Indeed, sir, so I must tell you what I suspect."

"What do you suspect, Monsieur?"

"That your ship was carrying gold bullion with your full knowledge and that Dalmas found out about it and was murdered for his pains and then Mornay was killed because Dalmas told him about the gold before he died."

"You're imagination is your greatest gift, Monsieur Inspector, but be warned, it might well lead you into difficulty" replied

Lefevre.

"I am a policeman, Captain, so therefore, by definition, I am always in difficulty" replied Hadley.

"You have not ever been in as much difficulty as you may be now."

"Why is that?"

"Because Monsieur Roguefort and his family, owners of my ship, are very rich and powerful people and will engage the finest Notaire's in France to defend their honour and integrity, they will not hesitate to destroy your career if they believe that they have suffered an injustice at your hands, Monsieur Inspector."

"Is that so, sir?"

"Oui, Inspector, that is so, do I make myself clear?"

"Perfectly, Captain, just perfectly" replied Hadley and he smiled to himself in the darkness of the Hansom cab.

CHAPTER 4

Hadley kept Captain Lefevre in custody over night, despite the Frenchman's protests of innocence and persecution by the police. The Inspector interviewed him the next morning but the Captain remained firm in his account of events and Hadley was forced to release him without charge. Hadley arranged passage for the Captain to Tilbury on a train from Liverpool Street at midday and then went to see Chief Inspector Bell.

"It has all been inconclusive, sir" said Hadley after he had sat down opposite the harassed Chief.

"Be specific, Hadley."

"Captain Lefevre is adamant that he had no knowledge of any gold aboard his ship, nor could he shed any light on the murders of his crew men."

"Do you suspect him?"

"Yes, I certainly do."

"Why?"

"Because Dalmas was murdered with a gold bar and that had to have come from the ship, and I believe that Lefevre knew all about it."

"Well keep at it."

"I will, sir."

"Inform me of all developments."

"Yes, sir" replied Hadley as he arose from the seat and went to the office door.

"And, Hadley…"

"Yes, sir?"

"Do follow up on the Hudson diamond theft, Mrs Hudson has sent a letter of complaint about slack policing to the Commissioner and he's not best pleased."

"Yes, sir."

Hadley and Cooper left the Yard and took a Hansom to the offices of Empire Shipping Agents in Tooley Street. The chief clerk, William Hammond, was Hadley's closest friend and the two men had known each other since school days.

"What brings you here today, Jim?" asked William as he

waved the two detectives to the straight back chairs in front of his desk.

"Information that only you can give, Bill" replied Hadley with a grin.

"I expect you'll invite Elizabeth and me to Sunday lunch as a reward then" replied Bill.

"Only if the information is any good!"

"I'm always happy to help you with reliable facts, Jim, as I tell all our friends, I'm known to the police" said Bill with a grin.

"Sunday lunch may be a possibility then" replied Hadley.

"I'll keep you to it."

"Right, now then, do you know shipping agents under the name of Johnstone and Bradley?"

"Never heard of them."

"I didn't think so."

"What's their address?" asked Bill.

"26, Tooley Street…"

"Good heavens, that's just up the way" interrupted Bill.

"Indeed it is."

"How long have they been there?"

"I have no idea but I'm sure they are a 'here today, gone tomorrow' outfit, but alas, now gone" replied Hadley.

"I can't help you then, Jim."

"No matter, they are just small players in a bigger game."

"I see."

"Now what can you tell me about a shipping company called Maritime du Provence, based in Marseille?"

"Now that does ring some bells, I'll have to look up the details for you but I can tell you that it has been rumoured, nothing more substantial than that so far, that one of their ships was suspected by the Turkish authorities, of transporting the proceeds of a robbery away from Istanbul."

"Go on, Bill."

"Well that's all I know really, Jim."

"What was stolen, Bill?"

"The Turks won't say, but the rumour is, that it was gold bullion."

"Bill, you're coming to lunch on Sunday!"

"My word, that was easy" smiled Bill.

"Now, get me everything you can, the ship involved, the Captain's name, where she put in after she left Istanbul…"

"Jim, it's only rumour" interrupted Bill.

"Bill, I love rumours!"

"As you will, call back tomorrow and I'll have as much as I can find for you."

Hadley and Cooper took a Hansom to the Kings Head pub in Whitechapel for an early lunch. The bar was busy as usual and the detectives ordered pints of stout from the busy girls behind the bar as well as pork pies and pickles. They settled at a corner table and waited for Vera to bring their lunches and Agnes to arrive. They had finished eating and were on a second round of stout when the formidable lady pushed her way into the bar accompanied by Florrie Dean.

"Hello, Jim… Sergeant" Agnes smiled and Florrie curtseyed.

"Ladies, please join us, Sergeant, do the honours, if you please"

"Two sixpenny gins?" asked Cooper with a smile.

"You're my favourite Bobby, Sergeant" said Agnes.

"Mine too" added Florrie and Cooper blushed slightly before he made his way to the crowded bar.

"He's a diamond, Jim" said Agnes.

"He is. Now, two nights ago, one of the girls arrived at the scene of a murder…"

"Molly Barnet" interrupted Agnes.

"Yes, she gave her name and her address as 34a, Gypsy Lane to the constable at the time, I want to speak to her, Agnes."

"She'll be at home this afternoon, I expect" said Agnes.

"Good, I'd like you to come with me."

"Why, Jim?"

"Because she may be nervous if the Sergeant and I call unexpectedly, and I want Molly to feel relaxed when I interview her."

"I see."

"As you know her, she'll have confidence with you there, and if you can tell her that I'm not too bad, as policemen go…"

"Jim, I couldn't possibly say that" she laughed as watched Hadley's face drop.

"Very amusing, Agnes, now then, if I could ask Florrie here to keep my Sergeant company for a while, I'd be very grateful" Hadley smiled.

"Oh, yes, sir, leave him to me" said Florrie with a big smile as Cooper arrived back with the two gins.

"There you are, Sergeant, I've made arrangements for you to keep Florrie company after lunch whilst I go with Agnes to speak to Molly Barnet" Hadley beamed and Cooper smiled.

"Very good, sir."

"And you are to remain here until I return, Sergeant, it shouldn't take long."

"Yes, sir."

"Oh, Jim, you are a prude" said Agnes.

"No I'm not, I'm just guarding my junior officer's moral standing" replied Hadley and they all laughed.

It was after two when Hadley and Agnes left the pub and made their way, a little unsteadily at times, along Thames Street and down Gypsy Lane. Hadley knocked at the door of 34a, and it was opened by a small, dark haired young woman of about twenty.

"Yes, sir?" she asked nervously before she caught sight of Agnes and then the woman relaxed visibly and smiled.

"Molly Barnet?" asked Hadley.

"Yes, sir."

"I'm Inspector Hadley…"

"I know who you are, sir, I've seen you with Agnes lots of times" she interrupted.

"Ah, good, now may I come in and speak to you for a moment?"

"Yes, sir, don't mind the place it's a bit of a mess just now" she replied as she stood back and allowed Hadley to enter the small room. Agnes followed and Molly closed the door before inviting them to sit on the only two chairs in the untidy room. Molly sat on the bed and asked "is this about the murder of that sailor the other night?"

"Yes, Molly, it is."

"Well, as I told the constable at the time, I don't know nothin' and I didn't see nothin', either."

"I'm sure, Molly, but I'd just like you to tell me exactly what happened, in every small detail, if you please" said Hadley with a smile. Molly looked apprehensive for a moment and then Agnes spoke to reassure her.

"Molly, this is very important and if you can take your time and tell Jim everything that you saw, I know it will help catch the person who did this awful thing, and then we'll all be a lot safer." Molly nodded and smiled.

"It was about one o'clock, I think, I was in bed and almost asleep, my last gentleman had been gone for about half an hour or so, when I heard voices, men's voices, and I couldn't make out what they were saying…"

"Were they speaking a different language?" asked Hadley.

"I don't know, sir, then the voices got louder and they began to shout, but I couldn't understand what they were saying, then one of them screamed out and it all went quiet."

"What happened next?"

"I was frightened, sir, but I decided to have a look and I got up, went to the door and opened it…"

"What did you, see?" interrupted Hadley.

"A man laying in the gutter, sir, and he saw me and waved at me, then he said something…"

"What did he say, Molly?"

"I couldn't understand him, it sounded like 'feather', sir."

"Lefevre, perhaps?"

"Might have been, sir, then he sort of wriggled and lay still, then I screamed and someone came and others went for a constable, I told him everything I've told you, sir, and he wrote it all down in his notebook."

"I know, Molly, I've seen his notes."

"That's all I can think of, sir."

"Thank you, Molly, you've been very helpful" Hadley smiled and Molly smiled back.

Hadley and Agnes made their way back to the Kings Head in silence and other than thanking her for her assistance no conversation passed between them. Hadley was deep in thought and when he entered the bar and saw Cooper laughing whilst gazing into the eyes of Florrie, he was not amused.

"Come along, Sergeant, we have serious work to do."

"Right, sir" replied Cooper as he stood up immediately.

"Thank you, ladies, for all your help today, we will see you again soon, no doubt" said Hadley before striding out of the bar as Agnes and Florrie said 'goodbye'.

They took a cab to Lipton Street and stopped outside the faded shop front of Charles Benton, purveyor of fine jewellery and well known fence.

"Cabbie, please wait, we will not be long" said Hadley as he stepped down from the Hansom and the driver nodded. The two detectives entered the gloomy interior and as the door bell stopped clanging, Charlie Benton pushed aside the heavy velvet curtains at the back of the shop and entered smiling when he saw Hadley.

"Afternoon, Jim, what brings you and the boy here, as if I didn't know" he said as he rubbed his unshaven chin. Hadley smiled and replied "information, Charlie, as you so rightly know."

"Come on through" said Charlie as he turned and led the way into his untidy office behind the curtains. He waved the two detectives to the seats by his desk and slumped down in his high backed leather chair, which creaked with his weight.

"There's been a robbery in Cavendish Square, and a diamond necklace with matching ear rings have been lifted" said Hadley.

"I heard that something had happened" replied Charlie with a grin.

"They're known as the 'Hudson diamonds', and I should imagine that a professional would break them up before trying to pass them on" said Hadley.

"You're always right, Jim" nodded Charlie.

"In all the years you've known me, have I ever been wrong?" Hadley asked with a grin.

"I hope you're paying attention to all this, Sergeant" said Charlie.

"Yes, of course, sir" replied Cooper.

"Watch, listen and learn, my boy" nodded Charlie.

"Well, Charlie, what do you know?" asked Hadley.

"Not a lot at the moment, Jim, but I'll keep this old ear to the ground" he replied as he pulled at his left ear lobe.

"I'll call again in a day or so, Charlie."

"Right, Jim."

"This is an urgent case, Mrs Hudson wants her diamonds back

by Christmas to wear at her party and she's already written to the Commissioner complaining of slack policing" said Hadley and Charlie laughed out loud at that.

"My God, Jim, how the upper crust carry on, they'll be the death of us all" he chuckled.

"Do your best, Charlie, Christmas is only a month away."

"And if you don't recover the diamonds by then, you'll be roasted along with the chestnuts!" he laughed and Cooper smiled.

"How right you are, Charlie."

The Hansom rattled over the cobblestones and eventually stopped outside number 12, Cavendish Square, allowing the detectives to alight in the misty, grey November evening. They were admitted into the hall by Wilkes, the butler, where they waited for a few minutes before being shown into the spacious drawing room.

"The police, sir" announced Wilkes with a slight nod of the head. Anthony Hudson was a tall, elegant and well dressed man, standing with his back to the fire as Hadley stepped forward.

"About time too, well, better late than never" said Hudson with a grimace.

"Good evening, sir, I am Inspector Hadley and this is Sergeant Cooper of Scotland Yard…"

"Do you know that my wife has written to the Commissioner, complaining, rightly so in my opinion, about the serious lack of interest in this case?" interrupted Hudson.

"I was advised of that fact by Chief Inspector Bell today, sir" replied Hadley and Hudson looked down at his wife seated on a chair close by.

"Your letter seems to have the desired effect, my dear" said Hudson and his wife smiled.

"Indeed" she said.

"Well, what progress?" asked Hudson.

"We have started enquiries with reliable contacts…"

"Have you no suspects, Inspector?" interrupted Hudson.

"Not yet, sir, these are early days in the investigation…"

"There's no time to lose, Inspector, I want the diamonds returned before very much longer so my wife can wear them at our Christmas party!" interrupted Hudson.

"So I understand, sir, but I have to advise you that these

investigations take time…"

"Time is not what we have on our side, Inspector."

"It never is, sir."

"Well, it seems to me that this slack approach of yours will certainly not bring the results we expect" said Hudson.

"Sir, with respect…"

"I can tell you, Inspector, if I was as relaxed in my duties at the Bank, why, the whole system would collapse, and where would we be then I ask?"

"I have no idea as I am not a banker but a professional policeman, who spends every hour of every day tracking down thieves and murderers before bringing them to face justice in the courts."

"I don't care for your tone, Inspector."

"I regret that, sir, but nevertheless, I have told you the truth and while it may appear to your untrained eye and supreme lack of knowledge in police methods that I and Sergeant Cooper are doing little to recover the stolen diamonds, the very opposite is the fact."

"Really, Inspector, you overstep the mark!" exclaimed Hudson.

"I normally do, sir, that's why I am so successful in bringing criminals to justice!"

"This is intolerable, my wife and I are having dinner with Sir John Simmons, chairman of my Bank tomorrow evening and as he is a very close friend of the Commissioner, I shall relate to him your intemperate outburst in front of my wife."

"As you please, sir, but I can assure you that it will not catch the thief or recover your diamonds any quicker, in fact, it will probably slow the investigation quite considerably" replied Hadley.

"How so?"

"The Commissioner, on hearing your complaint from Sir John Simmons, will call for a full investigation into my conduct and methods, I will be taken off the inquiry, another officer will be appointed to continue with the case and of course, he will have to start all over again" smiled Hadley whilst Cooper put his hand over his face to hide his grin.

"Nevertheless, I shall make my views known over dinner with Sir John."

"Your decision, sir, but the wrong one. Now, I am sure that the thief is an amateur…"

"How can you be sure?" asked Mrs Hudson as her husband was still lost for words after Hadley's rebuke.

"Because the lock on your scullery door is the standard patch type which is relatively easy to pick, and a professional would have done that rather than forcing the lock, damaging the wood work and making an un-necessary noise, the professional would have possibly locked the door behind him after he gained entry and then gone to the front door and opened it, leaving it slightly ajar for his hurried escape. He then would have searched upstairs for the diamonds before leaving as silently as he came."

"Good heavens" said Hudson.

"The amateur, however, broke in and stole the necklace and made off, for which we must be thankful" said Hadley.

"Thankful?" queried Hudson.

"Yes, sir, you see, a professional would know that the diamonds are so famous" at that Mrs Hudson preened "and are almost impossible to sell, no fence or buyer would take the risk of acquiring them, so the professional would have them cut up into small pieces before trying to dispose of them." On hearing that Mrs Hudson let out a wail of despair and started to cry.

"Calm yourself, my dear, the Inspector has told us that it was an amateur thief" said Hudson in a comforting tone.

"Quite so, sir, the amateur will endeavour to sell the diamonds quickly and when he does, that's when we'll catch the miscreant" smiled Hadley.

"I do hope you're right, Inspector" wailed Mrs Hudson.

"I know I'm right, Madam, now, if you'll excuse me, the Sergeant and I will leave now and will be in touch as soon as anything develops" smiled Hadley before wishing the banker and his wife 'goodnight'.

Hadley arrived home in the dark and was relieved to be there. Alice had a roaring fire in the parlour and dinner almost ready for them all. Hadley kissed his wife and said "I saw Bill today and I've invited him and Elizabeth to lunch on Sunday."

"Oh, that's lovely, Jim, it's a while since we've seen them" Alice replied.

"Yes, my dear, and I'd like something special for lunch as Bill has been very helpful to me."

"Right, I know he likes a good cut of roast beef, so that's what I'll get" she said.

"And a fine bottle of wine if you please" said Hadley.

"Anything else, master?" she giggled.

"Yes, I'll tell you later in bed!"

CHAPTER 5

It was pouring with rain when Hadley arrived in his office the next morning and only a steaming pot of George's tea helped the Inspector to regain his well being.

"I hate this time of year, Sergeant, it's wet, cold and gloomy."

"Yes indeed, sir, but it'll soon be Christmas and then we're into the new year" replied Cooper cheerily.

"Yes, and wonder what 1881 will have in store for us?"

"More of the same, sir."

"Sergeant, I believe that you are really enjoying all this" smiled Hadley.

"I certainly am, sir."

"Good, well it's all report writing and case review up until lunchtime, that will stop your enjoyment!"

"Yes, sir."

"Then we're off to see my friend Bill in Tooley Street, I am anxious to know what he has found out about our French friends." The two detectives, aided by George, sifted through the evidence of the 'Arabesque' murders and the Hudson diamonds theft. As usual there were more questions than answers and Hadley decided by midday that he had had enough of making notes whilst talking endlessly about possibilities and suggested an early lunch. They took a Hansom to the Crown Inn, situated in the Strand. Cooper paid the cabbie whilst Hadley bought a paper from a nearby news boy. He studied it for a moment before Cooper joined him.

"They're at it again, Sergeant."

"Really, sir?"

"Yes, listen to this 'Hudson diamonds stolen from Cavendish Square.... police slow to respond to violent robbery... Mrs Rowena Hudson, owner of the famous necklace, says that the police are baffled... Mr Anthony Hudson, a prominent City banker, has offered a reward for their recovery in time for Mr and Mrs Hudson's high society party at Christmas…"

"Unbelievable, sir."

"Yes, indeed, Sergeant, you'd better buy me a pint of stout and a good lunch before I get hungry as well as angry." Cooper smiled and followed Hadley into the crowded, smoke filled bar.

It was just after two o'clock when they arrived at the office in Tooley Street and Bill greeted them with a smile and said "I've some interesting information for you, Jim."

"I'm listening, Bill, take notes please, Sergeant." Cooper nodded and produced his notebook and pencil.

"Apparently, a brig called the 'Arabesque', belonging to Maritime du Provence, loaded a cargo of carpets, machinery and miscellaneous items in Istanbul at the beginning of September." Hadley raised his eyebrows on hearing that.

"Did she indeed" he whispered.

"The captain was Pascal Dalmas, a French national from Marseille…" Hadley's eyes opened a little wider at that.

"The brig then put in at Naples, where some of the cargo was off loaded and a cargo of wine taken on…"

"Tell me, Bill, was any of the machinery off loaded there?"

"No, Jim; she then sailed to Genoa, that's where all the machinery was off loaded and more wine taken on board before she finally arrived in Marseille."

"This is beginning to be very interesting" mused Hadley.

"Then the 'Arabesque' remained in Marseille for several weeks, which is unusual in itself, before a cargo of wine, tobacco and machinery was loaded and she sailed to London with a Captain Lefevre in command."

"Captain Dalmas was relieved and replaced by Lefevre then?"

"Apparently so."

"When a ship enters a port like Marseille, do the authorities check the cargo?" asked Hadley.

"Yes, normally when a vessel arrives they do so, to collect any duty payment, but not often when it sails" replied Bill.

"Is there any indication that the machinery off loaded in Genoa is the same that was loaded in Marseille before the 'Arabesque' sailed for London?"

"I've no idea, Jim, but why would they want to do that?" queried Bill.

"So the authorities in Marseille would not find anything untoward in the cargo of machinery when the ship arrived, Bill."

"So, you think the crates containing the machinery was transported over land from Genoa to Marseille?"

"It is a possibility; that would explain why the 'Arabesque' remained in Marseille for the unusually long time" replied Hadley.

"Well, that would tie in with the rumours about the bullion theft" said Bill.

"Tell me about that."

"Apparently a large French company called 'Istanbul Industrie S.A', operates a manufacturing business in Istanbul, making all types of water pumps, some for marine purposes and others for land irrigation, and it is owned partly by the Roguefort family, who also own Maritime du Provence" said Bill.

"Yes, I know, Captain Lefevre has told me that they are rich and powerful" said Hadley.

"Too true, Jim, the head of the family is Michel Roguefort, apparently he runs everything like a dictator…"

"A Napoleonic disposition then" smiled Hadley.

"Yes."

"We're good at defeating dictators, especially Napoleonic ones" said Hadley and they all smiled.

"So, the rumour is that an undisclosed amount of gold was stolen from an Istanbul Bank and the Turkish authorities have been pretty tight lipped about the incident" said Bill.

"Why?"

"I've no idea, Jim, but it seems for some reason they want to keep quiet about it."

"Very strange!"

"And the robbery took place at the very time that the 'Arabesque' was in Istanbul."

"Go on."

"Rumour has it that she sailed within a day or so of the theft" said Bill.

"With Captain Dalmas in command" mused Hadley.

"Yes, it appears that he was replaced once the 'Arabesque' had reached Marseille."

"This is all very suspicious, Bill, and I've let the prime suspect sail away to Rotterdam" said Hadley.

"Good heavens" murmured Bill.

"Yes, Dalmas was the first mate of the 'Arabesque' and his body was discovered lodged in the pier structure at Charlton wharf…"

"Dear God."

"According to the pathology report, he'd been murdered with a gold bar, before his body was flung in the river" said Hadley and Bill's mouth opened in astonishment.

"A gold bar?"

"Yes, and then his replacement, Jacques Mornay, was stabbed to death in Whitechapel."

"There is a lunatic at large, Jim" said Bill.

"Possibly, but I believe it is more likely that Lefevre is attempting to annihilate anyone who knows anything about the gold bullion that was stolen in Istanbul."

"My God" whispered Bill and they all remained silent whilst Hadley gathered his thoughts.

"The gold is in those machinery crates, I'm sure of it" Hadley said with conviction.

"Are we off to Liverpool now, sir?"

"Yes, Sergeant, we are."

"Good luck then, Jim."

"Many thanks for all your help, Bill" said Hadley.

"My pleasure, Jim" smiled his friend.

"I told Alice that you and Elizabeth were invited to lunch on Sunday and she looks forward to seeing you both" said Hadley.

"That's very nice, Jim."

"Say about midday, then we can raise a glass or two before lunch is served" Hadley smiled and Bill nodded.

"Capital, Jim, I look forward to seeing you if you are back from Liverpool by Sunday."

"It's only Wednesday, Bill, so you can rest assured."

"I've heard that before" replied Bill and they all smiled.

Hadley returned to the Yard to inform Chief Inspector Bell of the developments whilst Cooper went to Kings Cross and St. Pancras main line stations to make inquiries about the goods traffic that had been sent to Liverpool since Johnstone and Bradley had collected the crates from Charlton wharf.

"What you're telling me is quite unbelievable, Hadley" said the Chief Inspector with a puzzled look.

"I realise that, sir, but I must tell you that I am certain that stolen gold bullion has been hidden in those crates of machinery and someone is going to eventually collect it."

"Well, I understand that Hadley, but why haven't the Turkish authorities made it known that this gold has been stolen?"

"I have no idea, sir."

"And you think Lefevre murdered both his crew men?"

"Yes, sir, I do."

"Because they knew about the gold?"

"Yes, sir."

"And you had him in custody, then released him so he could sail off to Rotterdam?"

"Regretfully, sir."

"I hope you are right about all this" said Bell.

"I'm sure, sir."

"So you'll want to get off to Liverpool once again I take it?"

"Yes, sir, and I've already telegraphed Inspector Dunton up there and asked him to check on freight from London."

"I hope this is not another wild goose chase, Hadley."

"No, sir."

"The Commissioner will want to know what you are doing up there whilst the unsolved theft of Mrs Hudson's diamonds is causing her social life to collapse all around her."

"Yes, sir, but…"

"All London society is talking about it, you know" interrupted Bell.

"I do realise how important that case is, sir, and I think that in the circumstances, it might be better if a more experienced officer than myself were appointed to take over the investigation" said Hadley hopefully.

"I've no one that I can spare, Hadley" replied Bell as he glanced at the pile of papers on his desk in front of him.

"Surely, someone, like Carstairs, for instance, he's had a lot of experience…"

"Hadley, the answer is 'no'!"

"Very good, sir."

"Now keep me informed by telegraph of all events in Liverpool" said Bell as he returned his gaze to the papers in front of him. Hadley nodded and mumble "sir" as he left the office.

Cooper arrived back in the office just in time to join Hadley for a pot of George's tea.

"I've discovered that the crates from the 'Arabesque' were delivered by our bogus shipping agents to the goods depot at Kings Cross and the paperwork ties up with Maritime du Provence" said Cooper.

"Well done, Sergeant."

"And they are marked for collection at Liverpool by agents calling themselves Garstang and Fletcher."

"Now we're getting somewhere, Sergeant."

"The goods carriage has been paid forward, so the Liverpool agents have only got to sign for them" said Cooper.

"Any clue as to the final destination?"

"No, sir."

"In that case we'll have to follow them."

"Right, sir."

"Go home and pack a bag, Sergeant, we're off to Liverpool tonight."

"Yes, sir."

"George" Hadley called out.

"Yes, sir" replied the affable clerk from his small adjacent office.

"Get me the times of the express trains to Liverpool tonight, please."

"Right away, sir."

"I'll send another telegraph to our friend up there, Inspector Dunton, to let him know we're on our way" said Hadley.

"He'll be surprised to see us again so soon after our last visit" said Cooper with a grin.

"Yes, indeed, but at least you will be fit enough to assist me this time" replied Hadley as he tried to keep a straight face.

"It was not my fault that Richard Nevers shot me, sir."

"Quite so, Sergeant, now get off home, pack a bag and meet me back here as quick as you like" replied Hadley with a smile.

The two detectives caught the seven o'clock express from Kings Cross and settled down in the compartment for the journey ahead. As they were alone as far as Crewe, when a portly lady accompanied by a tall thin man joined them, they were able to discuss the case so far and make plans to follow the crates and arrest all those concerned. When the train pulled into Liverpool station Inspector Edward Dunton and a police constable were there to meet the detectives.

"Pleased to see you both again, Jim" said Dunton.

"Likewise, Edward, and thank you for meeting us" replied Hadley and Cooper nodded and smiled.

"Not at all, now let's get you back to the station so you can tell me all the details of your investigation" said Dunton.

"Right, Edward, but first we have to find lodgings for the night" said Hadley.

"Jim, it's all taken care of, it's called northern hospitality" smiled Dunton as he put a comforting hand on Hadley's shoulder.

"Thank you, Edward."

"Now let's get back and have a hot cup of cocoa with something in it to keep the cold out!"

When they were alone in the Inspector's office, nursing steaming mugs of cocoa with a dash of brandy, Hadley relayed the facts of the case and watched as Edward's eyes opened further at each revelation.

"Good God, Jim, this is big as well as international" whispered Edward Dunton.

"It certainly is, now we have to work closely together on this and I want everything kept secret" said Hadley.

"Right, Jim, so far I've had two plain clothes men checking the freight as you requested and the crates have arrived."

"Have the crates been collected yet?"

"No."

"Good. Now you must have a support officer who you can trust as well as two constables."

"Yes, Jim."

Then Hadley laid out his plans to Inspector Dunton, who took a neat nip of brandy at the end of it all. Then the two detectives were taken to a clean, warm lodging house, close to the police station for the night, where they drifted off into deep sleep.

It was just after eight the next morning when they arrived back in Inspector Dunton's office. After asking about their nights rest and comfort, Dunton introduced a tall, slim young man who was smartly dressed.

"This is Sergeant Harris, my trusted right hand man, Jim."

"Pleased to meet you Sergeant" said Hadley.

"Likewise, sir, it's not often we get the chance to work with Scotland Yard and I'm looking forward to it" smiled Harris as he shook hands with Hadley and then Cooper.

"Now then, I do not know how much Inspector Dunton has told you, but suffice to say, this is a very important investigation and it could be dangerous" said Hadley.

"Yes, sir, I am aware of that" replied Harris.

"And it is imperative that not a word of this operation should be discussed with anybody outside this office" said Hadley firmly.

"I understand, sir."

"Good, now the first thing is to go to the goods depot and await the agents who will collect the crates" said Hadley.

"I've detailed two reliable constables as you requested, Jim, do you want them to accompany us now?" asked Dunton.

"No, not yet, Edward, they'll be needed a little later on."

"Right, Jim."

The four detectives set off in a hired trap to the Goods Depot, where they made their way to the office of the manager, Mr Ernest Tibbs. The two plain clothes officers confirmed that the crates were still awaiting collection and Tibbs looked surprised when the four policemen entered his paper strewn office. After introductions, Dunton asked to see the paperwork covering the crates of machinery that had arrived from London. Mr Tibbs duly obliged and Dunton showed Hadley when he had read the shipping notes.

"To be collected by Garstang and Fletcher for onward shipment" said Hadley softly as he read the notes.

"Where to, I wonder?" queried Edward.

"That's the key to all this" replied Hadley.

"What now, Jim?"

"Let us inspect the crates" said Hadley.

"Mr Tibbs, please lead the way" said Dunton and the manager nodded before leading them out onto the loading bay area.. There were three wooden crates, each about three feet long, two feet high and about the same dimension width wise, stencilled with the words 'marine pumps' and 'Maritime du Provence'. There were paper labels stuck on the lids which read 'London to Liverpool by rail'. Hadley looked closely at the well made crates with wood screws holding the lids in place.

"Normally crates like this are nailed together for transporting machinery, these look as if they have been very carefully made" said Hadley.

"Are we going to open them, sir?" asked Cooper.

"Not yet, Sergeant."

"So, we wait for the agents to collect them" said Dunton.

"Yes, we do Edward, now, Mr Tibbs…"

"Yes, sir?"

"We shall remain hidden in your office until the crates are collected" said Hadley.

"Very good, sir."

They waited until nearly midday before two men arrived with the paperwork to collect the crates. They were both in their thirties, looked well built and dressed quite smartly, making a good impression on Mr Tibbs who, on their signatures, released the crates to them. They were then hoisted up on a small jib crane by a rail worker and loaded onto a four wheel open wagon. With thanks and a wave the two agents climbed up onto the wagon and one slapped the reins for the horse to walk on, pulling out into the busy street. Hadley and the others gave it a few moments before thanking Mr Tibbs and following the suspects.

"Edward, we'll walk and you two will follow on in the trap" said Hadley to the Sergeants.

"Right, sir" nodded Cooper..

"If they start to pull away from us you take up the chase, but don't get too close" said Hadley

"Yes, sir."

The two Inspectors walked casually along the street whilst keeping the wagon in view with the trap following at a discreet distance. It was a cold but bright day and Hadley was enjoying the walk. He and Dunton chatted amiably about events and Hadley reminded the Inspector about his invitation to London when they last met. Dunton said that he and his wife looked forward to a visit sometime in the Spring, when duty allowed. They followed the wagon along the streets towards the dock area and as they approached one of the quays, the wagon turned abruptly into an alleyway and disappeared. The Inspectors hurried to the corner of a building by the alley and peered round just in time to see the wagon entering a small yard at the end. When the horse had pulled the four wheeler in, one of the men jumped down and closed two, high wooden gates blocking the wagon from view.

"Now what, Jim?"

"We'll make sure that there is no other exit then watch and wait until they leave, then we go in" replied Hadley.

"It could be a long wait, Jim."

"Not to worry, we'll take it in turns, now then, is there a pub close by?"

"Yes, Jim" Dunton laughed.

"Good, I'm hungry and you can show me some more of your northern hospitality and buy me lunch!" said Hadley and Dunton smiled.

"I'll tell the Sergeants to take first watch then" said Dunton.

"We work well together, Edward" smiled Hadley as the trap arrived with Cooper and Harris.

It was just an hour later, when the Inspectors had finished their lunch of pasties washed down with stout in the 'Ferryman' pub, that Cooper entered the bar with the news that the two men had left the yard and gone down towards the quay.

"Edward, send Harris back to the station to collect the constables as well as crowbars and large screwdrivers, we may not have much time!" exclaimed Hadley.

"Right" replied Dunton as they all hurried out of the bar. Harris was despatched with all speed whilst the detectives walked down the alleyway to the gates. They were locked and Hadley assumed that a simple patch lock was holding the gate against the other which had a large bolt dropped down into the cobbles.

"Can you open that, Sergeant?"

"If you'll give me long enough, sir" replied Cooper.

"No time, I'm afraid, Sergeant, you'll have to climb over and lift the bolt."

"Right, sir."

"I'll give you a leg up, Sergeant" said Hadley as he bent forward and cupped his hands for Cooper. The Sergeant placed his foot in the Inspector's hands and as he stepped up Hadley flexed his broad shoulders and heaved Cooper up allowing him to clamber over the gate and drop down the other side. Cooper unbolted the gate and swung it open, allowing the two detectives to enter the yard. The wagon stood close to a dilapidated wooden building, the horse had been released from its harness and was standing in a shelter munching hay.

"Quickly, Sergeant, search the building and see what you can find" said Hadley and Cooper nodded.

"Now, Edward, let's examine these crates." The two Inspectors climbed up onto the wagon and removed an old tarpaulin that had been hastily thrown over the crates. Hadley looked carefully at the lids and knew that these well made wooden boxes held more than marine pumps. It seemed an age before Harris arrived with two constables in the trap.

"Quickly, lads, get these lids unscrewed" said Dunton and the constables set about the task with vigour. The first lid was freed as Cooper returned from his search of the building and Hadley started pulling the straw from around a large, grey marine pump.

"Did you find anything of interest, Sergeant?" asked Hadley.

"No, sir, it's all pretty derelict" replied Cooper.

"As I thought, now, help me clear all this damned straw!" As they emptied the crate the constables removed the screws from the remaining two and started to clear them of the straw packing. The policemen gazed down at the three marine pumps that were tied down in each crate and remained silent.

"Well, nothing there, Jim" said Dunton.

"Let's lift these pumps out" said Hadley. They untied the holding ropes and the two Sergeants aided by the constables struggled to lift the heavy pumps from the crates. When they were all empty, Hadley examined the bottom of each crate to look for fixings that would indicate a false bottom, but there were none.

"Perhaps what we're looking for is in the pump" said Dunton.

"No, Edward, I don't think so" replied Hadley. They fell silent whilst Hadley thought for a moment.

"Turn the crates upside down, lads" he said and the constables did as he requested and needed help from the Sergeants as the crates themselves were surprisingly heavy. A neat row of screws in the base of each were quickly removed and when the solid, hard wood covers were removed, bundles wrapped in newspaper were revealed. Hadley picked one up and unwrapped it slowly. A bright bullion bar of gold shone in the afternoon sun and all the officers gasped as the Inspector held it up. Hadley felt greatly relieved.

"Quickly, lads, unpack each box, get the gold into the trap, and then put everything back as it was, I do not want our friends to know that we've been here!" exclaimed Hadley in a triumphant tone.

CHAPTER 6

Hadley, Dunton and the two constables returned to the police station whilst leaving Cooper and Harris on surveillance duty near the yard. The gold bars were brought into Dunton's office by the constables and placed on the floor. Twenty bars had been concealed in each crate and the detectives gazed down at a pile of sixty on the polished wooden floor.

"Worth a guinea or two, I suspect, Jim" said Dunton.

"Yes, indeed, Edward, now all we've got to do is find out where this little fortune was going, arrest our two agents who collected the crates and get the gold back to London" said Hadley.

"Right, we've got some empty wooden ammunition boxes in the armoury, you can have those to transport this lot back to the Yard" said Dunton.

"I'll telegraph my Chief and let him know what has happened and I'll request that four constables meet us tomorrow in a suitable wagon at Kings Cross."

"I suppose you'll need some of my lads to accompany you down on the train?"

"Yes, please, Edward."

"Right."

"Now we have to wait to see where those crates go next" said Hadley.

It was six o'clock exactly when Harris, flushed and soaking wet from the rain that had just started to fall, rushed into the office and announced that the wagon with the crates was about to move.

"This is it, Jim."

"Bring your two constables, Edward, this might get ugly!" Within minutes the five policemen were in the trap and heading back to the alleyway where Cooper was standing in the rain.

"I think they're coming out any moment now, sir" said Cooper.

"Right, Sergeant, now Edward, keep the constables out of sight whilst we follow the so called 'agents'." Orders were given and the policemen dispersed amongst the rain soaked people hurrying back from work. Hadley and the others did not have to wait long before the gates of the yard swung open and the wagon appeared in the gloom. It came to the road and turned left towards the quays and the policemen followed in the trap at a distance. Eventually the wagon entered a large shipping warehouse close to the quayside. Alongside was moored the passenger steamship 'American Spirit' out of Boston and Hadley's mind began to race with possibilities.

"They're shipping it to America, Edward" he whispered.

"Good heavens, you're right, Jim." They waited outside the open doors of the warehouse whilst observing the two men inside talking with cargo loaders, illuminated by the flickering gas lamps. Hadley watched as the crates were unloaded by jib crane and placed on the floor with others, obviously awaiting loading onto the 'American Spirit'. Hadley waited until he saw paperwork being exchanged between the agents and a sombre looking man with a clipboard.

"Get ready, Edward, I think it's nearly time to go!"

"Right, lads, wait for it and be ready in case it gets rough!" said Dunton. Hadley waited for a few moments longer and then gave the order to arrest the agents. Harris and Cooper were away like greyhounds and as they closed in on the men, they turned to face the policemen. Cooper shouted "police, you're under arrest!"

"Are we, by God!" replied one of the men as he took a swipe at Cooper and missed whilst Harris pushed the other man to the floor and fell upon him as he struggled to get away. The constables arrived at that moment and added their weight to the melee whilst Hadley and Dunton arrived, slightly out of breath. The two men were quickly overpowered and handcuffed whilst the cargo loaders looked on, open mouthed with astonishment.

"Well, done, lads" said Hadley as the sombre man with the clipboard approached.

"What's all this then?" he enquired.

"Police business, sir, I'd be obliged to see all the documents that refer to those three crates that have just been unloaded by these men" said Hadley firmly.

"And you are?" enquired the sombre man.

"Inspector Hadley of New Scotland Yard, in London."

"I know where it is, Inspector, we're not all uneducated heathens up here you know!"

"Indeed, sir, now if you'll kindly show me the paperwork"

Hadley smiled.

"Here" and the sombre man handed Hadley the clip board as the agents were taken out to the trap by the four officers and driven away in the rain. Hadley looked for their names on the loading sheet and found them almost at the bottom. He read it out loud "three crates of marine pumps from Maritime du Provence, Marseille, delivered by Garstang and Fletcher, shipping agents, … destination Boston, U.S.A. by sea aboard SS 'American Spirit', departing midday, tomorrow, to be collected by American First Line Shipping Agents on arrival."

"You were right, Jim" said Edward.

"Are you going to hold these crates back, Inspector?" asked the sombre man.

"No, sir, please load them and let them go on their way" replied Hadley with a smile.

"Thank you" said the man, Hadley then made notes of the relevant details before handing the clipboard back to the dour individual.

"Right, Edward, I think we can commandeer the agents wagon and return to the station" said Hadley.

Garstang and Fletcher were in the interview room with Cooper and Harris awaiting the Inspectors arrival. Once out of their wet great coats, the Inspectors stopped for a pot of tea before proceeding to the room where the bedraggled agents sat with long faces.

"I'm Inspector Hadley and this is Inspector Dunton…"

"We know who you are" interrupted the bigger of the two men.

"And you are?" asked Hadley.

"I'm John Fletcher and he's Robert Garstang, we're shipping agents and you are making a big mistake!" said Fletcher.

"Really?"

"Yes, we're bona fide agents, with offices in the Huyton Road, carrying out delivery instructions from agents in London" said Fletcher.

"And who might they be?" asked Hadley.

"Johnstone and Bradley of Tooley Street" replied Fletcher.

"Can you prove that?" enquired Hadley.

"Yes, I have their instructions that arrived in the post today" said Fletcher and he pulled a limp piece of paper from his jacket pocket and handed it to Hadley. The Inspector looked at it for a moment then read out aloud "To Fletcher and Garstang, shipping agents, Huyton Road, Liverpool, Dear Sirs, please be good enough to act upon the following instructions, a consignment of three packing cases, marked 'Maritime du Provence, marine pumps', will arrive by goods train from London, collect the aforementioned cases and hold them securely before delivering them to quay five, Liverpool docks for loading on to the SS 'American Spirit' bound for Boston, America, where they will be collected by American First Line Shipping Agents, ensure you mark the cases for their attention, we are pleased to enclose five pounds for your services and can assure your goodselves that once we are advised by American First Line that the cases have arrived safely, then we shall be despatching more items for your attention, yours faithfully etc., Johnstone and Bradley." Hadley looked up, his mind racing.

"I think we had better have a word in my office, Inspector" said Dunton.

"Indeed" replied Hadley.

"Does that mean we're free to go?" demanded Fletcher.

"No, sir, most certainly not" replied Hadley before he followed Dunton out of the room.

Dunton sat behind his desk whilst Hadley paced up and down.

"Do you think that there's more gold on its way, or was line in the instructions about more work a bluff, to make sure these men delivered the cases?" asked Dunton.

"I think it's a bluff, a forward fee of five pounds is a great deal of money for a simple collection from the station and delivery to the docks" replied Hadley.

"Certainly is."

"And the thought of more easy money would ensure that everything went according to plan" mused Hadley.

"Whoever sent this gold originally was taking a risk though" said Dunton.

"Yes, Edward, I'm not a gambling man myself but I can recognise the weakness in others."

"Indeed, I'm sure Fletcher and his partner have no idea about the gold" said Dunton.

"Obviously."

"What do you intend to do with them?"

"Charge them with affray and resisting arrest, get them photographed then release them on police bail" replied Hadley.

"Right, and we'll keep an eye on them from now on."

"Yes, and a discreet word to Mr Tibbs at the goods rail depot, to advise you of any more crates to be collected by Fletcher and Garstang" said Hadley and Dunton nodded.

The puzzled agents were later released, anxious to know why they had been arrested so forcefully and by so many senior officers. Hadley informed them that it was all part of a customs investigation into the non payment of duty on items shipped in by Maritime du Provence. They seemed content with the explanation and Hadley assured them that they were not implicated in any criminal activity. They both looked relieved as they left the station and climbed up on their wagon in the pouring rain.

The next morning the gold bars were packed in the old ammunition boxes and were taken to the station in time to catch the express to London. Inspector Dunton provided four constables to accompany Hadley and Cooper on the journey to Kings Cross. It had been arranged for the party to travel in the guards van with the gold, well away from curious passengers.

"Well, Edward, I must thank you for all your help in this investigation, I will certainly keep in touch and let you know the outcome of it all" said Hadley as he boarded the guards van.

"Yes, Jim, I look forward to hearing from you in due course" replied Dunton with a smile.

"As it is unlikely that I will see you before Christmas…"

"You never know, Jim" interrupted Dunton with a smile.

"True, Edward, even so, I wish you and your wife the very best for the season" said Hadley.

"Thank you, Jim, Christmas greetings to you and yours" replied Inspector Dunton as Sergeant Harris smiled and waved. Just then the guard blew his whistle and waved his green flag before stepping up into the van. The engine blew steam and the couplings clinked as the power was applied, moving the train forward on its express run to London. Hadley sat back in the seat next to Cooper, opposite the small window, feeling relaxed and comfortable at their success.

"A good outcome, Sergeant."

"Yes, sir."

"And you didn't get injured during the arrest."

"No, sir."

"Let us hope that we always keep it that way." Cooper laughed at that and the four constables sitting opposite all smiled. The journey was un-eventful and Hadley used the time to think about his next move. The gold was recovered and the master mind behind the crime was totally unaware of that fact. Hadley reasoned that once the thief discovered that the bullion was missing, they would have to show their hand, or, alternatively, take no further interest in it. Somehow he thought that was unlikely, and Garstang and Fletcher would be the first to fall under suspicion. It promised to be a very interesting case. He knew that he had to inform the Boston Police Department and ask for their co-operation in tracking down the final destination of the crates. He wondered if there was more bullion to be despatched from London to Liverpool and he realised that unless the Turkish authorities admitted the theft and disclosed how many gold bars were stolen, would he know for certain.

The train pulled into Kings Cross and when all the passengers had cleared the platform, the constables un-loaded the ammunition boxes onto trolleys which were then brought to the concourse. Cooper went ahead and found the constables from the Yard and they took over from their Liverpool colleagues, wheeling the boxes out to the four wheeler. Hadley thanked the constables for their help before wishing them a safe return to Liverpool. As soon as they arrived back at Scotland Yard, Hadley went up to Chief Inspector Bell's office. The Chief waved Hadley to a seat and looked hard at the Inspector.

"Well, Hadley, let's have it."

"We followed the crates and opened them…"

"And?"

"We recovered sixty gold bars from the false bases…"

"Good God!"

"We re-packed the crates and allowed them to continue on their journey to Boston on board the 'Spirit of America', which sailed from Liverpool today, sir."

"Where's the gold now?"

"Downstairs in my office, sir."

"Hadley, are you completely mad?"

"Hopefully not, sir."

"We can't have gold bullion on the premises, for security's sake we must get it to the vaults at the Bank of England!"

"Yes, sir."

"Organise that immediately whilst I inform the Commissioner of what's happened."

"Yes, sir."

"Any arrests?"

"Yes, two men, Garstang and Fletcher, they're bona fides shipping agents" replied Hadley.

"Good, keep them in custody."

"They've been released on police bail, sir."

"What! You've let them go?"

"Yes, sir."

"Why?"

"They're innocent men, sir."

"Good heavens, man, it's better that we hold innocent men in custody than release suspects into the world at large!"

"Possibly, sir."

"Now, as soon as you've taken the gold bullion to the bank, get along to Cavendish Square and calm the Hudson's down, they're making the Commissioner's life a misery. And have full reports on both investigations on my desk by lunchtime tomorrow so I can inform the Commissioner at our formal three o'clock meeting."

"Yes, sir."

Hadley returned to his office, ordered a pot of tea from George and told Cooper what the Chief's instructions were for the investigations. It was late afternoon before they set off to the Bank of England, with the gold in a four wheeler, and the necessary official paperwork with attendant constables. It took an age to go through the process of lodging the gold in the vault and Hadley breathed a sigh of relief when the operation was concluded. He sent the constables back to the Yard whilst Cooper hailed a Hansom to take them to Lipton Street.

Charlie's shop was gloomier than usual in the grey November afternoon and he did not seem overjoyed to see the two detectives.

"No news, I'm afraid, Jim."

"Nothing at all?" asked Hadley.

"No, it seems to have gone quiet, Jim, and that makes me very suspicious" said Charlie as he bent forward over his untidy desk and scratched the stubble on his chin.

"I'm listening, Charlie."

"Well, for a start, lifting sparklers like the Hudson diamonds, normally leads to rumours and they're 'aint none!"

"Go on."

"A professional would have got rid of them by now to some underhand cutter in Hatton Garden to break them up and would be passing the word of his success over a few drinks, somewhere about here" said Charlie.

"With a pocket full of money" said Hadley.

"Yes, Jim, but as I say, nothing and I would have heard, believe me."

"And an amateur, a chancer, wouldn't know what to do with such valuable lift."

"True, he'd have panicked, and then we'd all have known, quick as you like."

"What do you think, Charlie?"

"Could be a fraud, Jim."

"Inside job for the insurance?"

"Crossed my mind, Jim."

"It will now cross mine, Charlie."

"I'll keep the old ear to the ground, so come and see me next week" said Charlie and Hadley nodded before saying 'goodbye' to the old man. The detectives hailed a cab which hurried them along the busy, gas lit streets to Cavendish Square.

The butler made them wait in the hallway whilst he informed Mr Hudson of their arrival. He eventually re-appeared and announced "the master will see you now." The two detectives were ushered into the spacious and well lit drawing room where Mr and Mrs Hudson were in the company of a strikingly beautiful young woman and a smartly dressed, dark haired man of 'Mediterranean' appearance. Mr Hudson stood with his back to the roaring fire whilst Mrs Hudson sat with the female guest on a plush couch and the man sat opposite in a wing backed chair.

"The police, sir" announced the butler with disdain.

"Good afternoon, Mr Hudson…. Madam" Hadley smiled and gave a little bow.

"I hope it is, Inspector" replied Hudson.

"Indeed, sir."

"What news then?" asked Hudson impatiently.

"I wonder if you would prefer our discussions to be in private, sir?" asked Hadley.

"Oh, no, Inspector, we all want to hear your news" said Mrs Hudson.

"As you wish, Madam" replied Hadley with a slight nod of his head.

"I do wish it, and so do our guests, Count Castellini and his wife will be enthralled by what you have to say" said Mrs Hudson.

"Really, Madam?"

"Yes, the Count and Countess are very renowned in France and share a fascination with Scotland Yard" replied Mrs Hudson, enjoying the limelight.

"I am pleased to hear it."

"Indeed you should be, the Count has connections of the highest order with the police in Genoa and the Countess is a member of the famous Roguefort family, they're in shipping, but I don't expect you've heard of them, Inspector" preened Mrs Hudson.

"On the contrary, Madam, I know that Monsieur Michel Roguefort is the head of that auspicious family…"

"He is my uncle" interrupted the Countess in a delightful French accent, whilst Mrs Hudson looked stunned.

"You surprise me, Inspector" said Mrs Hudson.

"I often surprise people, Madam, sometimes in the most unexpected way" smiled Hadley whilst Cooper tried to hide his grin. Mrs Hudson was not amused and fixed the Inspector with a sharp stare.

"Really" she said in a flat tone.

"As you are famous in the world of shipping, Countess, you probably know Mr Robert Walker of the Walker Shipping Line" said Hadley.

"Oui, I do."

"That gentleman is presently staying in London with Sir Robert Cavendish" said Hadley and that caused a look of horror on the face of Mrs Hudson.

"You seem remarkably well informed about society, Inspector" said Mrs Hudson.

"We do our best to keep ourselves up to the mark, Madam" replied Hadley.

"Indeed" she glared.

"My wife and I are travelling to Boston for Christmas and we shall be calling on the Walker family whilst we are there" said the Count in a thick Italian accent.

"How very nice, sir, do you plan to stay long in Boston?" asked Hadley, his mind racing with the information he had been given by the Count.

"Our return from America is not yet finalised, we have to visit many of our family's friends in Boston, you understand" replied the Count with a smile.

"Indeed, sir" replied Hadley.

"Let us get back to the matter in hand, Inspector" said Mr Hudson in an impatient tone.

"Of course, sir, we have been making progress with the investigation and this very afternoon we had discussions with our undercover agent…"

"Yes, yes, Inspector, but what I want to know is, are you any closer to recovering my wife's jewellery?" interrupted Mr Hudson.

"Closer than we were, sir."

"Well I've offered a substantial reward…"

"So I understand, sir" interrupted Hadley in a sharp tone.

"You sound as if you don't approve, Inspector!"

"Not for me to comment, sir."

"Well somebody has got to do something positive" said Hudson angrily.

"We're always taking positive action, sir."

"My wife has simply got to have her diamonds to wear at our Christmas party, so, I have advised my contact at Lloyds, who insure the jewellery, to prepare to meet my claim and I have advised Asprey's to select diamonds to make an exact copy of the stolen necklace, and it must be ready by Christmas" said Mr

Hudson firmly and his wife preened herself on hearing that.

"I understand, sir."

"Do you, Inspector, as I sometimes wonder!" Hadley waited for a few moments before replying, conscious that everyone's eyes were upon him.

"I think that our discussions are finished for the moment, sir, so I wish you all good evening and I will be in touch as soon as I have something to report."

"The Commissioner will hear of your lamentably slow progress, Inspector."

"Indeed, I am sure that is so, sir, but he's used to it" replied Hadley and he gave a slight nod of his head. He and Cooper left the room with Hudson and his wife open mouthed with astonishment.

In the Hansom, as it made its way through the dark, busy streets to the Yard, Hadley discussed the information that the Count had given away.

"They're off to Boston for a golden Christmas, Sergeant."

"Or so they think, sir."

"Precisely, now, are they the masterminds behind all this or is it controlled by Michel Roguefort himself, and they are just players in this tomfoolery?"

"That will take time to investigate, sir."

"Indeed it will, and we must start by contacting our opposite numbers in Genoa and Boston."

"Right, sir."

"We'll ask the Chief Inspector to do that, he's good at paperwork, that's why he's a Chief." Cooper laughed out loud and Hadley smiled to himself.

"What about contacting the Turks, sir?"

"This is a tricky situation and I think I'm going to have to ask the Commissioner to do that through our embassy in Istanbul."

"What if the Turks deny all knowledge of the theft, sir?"

"Hard to say, but if they do, the Bank of England will have acquired more gold reserves and I'm sure that they will agree that you can never have too much gold" replied Hadley and Cooper laughed. They remained silent for a while, each deep in thought, as the Hansom continued its journey along the damp, cobbled streets.

"This Hudson case is an unwanted distraction, sir."

"It is, unless it is linked in some way, Sergeant."

"How can that be possible, sir?"

"I don't know yet, but I have some thoughts on the matter."

"Such as, sir?"

"Mr Hudson is in a damned fine hurry to get an identical necklace made using the insurance money."

"Yes, sir, he wants it for Christmas, he's said that clearly."

"I know, but I'm suspicious and possibly Charlie is right, it is an insurance fraud."

"Really, sir?"

"Yes, if he has taken the original necklace, he will be able to have it cut up and the diamonds sold piece meal."

"Yes, indeed, sir, but how might that be connected to the gold robbery?"

"I'm not sure yet, Sergeant, but I am giving it a great deal of thought, it is such a coincidence that the Count and his wife are staying with the Hudson's, prior to their trip to Boston."

"I wondered about that, sir."

"Good man, keep wondering" said Hadley with a smile as the Hansom pulled up outside the Yard. They worked for several hours writing reports on both cases, stimulated by pots of George's tea. It was after eight o'clock when they all said 'goodnight' and left the office to return to their respective homes.

Alice made her husband welcome with a warm kiss, a roaring fire in the parlour and a late supper of beef stew with dumplings. After the meal and several pints of stout the weary Inspector spent a little time talking to his children before they retired. It was passed eleven o'clock when Hadley finally slipped into bed with his wife.

"Only God knows what I would do without you, Alice" he said as he snuggled up to her in their warm bed.

"It's nice to be appreciated, my dear" she replied before kissing him gently on his lips as he closed his eyes and drifted off into a deep sleep.

CHAPTER 7

Hadley arrived at the Yard by eight o'clock and was pleased to see Cooper at his desk going over the reports written the previous night.

"Any further thoughts on what we've prepared for the Chief, Sergeant?"

"Not really, sir."

"In what direction do you think our investigations should now move?"

"We should try and ascertain when the Count and his wife are leaving for America, just in case they are delaying the trip for some reason…"

"Well done, Sergeant, my thoughts precisely" interrupted Hadley and Cooper smiled.

"I think we should also make inquiries at the jeweller's to see exactly what Mr Hudson has ordered for a replacement and we should contact the authorities in Rotterdam to find out what Captain Lefevre has been up to, sir."

"We will ask the Chief to do that, it will take his mind off the Hudson case for a moment" Hadley smiled.

"Right, sir."

A pot of tea was ordered from George whilst Hadley made plans for the rest of the day.

The reports were placed on the Chief Inspector's desk at midday by Hadley, who thought that the poor man looked decidedly harassed.

"I hope to God you recover the Hudson diamonds in the next week or so, Hadley, she's driving the Commissioner mad with daily letters of complaint about police inactivity!"

"I believe she has a touch of Lady MacBeth about her, sir."

"What a dreadful thing to say, Hadley!"

"Yes, sir, but regrettably true" replied the Inspector.

"It will be the end of the month soon and then only twenty five days to Christmas" said Bell as he clasped his hand to his worried brow.

"Yes, indeed, sir, but although I appreciate the seriousness of the diamond theft and the effect it will undoubtedly have on London society, I think that the bullion case with the murders of two men is even more serious" said Hadley.

"Nonsense, man, how can the death of two drunken French sailors possibly compare with the theft of valuable diamonds from the home of a renowned London Banker?"

"But, sir…"

"Enough, Hadley, you must understand the position of the Commissioner in all this and besides, we've recovered the gold and have it safe in the Bank."

"True, sir, but…"

"No 'buts' today, Hadley, leave me to read your reports and worry about all the consequences, the Press are having a field day with this, so you had better be quick about recovering the diamonds or at least make some arrests!"

"Yes, sir."

"The Commissioner demands action!"

"Yes, sir, but I must advise you confidentially, that the theft may be an insurance fraud." Chief Inspector Bell sat back in his chair with a stunned look on his face, mouth wide open.

"Good God, man, do you know what you're saying?"

"I do, sir, and I'll keep you informed of all the developments as they occur, meanwhile, after you have read my full report and recommendations, please contact the Turkish authorities through our Ambassador in Instanbul, the Boston Police Department and the harbour authorities in Rotterdam, good day, sir" Hadley smiled and left the office before the Chief could reply.

The detectives took another early lunch at the 'Kings Head' in Whitechapel, where the bar was unusually busy due to the incessant rain and cold wind that whipped around the cobbled streets outside.

"Two pints of stout and hot pasties today, Vera" said Hadley as he and Cooper at last reached the bar. The bar maid nodded as she handed a lighterman his wet change before pulling the stouts and said "I'll bring the pasties over in a minute."

"We will never find anywhere to sit, sir" said Cooper.

"Alright, Sergeant, pay Vera and we'll stand here and have lunch." Cooper nodded and felt for the money in his pocket. They supped at the stout and Hadley nodded to one or two of the men he recognised before the hot meat pasties arrived. They had just finished eating when Agnes and Florrie arrived in the smoke filled bar. Agnes saw Hadley and pushed her way through the customers with Florrie in tow.

"Hello, Jim… Sergeant" she smiled.

"Hello, my lovely ladies, how are you today?" Hadley beamed as Agnes smiled and did a little curtsey.

"All the better for seeing you both" she replied.

"That reply calls for two sixpenny gins, Sergeant, if you please." Cooper smiled, nodded and waved at the overworked Vera.

"Thanks, Jim" said Agnes.

"It's a cold day out there and you both look pale, I think you could do with hot pasties to warm you up" said Hadley as he reached into his pocket for some coins.

"Oh, thank you, Jim, you are a sweetheart" said Agnes and Florrie smiled.

"Sergeant, ask Vera for two pasties" and the Inspector handed two shillings to an amazed Cooper who stared at the coins.

"Right, sir."

"Now ladies, any news for me?" asked Hadley.

"No, not really, Jim, except Florrie heard one of the girls say that her bloke had done a little job up west for some gent and been handsomely paid for his troubles" replied Agnes.

"Tell me more, Florrie dear" Hadley smiled as Cooper handed the gins to the women. Just then someone at the bar pushed against Agnes who became squashed up against the Inspector and he felt her well rounded bosoms through his coat.

"Oh, my, this is cosy, Jim" she smiled.

"Now, now, Agnes, behave, I'm a married man you know" he smiled and Cooper laughed.

"I know, I know, Jim, you never let me forget" she replied.

"And if I wasn't married, Agnes, you'd be the very first lady in my life with Florrie a close second" said Hadley and he winked at Florrie who blushed.

"Oh, you are awful, Jim" said Agnes with a laugh before she sipped her gin.

"Now tell me, Florrie, about this bloke who did this job" said

Hadley.

"Well, it's only what I heard, I don't know the truth of it" said Florrie.

"Never mind, dear, just say what you heard."

"It's Betsy Woodman's bloke, Harry, it seems someone asked him to go up west to this posh bloke's house and pretend to break in" she said plaintively.

"Go on, Florrie."

"That's all I know, sir, honest, I swear" she replied.

"That's alright, now then, where will we find this 'Harry'?" asked the Inspector.

"Normally he drinks in the 'Blind Beggar' but I've not seen him recently" replied Florrie.

"Will Betsy Woodman know where he is?"

"Yes, I think so."

"Take us to Betsy after lunch, if you please" said Hadley.

"No, I can't do that, she'd know that I'd snitched on her" replied Florrie nervously.

"Right, just tell us where she lives" said Hadley.

"She's got rooms at number twelve, in Gypsy Lane."

"Is that where she entertains gentlemen?"

"Yes."

"The Sergeant and I will call upon her later" said Hadley.

"Lucky girl" murmured Agnes and Hadley heard her comment and cocked his head to one side and gave Agnes an old fashioned look with his twinkling blue eyes. The hot pasties arrived and the two women devoured them with relish. They stayed chatting for a while and Hadley treated them all to another round of drinks before giving Agnes a quick kiss on the cheek and pressing a guinea into her hand, whispering "take care of yourselves".

Hadley knocked on the door of number twelve, Gypsy Lane and waited for it to open. It was a while before he heard movement and then the door opened just a little, a pale faced woman peered out.

"Yes?" she asked.

"Are you Betsy Woodman?"

"Yes" she replied and looked both men up and down before swinging the door wide open.

"I'm …." began Hadley.

"Never mind who you are dear, just come on in, I never normally give relief to more than one gent at a time, but I'll make an exception today, it'll cost you double, mind" she grinned.

"I'm afraid you misunderstand" said Hadley as he stepped through into the small, untidy room, followed by Cooper.

"No dear, there's no misunderstanding, I know what you gents are after, so let's get down to the business in hand, I normally charge seven and six for…"

"We're police officers…" interrupted Hadley.

"Oh my Gawd!" shrieked Betsy as she put her hand over her mouth.

"I'd like you to help us with our inquiries" said Hadley as Betsy sank down on to the unmade bed in the corner.

"I don't know nothing, sir, I'm just a woman…"

"I know what you are Betsy Woodman, but I'm here to find out about a man called 'Harry', do you know him?"

"You mean my Harry?"

"Yes."

"What's he done now?"

"Nothing serious, I only want to speak to him to eliminate him from my investigations."

"Well, his name is Harry Grover, he works down the docks" she replied.

"Does he live here with you?"

"Sometimes, but I've not seen him for days now, so I don't know where he is" she said in an anxious tone.

"I've been told that he did some work for a gentleman who lives in the west end, what do you know about that?"

"Nothing really, he said some bloke in the pub asked him to go up west and meet a gent who wanted a locked door opened, that's all I know" she replied.

"Did he meet the man?"

"Yes, and he got handsomely paid for his troubles" she replied.

"Then Harry disappeared?"

"As I said, I haven't seen him since, I've got an idea he's gone back to his wife 'an kids in Bermondsey" she said glumly.

"Do you have the address?"

"No, for Gawd's sake, why would I have it?" she asked in an angry tone.

"Indeed, well, Betsy, thank you for all your help" said Hadley.

The two detectives left Betsy Woodman and walked quickly up the Lane before turning into Thames Street, where Cooper hailed a cab.

"Where to, sir?" asked the cab driver.

"Asprey's in Bond Street, if you please" said Hadley as he stepped up into the Hansom.

When they were on their way, Hadley said " I think it's time we confronted Mr Hudson with some facts and see if we can flush him out."

"You think he's planned an insurance fraud, sir?" asked Cooper.

"Possibly, Sergeant, and we may know more when we've made inquiries at the jewellers."

They arrived in the prestigious shop where a delicate, well spoken young man approached them.

"May I help you gentlemen?" he enquired in a soft, hushed voice.

"Yes, we'd like to see the manager please" replied Hadley.

"In what connection, sir?"

"Theft and possibly fraud, we're police officers from Scotland Yard, so, please let the manager know we are here" replied Hadley as the young man recoiled visibly at the very notions of criminal activity.

"Please wait here, I'll see if Mr Digby is free" he stammered. The detectives looked around the shop and were impressed by the velvet pads full of glittering diamond rings, brooches and necklaces displayed in splendid cabinets.

"Not a shop to bring your wife to if you are only on policeman's pay, Sergeant."

"No, sir, the visit would surely end in her disappointment" replied Cooper and Hadley laughed just as Mr Digby approached.

"Can I help you, gentlemen?" he asked nervously.

"I hope so, Mr Digby, do you have an office where we may discuss matters?"

"Yes, of course, please follow me." The detectives followed the manager upstairs to a spacious office which was neat and tidy.

Hadley made the introductions and Digby waved the officers to plush seats opposite his large desk.

"You may have read in the Press that the Hudson diamonds have been stolen" said Hadley.

"Yes, Inspector."

"Now, Mr Hudson has told me that he plans to order a new, identical necklace from Asprey's, to be ready for his wife to wear at their Christmas party, can you confirm that, Mr Digby?"

"Yes, Inspector, that is so" replied the manager.

"Mr Hudson has said that he has instructed you to start selecting the diamonds, is that true?" Mr Digby looked uncomfortable at that and began to sweat a little.

"Well…" he began and Hadley knew that something was not quite right.

"Go on, Mr Digby" said Hadley.

"I can't say any more, Inspector, we pride ourselves at Asprey's on our client confidentiality…"

"Do you, sir, well I can inform you that at the Yard, we do the same."

"Really?"

"Yes, we try and keep the names of people that we arrest for obstructing police inquiries in confidence!"

"Oh, dear God" whispered the manager.

"But the Press always seem to find out, then it's all over the newspapers" said Hadley with a devilish smile.

"Oh, dear, oh, dear… look, Inspector, you must understand my position…"

"What position is that, sir?"

"I have our clients to think of…"

"The courts take a very dim view of anybody who attempts to pervert the course of justice" said Hadley, turning the screw.

"Oh, dear God…"

"And I don't hesitate to drag those miscreants in to face the judges, who are always less than lenient in the matter." At that, Mr Digby began to mop his forehead, which was bathed in sweat.

"This will be the end of me, oh, dear God" he wailed.

"Come, come, Mr Digby, telling the truth never harmed anyone" said Hadley and he waited for the terrified man to compose himself.

"Mr Hudson came to the shop and did as you say, but he asked me to make replicas of the stones…" and he then hesitated for a moment, whispering "in paste…"

"Tell me everything, Mr Digby, and leave nothing out" said Hadley in a menacing tone.

"Well, as I say, he asked me to replicate the stones in paste and mount them identically as the original, his reason was that some thief or other would surely break into his home once again and steal the necklace, he said that as the police were so hopelessly inefficient that the thief would never be caught, so he was determined that no miscreant would ever profit again from his misfortune" said the manager, now sweating profusely. Hadley sat stony faced for a while as the criticism of his profession sank in and then said "go on, Mr Digby."

"There's no more to tell, Inspector…"

"Are you certain, sir?"

"Yes, he just said that he wanted the necklace ready for his collection on the twentieth of December."

"Thank you for your assistance, Mr Digby."

"My pleasure, Inspector."

"I would be obliged if you would keep our conversation strictly confidential, sir" said Hadley in a forceful tone.

"Yes, of course, Inspector, you have my word" stammered the relieved manager.

"Good day, sir" smiled Hadley as he stood up and left the office, followed by Cooper.

Outside the shop, Cooper hailed a cab and asked Hadley "where to, sir?"

"Number twelve, Cavendish Square, Sergeant."

"Right, sir."

"I think it is now time we had a few words with Mr Hudson."

"Yes, sir."

The butler opened the door and when he saw the detectives, took a deep breath before asking "may I help you, gentlemen?"

"Yes, I'd like to see Mr Hudson, please" replied Hadley.

"I'm afraid you can't, sir" came the haughty reply.

"And why is that?"

"The Master and Mrs Hudson are not at home."

"Where are they?"

"They have retired to their house in the country for the weekend, sir."

"I'd be obliged to know where that is."

"The Master owns Pangbourne House, on the river at Pangbourne" replied the butler.

"That's in Berkshire."

"I believe it is, sir."

"When do you expect Mr and Mrs Hudson to return to London?" asked Hadley.

"I can't say for certain, sir, possibly Tuesday or Wednesday of next week."

"Has the Count and his wife joined them at Pangbourne?"

"They have, sir, along with other guests."

"Do you know who?"

"No, sir, but I am sure that they will be prominent people in London society" replied the butler in a haughty tone.

"Thank you for your help" said Hadley.

"Will there be anything else, sir?"

"Not for the moment, good afternoon." The butler slammed the door as Hadley and Cooper turned and walked down the steps to the pavement.

"What now, sir?"

"Back to the Yard, Sergeant, and while I tell the Chief what our inquiries have revealed, you'll find out the times of trains from Paddington to Reading and George can make a pot of tea!"

"Are we going to Pangbourne tonight, sir?"

"No, Sergeant, we'll set off first thing tomorrow, and that will do nicely."

"Right, sir" replied Cooper with a smile and Hadley gave him a wink.

Chief Inspector Bell face was contorted with a mixture of fear and misunderstanding as Hadley told him of his suspicions.

"But the man is a leading Banker, a pillar of London society connected at the highest level…" wailed the Chief.

"I realise that, sir, but I believe that Mr Hudson is attempting to carry out an insurance fraud…"

"Why, in heavens name?"

"I don't know, sir."

"The man is reputed to have a substantial fortune, why on earth should he do such a thing?" demanded the Chief as he looked from side to side, hoping for an inspirational answer.

"I really can't say, sir, but I do know that crime is not the monopoly of the poor."

"Hadley, if you're wrong about this, you'll have to consider your position, you do realise that, don't you?"

"Possibly, sir."

"No 'possibly' about it, Hadley, the Commissioner will demand your head on a plate, and probably mine too!"

"I am sure that is true, sir, but I have to do my duty as I see it, and I would be failing if I did not follow the investigation to the very end" said Hadley.

"Oh, God, if only I'd given this case to someone else…"

"I did ask to be relieved of it, sir…"

"I know, I know, you don't have to remind me" interrupted the Chief testily.

"I believed that the gold bullion murder case was more than enough for Cooper and me to contend with at the moment, sir" said Hadley.

"Yes, yes, but we're woefully stretched as usual and sacrifices have to be made."

"Indeed, sir."

"What do you plan to do next, Hadley?"

"Go to Pangbourne tomorrow, sir, and see what Mr Hudson has to say when I confront him."

"Oh, dear God!"

"I'll be discreet, sir."

"You do know that I don't sleep anymore?"

"I was not aware of that, sir."

"Well, you know now, Hadley!"

"Yes, sir."

"Please leave me and let me worry about this in peace."

"Yes, sir."

Hadley returned to his office, sat behind his desk, and whilst sipping tea discussed the plans for the journey and the Hudson interview.

"We'll catch the eight thirty from Paddington and then take a four wheeler out to Pangbourne, Sergeant."

"Yes, sir."

"So we'll meet at the station ticket office at eight o'clock sharp."

"Right, sir."

"Now once we get to Pangbourne we'll have to be very discreet and the questioning will have to be diplomatic in the extreme."

"Of course, sir."

"Take everything down in your notebook, Sergeant."

"Yes, sir."

"Don't miss one word."

"I won't, sir."

"And the Count and his wife are sure to be there, so keep a careful eye on them."

"Yes, sir."

"Good man."

"Will be coming back to London, Saturday afternoon, sir?"

"Without doubt, Sergeant, I will remind you that I'm entertaining my friend, Bill and his wife for lunch on Sunday."

"Yes, sir."

"I'm not missing that, whatever happens!"

CHAPTER 8

The detectives arrived at Reading station at ten o'clock and hired a four wheeler to take them out to Pangbourne. The weather was fine and they both enjoyed the unhurried journey, admiring the gentle, green hills that surround the meandering River Thames as it flows down towards London.

"This is very pleasant, Sergeant."

"Indeed, sir."

"We should have more days out like this."

"Only if duty allows, sir."

"Yes, I really think that I should get the Chief Inspector out with us, I'm sure it would calm his nerves."

"Not always, sir" replied Cooper and Hadley laughed.

"No, I suppose you're right, he'd hardly approve of Agnes, Florrie and dear old Charlie."

"No, sir, and he'd frown at early lunches in the 'Kings Head'" grinned Cooper.

"Possibly."

As they reached the outskirts of Pangbourne, the driver turned off the Oxford Road onto a narrow road that went up a gently sloping hill. The two horses pulled hard and the four wheeler eventually reached the top of the hill from where the view of the Thames valley was simply breathtaking.

"My word, look at that, Sergeant."

"Yes, sir, it's magnificent."

"England's green and pleasant land..." At that moment the four wheeler turned into a private driveway and through large wrought iron gates, standing open.

"This is Pangbourne House, gentlemen" said the driver as Hadley glanced at his fob watch. It was just after eleven o'clock.

"Just in time for tea" mused Hadley with a smile. The driveway swung round to the left and at that point the house came into view. It was a large Georgian, pillared house in the traditional style and as the four wheeler approached the steps to the portico, Hadley looked to his right to admire the spectacular view. They alighted and asked the driver to withdraw and come back at two o'clock sharp in order that they could catch the return train to Paddington at three thirty. With a nod the driver pulled away over the gravel drive as the detectives mounted the steps to the front door. They turned to admire the view once more before Cooper rang the bell for attention. Eventually the door was opened by a tall, gaunt butler, who looked them up and down before saying "tradesmen round the back" and Hadley realised that he must buy a new top hat and great coat to replace his battered and well worn items of clothing.

"I would like to see Mr Hudson, please" said Hadley, ignoring the remark.

"And who are you, pray?" asked the gaunt one.

"Inspector Hadley and Sergeant Cooper from New Scotland Yard, that's in London" replied Hadley as he watched the butler's face change to a pale shade of grey.

"I apologise, gentlemen, do come in and I will inform the master."

"Thank you" replied Hadley with a smile as he stepped into the marble floored hallway. The butler disappeared through double doors and the two detectives looked around at the opulence of Mr Hudson's country house. The large stairway, between two pillars, swept up to the next floor and a magnificent chandelier was poised above the centre of the hallway. Portraits of family members adorned the walls and cream drapes hung in profusion, gathered back with matching restraints giving a rich, warm feeling to the interior. French half tables were placed against the walls with mirrors above for effect and they gave an illusion of even more space to the grand entrance. The butler re-appeared and nodded "this way, Gentlemen." They followed him into the drawing room where the Hudson's and their guests were seated. The Count and Countess were there along with several others whom Hadley did not know. Mr Hudson stood up as the butler announced them and Hadley made a slight nod of his head.

"What the devil are you doing here, Inspector?" demanded Hudson.

"Good morning, Sir, Madam, I have some news concerning the robbery and as I promised, last time we met, that I would inform you immediately, I am pleased to do so" said Hadley.

"It must be very important to bring you all the way down from

London" said Mrs Hudson in a sarcastic tone.

"I think so, Madam, and of course, it saves you having to write to the Commissioner today" replied Hadley.

"Now look here…" began Mr Hudson.

"We have a prime suspect and expect to have him in custody very soon" interrupted Hadley and they both looked astonished at that.

"Really?" asked Mr Hudson in an anxious tone.

"Yes, sir, and it comes about after our intense and fast moving inquiries" said Hadley and Cooper smiled inwardly as he thought about Charlie, Agnes, Florrie and Betsy Woodman. Certainly the Inspector had a way with words as well as a lively imagination.

"Who is this damned fellow?" asked a red faced man, in his fifties with bushy, grey side whiskers. Hadley looked at the man for a moment before asking "may I enquire who you are, sir?"

"Inspector, you go too far!" exclaimed Mr Hudson.

"Indeed, sir, but just for the record."

"This gentleman is Sir John Simmons, chairman of our Bank" announced Mr Hudson as the red faced man preened.

"I am pleased to make your acquaintance, Sir John, and may I ask what the name of your Bank is?" asked Hadley.

"Why do you want to know?" inquired Sir John who now stood up, a little unsteadily and Hadley thought that the knight was probably more than partial to a drink or two.

"Just curious, sir."

"Well, you know what they say, curiosity killed the cat" replied Sir John with a grin.

"As I am not a cat, sir, I'm not unduly concerned at the moment" replied Hadley and Cooper tried to hide his grin by looking down at his notebook.

"You're damned impertinent, sir!" said Sir John as a grey haired woman sitting close tut tutted.

"Possibly, sir, but, for the record" persisted Hadley.

"Tell him, Anthony" said Sir John angrily.

"Sir John is the chairman of the Anglo American Bank in London!" said Mr Hudson angrily.

"Thank you, Sir, and is the bank affiliated with any other Bank, in America for instance?"

"Yes, Boston First National, if you must know" replied Mr

Hudson.

"Very interesting" Hadley smiled.

"Now then, Inspector… whatever your name is…" began Sir John.

"Hadley, Sir, James Hadley" interrupted the Inspector with a smile.

"Who is this miscreant you hope to arrest for this dreadful crime?" asked Sir John.

"His name is Harry Grover, Sir" replied Hadley and he watched Mr Hudson's face become suddenly pale.

"Is he known to the police?" asked Sir John.

"Oh, yes, Sir, we'll soon pick him up and when he comes under pressure from me, he'll furnish us with everything we want to know about the robbery" replied Hadley as he noticed the sweat on Mr Hudson's forehead and the impassive look on his wife's countenance.

"Is that so, Inspector?" asked Mr Hudson.

"Yes, indeed, Sir."

"How do you know he's not escaped abroad?" enquired Mrs Hudson.

"Because he's been seen in his usual haunts in Whitechapel with too much money in his pocket, spending it in the pubs, and his wife in Bermondsey is expecting him home any minute now, that's where my men will pick him up" smiled Hadley and he noticed the look of anxiety on the faces of both Mr Hudson and his wife. He thought 'they're both in this up to their necks'.

"Will you recover the diamonds?" inquired Sir John.

"Without doubt, sir, I believe that they are very close at hand" replied Hadley.

"Well, that's extremely good news" said Mr Hudson nervously.

"Indeed, sir, now, may I have just a quick word with you in private?" asked Hadley with a smile and he watched Mr Hudson blanche.

"Yes, yes, of course, Inspector, we'll go into the library" stammered Mr Hudson.

"Should I come too?" asked his wife nervously.

"No, Madam, that will not be necessary, thank you" replied Hadley which seemed to make her even more anxious. Hadley and Cooper followed the Banker out of the drawing room and across the hallway into the plush library. Mr Hudson sat behind a large desk and invited the detectives to sit opposite.

"Now, Sir, as I said a moment ago, we expect to recover the diamonds at any time now" said Hadley.

"That's good news, Inspector."

"Yes, it is, so you will not need to purchase the paste replicas that you've ordered from Mr Digby at Asprey's, Sir" Hadley smiled and Mr Hudson looked as if he had just been shot. They all sat in silence for several moments while the Banker attempted to get his thoughts in some form of order. Hadley decided to place the man under more pressure.

"As you may now realise, Sir, we are very thorough in our investigations and leave no stone unturned to get at the truth" smiled Hadley.

"Yes, indeed, Inspector, and you must be commended for your diligence" replied Hudson anxiously.

"Thank you, Sir."

"What happens next, Inspector?"

"We'll arrest Harry Grover, find out everything we want to know and when you return to London you can inform your insurers at Lloyds that an arrest is imminent followed by the recovery of the diamonds, Sir."

"Well, I hope it all goes to plan, Inspector."

"Oh, it will, Sir, I can assure you." Mr Hudson looked terrified and Hadley just sat in silence watching the Banker suffer. Before anything more was said the door suddenly opened and Mrs Hudson entered.

"I'm sorry to disturb you, but I must ask if you would like to stay for luncheon, Inspector?" she asked with a forced smile.

"How kind, Madam, the Sergeant and I would be delighted."

"Good, that's all arranged then" she said nervously as she looked at her husband for some clue as to what had transpired. Hadley watched them both and thought that his comment about Lady Macbeth was accurate. When she had left the room, Mr Hudson asked " is there anything else, Inspector?"

"Not at the moment, Sir."

"Good, will you join me in a sherry before lunch?"

"Certainly will, Sir."

"I thought you were not allowed to drink on duty, Inspector?"

"We're not, Sir, but we're off duty at lunch time."

"I'm slightly mystified, Inspector."

"Don't worry, Sir, believe me, it is a police matter, only understood by those in the force."

Mr Hudson looked confused as he led the detectives back into the drawing room. The guests looked at the Banker expecting him somehow to reveal what had been said privately. He just smiled and rang for the butler, who came quickly to the room and at his master's command, poured sherry for all the guests. Hadley watched Mrs Hudson carefully and noticed that she kept giving her husband, hard and imploring looks, to which he did not respond. The detectives sat quietly and listened to the general small talk, mostly from Sir John about the general state of the country coupled with falling standards in every walk of life, to which the captive audience murmured agreement at the appropriate moments. At last they were summoned for lunch and everyone followed Sir John and Mrs Hudson through to the spacious dining room. Hadley and Cooper were seated opposite each other at the bottom end of the table. The meal consisted of vegetable soup, followed by beef stew with apple pie and custard as desert. A full blooded Burgundy accompanied the meal and both detectives enjoyed a glass. The wine loosened tongues and Hadley, anxious to gain more information, listened to the Countess telling the guests about her impending trip to America. At the right moment when there was a pause in the conversation, he asked "when do you propose to sail to America, Countess?"

"In about a week's time, I think" she replied and paused for a moment and then said to her husband "when do we sail, Giovanni?"

"Next Saturday, at midday" he replied with a smile.

"Oh, oui, I remember now, it is Thursday that we have to meet our ship and then we go to America" she said loudly.

"Your ship, Countess?" inquired Hadley.

"Oui, it's coming from Rotterdam with some things for us to take to Boston" she smiled.

"Is it coming to London?" asked Hadley, his mind racing.

"Non, I don't know, where is it coming to, Giovanni?"

"I think it's docking at Tilbury, but Anthony will tell us,

because he's arranged everything" replied the Count as he looked at Mr Hudson who face became pale once more. Hadley looked at the Banker and smiled, waiting for the confirmation.

"Yes, it will dock at Tilbury, sometime on Thursday and then the captain will telegraph me at the bank when it has arrived" he said in an anxious tone.

"What's this you've arranged at the Bank?" asked Sir John as he fixed a disapproving gaze on Hudson.

"Er, just a little facility at the office to assist the Count and Countess, before they sail for America, Sir John" replied Mr Hudson with a smile.

"You can tell me all about it when I come to the Bank on Wednesday, Anthony" said Sir John firmly as Mrs Hudson looked anxiously at her husband.

"Of course, Sir John" he replied.

"Will you be going down to Tilbury, Countess?" asked Hadley.

"Oh, oui, I love to see our ships and meet the captains, they're so brave, you know" she replied sweetly.

"Indeed, Countess."

"Oui, Captain Lefevre is one of my favourites, he's coming from Rotterdam you know" she said and nodded her head.

"How nice" smiled Hadley.

"He's been sailing our ships for many years and my uncle says he's the best captain in the fleet" she smiled. The Burgundy had certainly made the Countess very talkative and Hadley saw that the Count along with the Hudson's were not best pleased that she was imparting so much information. Her husband attempted to change the conversation.

"Tell everyone how Captain Rousseau saved a Maltese ship from sinking outside the harbour at Valetta, my dear" said the Count.

"Oh, oui, it happened a year ago, and it was only the bravery of the captain that saved all the Maltese crew from certain death…" she began as Hadley had heard enough and looked at his pocket watch. It was almost two o'clock.

"Please forgive me for interrupting you, Countess, but we must leave now if we're to catch the train back to London" said Hadley and the Hudson's looked relieved.

"Yes, of course, Inspector, thank you for coming down with

such good news today" said Mr. Hudson.

"Thank you for your help, Sir, and for a splendid lunch, most kind" Hadley smiled as he stood and gave a little bow to them all. Mr Hudson followed the detectives to the front door and wished them a safe journey back to London. The four wheeler was waiting outside and the policemen climbed aboard before they set off for the station. Hadley remained quiet, deep in thought, all the way back to Reading, and Cooper knew that it was best to keep silent when the Inspector was pre-occupied. Once on the train and alone in a compartment Hadley asked " what did you make of that little masquerade, Sergeant?"

"As usual, sir, more questions than answers."

"Too true, I am just wondering what the links are between the Hudson's and the Count and his wife."

"Do you think the Count was responsible for the bullion robbery?"

"Possibly."

"And it is certain that Captain Lefevre will be back here on Thursday."

"Yes, Sergeant, and this time he's not getting away."

"And where are the diamonds, sir?"

"I think Mr Hudson has those safely under lock and key somewhere."

"Harry Grover hasn't got them, that's for sure, sir."

"That's for sure, sergeant, now, I want you to have a good rest tomorrow because next week will keep us on our toes, believe me" said Hadley.

"Right, sir."

"It could get very nasty."

It was just midday on Sunday when Bill and Elizabeth arrived at the Hadley home in Camden. With warm handshakes and gentle kisses on proffered cheeks they were made welcome by the Inspector and his wife. A roaring fire in the parlour greeted them and Hadley began pouring drinks for all as soon as Bill and his wife had taken off their coats.

"It's cold out there, Jim" said Bill.

"It's winter, Bill, and it will soon be Christmas" replied Hadley as he handed his friend a hot toddy.

"Cheers, nice to see you all" said Bill as he raised his glass. They all responded and Elizabeth gave a little chuckle, which amused the children. They were very fond of Elizabeth as she was a gentle and understanding woman with no airs or graces, just a caring person. She and Bill were happy and well matched. They had married later in life and had no children, so they doted on young Arthur and his sister, Anne.

Lunch was splendid and the roast beef with all the trimmings was particularly good. The full, rich Burgundy that accompanied the meal relaxed everyone and after the apple pie, followed by cheese and biscuits, Arthur prevailed on his father to tell stories about his days as a young constable.

"Must I?" asked Hadley.

"Yes, Papa" replied Arthur and Anne pleaded "yes, they're so funny."

"Funny 'ha ha' or funny 'peculiar'?" asked Hadley with a smile.

"Both, my dear" said Alice and they all laughed.

"Well" and Hadley paused for effect "I remember one of my first arrests in the Minories, just by the Tower, it was a man who was known to be a bit of a ruffian, he'd stolen some pocket watches from a jeweller's and run off, I was close by, and after being alerted by the shop owner, gave chase, the thief ran down towards the river with me chasing him, it was low tide and he jumped down into the mud and tried to get away but I caught him by a sewage pipe and bowled him over, he began to fight but in the end I managed to handcuff him."

"Were you covered in mud, Papa?" asked Anne.

"Mud and pooh from the sewage" replied Hadley with a grin.

"Oh, dear" said Elizabeth.

"And you've been up to your neck in it ever since!" Bill laughed.

"That's so true, Bill," replied Hadley and they laughed at that.

"Now, when I managed to get back to the station, they wouldn't let me in with my prisoner, because of the smell…"

"What did you do, Papa?" asked Arthur.

"I had to remain in the stable yard with the horses, handcuffed to the thief and wait for someone to hose both of us down with cold water!"

"Oh, dear" said Elizabeth.

"Then we had to take all our clothes off before being hosed down once again!" Both children were laughing at this as their imaginations ran riot.

"Then, with only towels to cover our dignity, I took the thief into the station and charged him with stealing the watches."

"Then what, Papa?" asked Anne.

"They sent my uniform down to the laundry and burnt the villain's clothes because they were rotten and falling to pieces" replied Hadley.

"What he do for clothes?" asked Elizabeth.

"The custody sergeant gave him a spare shirt and trousers from the stores and he stayed in those until after his appearance in court."

"What sentence did he get, Jim?" asked Bill.

"Three years hard labour."

"He got off light then" said Bill.

"Yes, the courts are becoming very lenient these days" replied Hadley.

"Indeed they are" said Bill.

"But the worse thing about it was, I was courting your mother and called that evening, Grand Mama kept complaining of a funny smell in the parlour whilst looking at me all the time!" said Hadley and they all roared at that.

Hadley told some more stories to entertain them and Jim related some of his experiences when he first went to sea as a cabin boy in the merchant marine. After a late tea, Bill and his wife said their 'goodbyes' and left the warm house to make their way home. Hadley settled down in front of the fire and fell asleep. He was woken by Anne kissing him on his cheek and whispering "goodnight, papa." He opened his eyes and saw his daughter before him, smiled and held her close, kissing her on her forehead.

"Goodnight, my little princess."

"Will you tell us more stories soon, Papa?"

"Of course" he smiled and his daughter gave him another quick kiss and left the room.

After a late supper Hadley and his wife retired to bed where he fell into a deep sleep, leaving his patient wife a little frustrated. She realised that he was under a great deal of pressure but knew that soon as it relented, her husband would meet all her needs.

CHAPTER 9

On Monday morning, Hadley and Cooper made detailed plans for the coming week before going over all the reports and evidence that they had to hand in both investigations. Hadley telegraphed Bermondsey police station at midday and requested that they try and find Harry Grover. He made it clear that he was wanted to help with inquiries at this stage and that he should be brought to Scotland Yard for interview, after his arrest. The detectives then left the office and went to the 'Kings Head' for lunch. The bar was less busy and after ordering their usual stouts and pork pie lunches they found a suitable table in the corner. It was just after one o'clock when Agnes and Florrie waltzed in. The women spotted them immediately and after the usual greetings, Cooper hurried off to the bar for two six penny gins.

"Have a good weekend, Jim?" enquired Agnes.

"Yes, after a trip down to Pangbourne on Saturday, I had a relaxing day at home with the family and friends" replied Hadley.

"You're a lucky man, Jim" she replied and Florrie nodded.

"Better be born lucky than rich" replied Hadley with a smile.

"Blimey, Jim, you're both and you don't know it!" exclaimed Agnes and Hadley laughed.

"Possibly, now then, I'm on the look out for Betsy's fellow, Harry Grover, so if either of you see him, let me know" said the Inspector.

"Jim, you won't believe this, but we've just come up from the 'Blind Beggar', and Harry is in there now with some of his mates, drinking away as if his life depends on it!" replied Agnes.

"Agnes, you're a treasure" said Hadley and leaned across giving her a quick kiss on the cheek as Cooper arrived back with the two gins.

"Say 'goodbye' to the ladies, Sergeant, we're off to the 'Blind Beggar' right now!"

"Why, sir?" queried Cooper.

"To arrest Harry Grover, if he's still there!"

"Right, sir."

As the Hansom hurried down the Whitechapel Road to the 'Blind

Beggar' pub, Hadley warned Cooper that the arrest could get out of hand and to be ready for all eventualities. When they arrived at the busy pub, they looked around the bar and spotted a group of men sitting at a table in the corner. The men were scruffily dressed and they had obviously had too much to drink. The person that appeared to be the centre of attraction was talking loudly and laughing too much. The detectives went to the bar and Hadley asked the bar man "is that Harry Grover over there?"

"Yes, sir, he's a regular, and he's been celebrating something for several days now" replied the bar man. Hadley nodded his thanks and made his way over to the men.

"Harry Grover?" Hadley enquired. There was a total silence for a moment and then Grover asked "who wants him?"

"I do."

"And who are you, mate?"

"I'm Inspector Hadley and this is Sergeant Cooper of Scotland Yard, Mr Grover." The man went pale on hearing that.

"What d'you want me for?" he asked anxiously.

"I'd like just a few words in private" replied Hadley.

"Is that all?"

"Yes, nothing serious, Mr Grover, so if you'll kindly come along with us now, I'd be obliged."

"Well, anything to oblige a couple of Bobbies, eh, lads?" he said and his drunken friends laughed whilst nodding their heads.

"Here's to you, Harry boy" said one as he raised his glass and was quickly followed by the others. Grover smiled, nodded and stood up, somewhat unsteadily and walked towards the door of the pub. Once outside, Cooper hailed a trap to take them to Scotland Yard. As the open trap pulled alongside the kerb and Hadley went to step up into it, Grover lashed out at Cooper and hit the Sergeant in the side of his head. Cooper stumbled as Grover attempted to run off but the Sergeant managed to hold on to his arm and swung the drunken man around. Hadley immediately jumped down from the trap and caught hold of Grover around his neck and forced the man to the ground.

"Now, Mr Grover, enough if you please, otherwise I shall be forced to use unpleasant methods to restrain you" said Hadley through clenched teeth.

"Alright, alright" replied Grover, somewhat shaken by

Hadley's reaction. Hadley and Cooper hauled Grover to his feet and bundled him into the back of the trap as the driver looked on, wide eyed with fright.

"Scotland Yard, driver, and hurry if you would" said Cooper. The driver nodded and set his horse off on a fast trot through the busy traffic.

Once in the interview room, Grover looked a sorry sight and was not very forthcoming with answers to Hadley's questions.

"Tell me again about the man who approached you in the pub, Grover" demanded Hadley.

"I told you more than once already, his name is Eddie, that's all I know, and says he's got a job for me up west, and if I do it right and keep my mouth shut, there's ten pounds in it for me, and that's a king's ransom, I'll be bound."

"Then what happened?"

"I went with Eddie and he showed me the place and told me that the gent who lived there wanted me to force the back door and leave it open."

"Go on."

"As I just told you, all I had to do was force the door and then scarper, and that's what I did."

"Did you get your ten pounds?" asked Hadley.

"Yeah, Eddie brought the money to the pub the next day and he told me that the gent was pleased and he'd won his bet."

"His bet?"

"Yeah, Eddie said the gent did it for a lark and had bet on it being done without no one knowing" replied Grover.

"Where was this house, Grover?"

"I dunno, up west somewhere, Eddie took me, he waited outside whilst I did the job."

"Right, Sergeant Cooper and a constable will take you to a house in Cavendish Square and I want to know if you recognise it, do you understand?"

"Yeah."

"When you get back, I'll have some more questions for you" said Hadley.

"Oh, Gawd" mumbled Grover.

"Then it will be necessary for you to point out this 'Eddie' character…"

"Oh, no, guv'nor, he swore me to keep me mouth shut and I'd rather go to prison than grass him up" interrupted Grover.

"We shall see about that" replied Hadley in a menacing tone.

"I didn't do nothing wrong, I just opened a door for Gawd's sake!" wailed Grover.

"So you say."

"Honest, guv'nor."

"Sergeant, keep him handcuffed all the time you are out and if he plays up, beat him hard" said Hadley.

"Right, sir."

"When you get back, put him a cell and come to the office."

"Yes, sir."

"Blimey, am I under arrest, guv'nor?"

"You certainly are!"

"On what charge?" asked Grover.

"I'm not sure yet, but I'll think of something by the time you return" replied Hadley as he strode from the room.

Hadley made detailed plans of his next moves to arrest Captain Lefevre as well as following the Count and his wife to Tilbury to meet the 'Arabesque'. It was after five o'clock when Cooper arrived back in the office and was just in time to share a pot of George's tea with Hadley.

"Grover recognised the house alright, sir" smiled Cooper as he sat down at his desk.

"I knew he would" nodded the Inspector.

"He said it was easy, Eddie told him it was all arranged and that the house would be empty as soon as the groom went out to the horses in the mews" said Cooper.

"It was arranged alright and no mistake" smiled Hadley.

"Time to tell the Chief, sir?"

"Not just yet, Sergeant, I want to find this 'Eddie' character, first."

"Right, sir."

"We'll let Harry Grover spend tonight in his cell and have words with him tomorrow morning, by then the alcohol should have cleared from his head and then we'll help clarify his thinking" said Hadley with a grin.

"Yes, sir" grinned Cooper.

"Now, these are the plans I've made for the week" said Hadley and he then proceeded to give Cooper all the details of the operation.

The next morning Hadley and Cooper went down to custody and interviewed a sober Harry Grover.

"Let us start all over again, Grover" said Hadley as he sat opposite the unhappy man.

"Honest guv'nor, I've told you all I know, on my life I have" wailed Grover.

"The only thing you haven't told me is the surname of 'Eddie' and where I can find him" replied Hadley firmly.

"If I knew, I'd tell you, honest, I just want to get out of here" said Grover.

"Not good enough."

"Me wife an' kids will be wondering where I am" said Grover in a plaintive voice.

"They'll have to keep wondering, because until I get some answers you're staying here, that is until I put you up in front of the magistrate" said Hadley.

"Oh, Gawd, not up before the beak, he'll deport me this time!"

"Save yourself, Grover, only you can." Harry Grover paused and gazed down thoughtfully at his clasped hands.

"This bloke comes into the Blind Beggar and he's asking about for a 'handy man' know what I mean guv'nor?"

"Yes, someone who is used to opening other people's doors without them knowing, normally at the dead of night" Hadley nodded.

"Exactly, guv'nor, well, one of my mates overhears this geezer and points him in my direction, so to speak…" Grover paused for a moment.

"Go on" said Hadley in a firm tone.

"Well, he comes over to me, offers to buy me a pint, an' I couldn't say 'no' could I?"

"I'd be surprised if you did, Grover."

"An' he says he's got a little job for the right man, an' I could be that man, well, what was I to do?"

"Carry on."

"I asked about the job and what was in it for me, and blow me down, he said that all I had to do was break a door in, then scarper, and after that, he'd pay me ten pounds!"

"Good money for an easy job then" said Hadley.

"On my life, the easiest money I've ever made, guv'nor" smiled Grover.

"So, you've never seen this man before?"

"No, guv'nor, he just said his name was 'Eddie', and he would take me to the house and wait while I forced the door and then he'd get me away, he said everything was arranged and that no one would be at home."

"Tell me again, when did he give you the ten pounds?" asked Hadley.

"The very next day, at lunchtime in the pub."

"Anything else?"

"He made me swear on my mother's life that I would not breathe a word of it to a living soul."

"You told me that this little caper was for a bet, is that true?"

"That's what Eddie said."

"Did you believe him?"

"I dunno, guv'nor, some of these toff's have got funny ideas."

"Was Eddie a toff?"

"No, don't think so."

"And you've never seen him before?"

"No, guv'nor."

"So you lied to me when you said he was often in the Blind Beggar?"

"Did I?"

"Yes."

"Well, in a manner of speaking…"

"Right, you'll stay in custody for a while longer whilst I make more inquiries" said Hadley and Grover hung his head. They left the unhappy man in the tender care of the custody sergeant and returned to the office.

Hadley mused for a while before announcing to Cooper "I think we'll have a photograph of Harry Grover and present it to the staff of the Hudson's household to see if it jogs any memories."

"Good idea, sir."

"Especially Mr Woods, the under groom."

"Right, sir."

"I just wonder if his name is Eddie" said Hadley as he sat back in his chair and gazed at the ceiling.

"If it is, it might be a coincidence, sir."

"Possibly" replied Hadley in a thoughtful tone before remaining silent.

"George!" he called suddenly.

"Yes, sir" replied the clerk from his office.

"A pot of tea and a photograph of Mr Harry Grover, if you please" said Hadley.

"Yes, sir, tea first I take it?"

"Yes, always, George, always."

After a late lunch at the Crown Inn on the Strand the detectives returned to the Yard where Hadley telegraphed the Police at Tilbury informing them of his arrival on Thursday. Then, with the sepia tint photograph of Harry Grover, they took a cab to Cavendish Square.

"The master and Mrs Hudson are still at Pangbourne, sir" said the butler after he opened the door to Hadley and Cooper.

"Indeed, I'm sure they are, but it is the household staff I wish to see this afternoon" replied Hadley.

"I cannot permit that without the master's permission" replied the butler.

"Well in that case, I'll arrest all the staff, including you, and question them at Scotland Yard, what do you think Mr Hudson would prefer, discreet inquiries here or at the Yard?" The butler went red in the face and Cooper thought the man was going to explode. However, he contained his anger and replied "do come in, gentlemen, if you would care to wait in the study, I'll gather everyone up."

"Thank you" replied Hadley as he stepped into the hallway and then followed the butler into the ornate room. The detectives waited some while before the butler re-appeared and announced "everyone is here and waiting in the hallway, sir."

"Very good, now, I'll start with you, if I may."

"Yes, sir."

"Have you ever seen this man before?" asked Hadley as he

produced the photograph of Grover. The butler peered at it and shook his head.

"No, sir, I've never seen him."

"Are you sure?"

"Positive, is he the thief, sir?"

"Possibly."

"What a dreadful looking person and to think he was in madam's bedroom, it doesn't bare thinking about."

"Quite so, now if you will please bring the staff in one by one and announce their names and their titles" said Hadley.

"Yes, sir" replied the butler and he seemed quite relieved. The housekeeper followed by each of the maids were announced and none of them recognised Grover. This was all a ploy to lull Woods into a false sense of security and when he was announced by the butler he looked a confident young man.

"Ah, Mr Woods, the under groom" smiled Hadley.

"Yes, sir."

"You discovered the break in on that infamous night."

"Yes, sir."

"Now just for the record, what is your full name?" asked Hadley.

"George Thomas Edward Woods, sir."

"Do some people call you Eddie?" at that Woods paled.

"No, sir."

"Honestly?"

"Honestly, sir."

"Perhaps this man does?" asked Hadley as he showed the photograph of Grover. At seeing Grover, Woods face went ashen and he started to sweat.

"I've never seen him in my life, that's the God's honest truth" Woods stammered.

"Mr Woods, if you're hiding the truth through misplaced loyalty, be assured that the consequences for you, if I discover that you have lied to me, will be more serious than you can imagine" said Hadley with menace. The young man became even paler and shook his head.

"No, sir, I've never seen that man before."

"Make a careful note, Sergeant, of Mr Wood's denial, if you please."

"Right, sir" replied Cooper.

"Now, Mr Woods, if on reflection you wish to talk to me in the strictest confidence, contact me at the Yard."

"Yes, sir, thank you, sir."

"That will be all for the moment."

"Yes, sir." The young man looked relieved and he left the room quickly.

Hadley thanked the butler for his assistance whilst Cooper went out into the Square to hail a cab.

As it rattled back towards the Yard, Hadley asked "what do you think, Sergeant?"

"He obviously recognised Grover, sir, and I'm surprised you haven't brought him in for further questioning."

"No, Sergeant, we'll let him sweat for a day or two, we've bigger fish to catch at the moment" replied Hadley with a grin.

Chief Inspector Bell sat impassive behind his desk and looked intently at Hadley.

"Are you really serious about the Hudson case?"

"Yes, sir, I have good reason to believe that it was planned as an insurance fraud, which, hopefully, I have now averted" replied Hadley.

"Well, I am staggered" said the Chief.

"Indeed, sir."

"Why on earth would the man do such a thing?"

"I really don't know, sir, but I am sure that the diamonds will soon re-appear…"

"Thank God for that, at least Mrs Hudson will stop writing to the Commissioner and London society can settle down and look forward to Christmas" interrupted Bell.

"Yes, sir."

"Well done, Hadley."

"Thank you, sir."

"Now if Mr Hudson has been warned off by your diplomatic moves, and we can cover the matter up, then we will all sleep easy in our beds" said Bell with relief.

"Yes, sir."

"Now what about the murder investigation?"

"I'm going down to Tilbury tomorrow night with Cooper to

await the arrival of the 'Arabesque' from Rotterdam on Thursday, then I plan to arrest Lefevre on suspicion of murder, sir."

"Good, let's get the devil firmly under lock and key before we find out the truth behind the matter."

"Yes, sir, but I must advise you there are further lines of inquiry involving Count Castellini and his wife…"

"They're not connected to these murders are they?" interrupted Bell.

"I'm not sure, sir…"

"Here you go again, Hadley, plunging me into a deep pool of worry once again because you're not sure!" interrupted the Chief.

"I'm sorry, sir."

"I mean, do you realise how important these people are?"

"I do, sir, but I must follow my lines and at present, I think that the Count and his wife may be implicated in the bullion robbery and hence the murders."

"Oh, dear God, will I ever live to see my pension!" mumbled the Chief.

"I am sure that Mr Hudson has been assisting the Count in suspicious financial arrangements, unknown to Sir John Simmons, chairman of the Bank, and that links Mr Hudson into further inquiries…"

"This is becoming a never ending nightmare, Hadley" interrupted the Chief.

"So it seems, sir."

"Well, I've heard enough now, put it all in your report and then get this Lefevre character into custody, I'm sure he's the villain of the piece."

"Yes, sir."

"I never did trust the French, they're our natural enemies you know, Hadley."

"Indeed, sir" Hadley smiled.

The next morning the two detectives completed full reports before interviewing Harry Grover once more.

"As you don't know Eddie's surname, give me a good description of him" said Hadley as he fixed Grover with a hard stare.

"He's about my height, with fair hair and a moustache" replied

Grover.

"What colour were his eyes?"

"For Gawd's sake, guv'nor, I don't know, I was in a pub, drinking an' it was dark."

"What about his clothes?"

"I dunno, he just had a black coat on and he was wearing a Derby hat."

"Anything else?"

"I can't remember, guv'nor, honest."

"If you see Eddie again, will you recognise him for certain?"

"Oh, yeah, on my life."

"Good, I will make arrangements for you to see him in due course."

"Oh, Gawd" mumbled Grover.

"Alright, against my better judgement, I'm going to release you from custody without charge for the moment…"

"Oh, bless you, guv'nor" interrupted Grover.

"But be aware, I shall be speaking to you again."

"Right, sir."

"Now stay out of trouble and get home to your wife and children."

"Yes, sir, thank you, sir."

The detectives enjoyed a late lunch in the Kings Head before catching the three thirty train to Tilbury from Liverpool Street station. As the train rattled along through the Essex countryside in the rain, Hadley sat quietly contemplating what would be the likely outcome of the arrest of Captain Lefevre. He planned to observe the Count and his wife covertly before moving in for the confrontation with Lefevre.

Inspector Peter Gray of the Essex Police was the officer who Hadley had telegraphed with all the details and he was waiting with Sergeant Richards for the detectives at Tilbury station when the train arrived. After introductions they went to the Police Station where Hadley went into further discussion with Inspector Gray.

"What we are investigating is most serious with international complications" said Hadley to the young Inspector.

"I understand completely" nodded Gray.

"We shall arrest Lefevre after the Count and his wife have left the 'Arabesque', I'd like two of your men to follow them whilst you and Sergeant Richards along with four constables assist Sergeant Cooper and myself when we board the ship."

"Right."

"I intend to wait in the Harbour Master's office at dawn for the arrival of the ship and we can direct our operation from there" said Hadley.

"Shall we be armed?"

"Yes, indeed, things may become distinctly un-pleasant aboard the 'Arabesque' when I arrest the Captain" replied Hadley.

"Would you prefer revolvers or rifles?" asked Gray.

"Rifles, if you please, they always look more menacing."

"Right, Inspector."

"Now, can you recommend a reasonable hotel for the night?" asked Hadley.

"Yes, the Crown and Anchor is the most comfortable with good food and a well stocked bar" replied Gray with a smile.

"That sounds most agreeable" replied Hadley.

"I'll send a cab for you at dawn to bring you to the station."

"Thank you very much."

"Tomorrow promises to be a busy day" said Gray.

"Indeed it does" replied Hadley.

CHAPTER 10

Hadley and Cooper arrived at Tilbury police station just after seven o'clock and were shown into Inspector Gray's office.

"A comfortable night at the Crown and Anchor, I trust?" asked Gray as he waved the detectives to a seat.

"Yes, thank you."

"We're all ready to go, Inspector."

"Excellent."

"Is there any last minute change of plan?" asked Gray.

"No, we are all set and we must take the day as it comes" replied Hadley.

"Good, now I took it upon myself to advise the Harbour Master, Mr Tom Wright, of our intentions and he will be giving us his full co-operation" said Gray.

"Excellent."

"Let's be away then" said Gray.

Tom Wright remembered Hadley from the previous incident with the 'Arabesque', and was all smiles when he met the detectives once more.

"This is just too exciting for words, it reminds me of my days at sea in the Navy" said Tom.

"Well, we'll try not to disturb you and your duties too much" said Hadley.

"You disturb away as much as you like, sir, it's a tonic to be involved with bringing criminals to justice" replied the old man.

"Your assistance is appreciated" said Hadley.

"Glad to help, sir."

"Have you any idea what time the ship may arrive?" asked Hadley.

"Possibly around mid morning, sir, with the tides as they are at present" replied Tom.

"Good, that gives us ample time to deploy our men" said Hadley.

"Indeed it does, sir."

"The constables as you see, are armed, and must be hidden from view" said Hadley.

"I've got the very spot for them, sir, downstairs in our equipment stores, there's a small window overlooking the harbour where they can watch for the ship and your signal to board her" said Tom, his eyes bright with the anticipation of action.

"Capital, Mr Wright."

"Call me Tom, Inspector."

"Thank you, Tom."

"Now I suppose you and Inspector Gray will want to remain up here with me" said Tom.

"Yes, please, it is important that we have an over view of the quay as we are expecting a man and a woman to arrive and go aboard the 'Arabesque'" said Hadley.

"Right, we'll get you sorted and ship shape before we get some tea organised for you all" said Tom and Hadley smiled.

After tea, served by young Charlie, Tom's assistant, the armed constables were deployed to the stores and two plain clothes officers were stationed in a warehouse by the quay along with a small trap. They all waited patiently until just after ten o'clock when suddenly the 'Arabesque' came slowly into view through the November mist.

"Here she is, Inspector!" exclaimed Tom, watching through his binoculars and hardly being able to contain his excitement. Hadley looked at Gray and nodded to him.

"Right, Sergeant Richards, go down and warn the constables that she is here and to be ready for action" said Gray.

"Yes, sir" replied the Sergeant and he was gone out and down the stairs in an instant just as a closed four wheeler arrived on the quay.

"That's good timing, sir" said Cooper as he nodded at the four wheeler.

"Indeed it is, Sergeant" replied Hadley.

The Count and the Countess alighted from the coach and stood watching the 'Arabesque' slowly making its way into the harbour.

"Are they your suspects?" asked Gray pointing at the Count and his wife.

"Yes" replied Hadley.

"I'll give a signal to my men in the warehouse and they will follow them until they are relieved by you" said Gray.

"Good."

"When she's moored up, I'll go and carry out my duties" said Tom and Hadley nodded.

Half an hour later the 'Arabesque' had moored by the quay and the Harbour Master went down with his paperwork to board the vessel. The Count and his wife waited until Tom had left the ship before walking up the gang plank to be greeted by Captain Lefevre. They then disappeared into the aft cabin as Tom returned to his office.

"Everything seems to be order, sir" said Tom waving his paperwork.

"I would have been surprised if it had been otherwise, Tom" replied Hadley.

"She's leaving later today, her next port of call is Nantes and her final destination is Marseille, sir" said Tom.

"Thank you, Tom."

They waited once more until, after about half an hour, the small jib crane on the 'Arabesque' was used to lift a heavy trunk from the cargo deck before swinging it out and placing it gently on the quayside where three crew men, off the ship, guided it safely down.

"I wonder what's in there, Sergeant" said Hadley with a smile.

"I can guess, sir."

"So can I."

The four wheeler moved forward and stopped very close to the trunk as another crew man joined the three and helped to lift the heavy trunk onto the platform at the back of the coach. It was then securely roped down.

"They can hardly lift it" murmured Hadley.

"It must be full of something heavier than lady's clothes" grinned Cooper.

The Count and his beautiful wife re-appeared on deck and with handshakes, followed by a little kiss on the cheek of Lefevre by the Countess, the couple left the ship. They climbed aboard the coach which set off at a brisk pace and Hadley watched as the plain clothes officers followed in the trap.

"Now let's see what Captain Lefevre has to say for himself" said Hadley as he made for the door.

"Take care, sir" said Cooper as he followed the Inspector.

"No, you take care, Sergeant, you're the one who usually gets shot!"

The detectives made their way down the steps and across the quay to the 'Arabesque' before walking briskly up the gang plank to the deck. Captain Lefevre saw their approach and with an angry expression, stepped forward to stop their further progress.

"Mon Dieu! You again, Inspector!"

"Yes, Captain Lefevre."

"What do you want this time?"

"To talk to you, Captain."

"I do not wish to talk to you, now leave my ship or I'll have you both thrown off into the harbour!" Lefevre shouted.

"Not an advisable course of action, Captain" replied Hadley as he waved for reinforcements and Gray with Richards followed by four armed constables rushed from the Harbour Master's locker room to the utter surprise of Lefevre. He stood open mouthed as the armed party raced up the gang plank and surrounded the astonished Captain.

"Mon Dieu! You English are mad!" he exclaimed.

"Possibly, Captain, now let's go to your cabin for a discreet conversation" replied Hadley. The Captain turned away and headed aft to his cabin followed by the detectives. Once in the cabin Lefevre turned and demanded angrily "what the devil do you want with me?"

"Captain Lefevre, I'm arresting you on suspicion of the murder of Pascal Dalmas…"

"You're insane!" shouted Lefevre.

"You will come with us for further questioning and…"

"Never!" interrupted Lefevre before he went to his desk and drew a Colt revolver from the top drawer and pointed it at the detectives.

"Captain Lefevre…"

"Get off my ship now!"

"As I said, you are coming with us to Scotland Yard…"

"I will not hesitate to use this if you don't leave!" interrupted Lefevre.

"If you discharge that weapon you may well murder one of us, but before you can fire again you will be overpowered and the armed officers outside will then arrive and arrest you without too much concern for your well being, so I advise you to put the weapon down and come quietly, sir." Lefevre stared hard into the eyes of Hadley and after a few moments of tension, slowly placed the Colt on the desk. Cooper sprang forward, picked up the weapon and stood back.

"Now, Captain Lefevre, shall we go?" Lefevre nodded and led the way out of his cabin back to the deck. He spoke briefly in French to a crew man, who nodded sheepishly, before walking slowly down on to the quay followed by the detectives and constables to a waiting police four wheeler. The detectives climbed aboard with their prisoner and set off to the Police station. Once there, Cooper went in to collect their overnight bags from the Inspector's office whilst Hadley waited outside, thanking Inspector Gray for all his assistance. Suddenly Cooper rushed out clutching the bags in one hand and waving a piece of paper in the other.

"Sir!"

"What is it, Sergeant?"

"A telegraph message from the Chief, sir" he replied as he handed the note to Hadley. The Inspector read it out aloud, "Hadley, return to London immediately, Sir John Simmons found dead this morning in the Anglo American Bank, Bell."

"This investigation is running deep, sir" said Cooper.

"It certainly is, Sergeant, let's be off to the station and catch the next train back!"

At Tilbury railway station the London train arrived and the detectives observed the Count and his wife boarding a first class compartment followed by the plain clothes officers. Hadley, Cooper and Lefevre travelled in a third class compartment at the rear of the train. Once they were on their way to Liverpool Street, Hadley told Cooper to contact the officers in first class and tell them the importance of keeping a constant surveillance on the Count and Countess until they reached their final destination, then one of them was to contact them at the Yard. Hadley guessed that the Castellini's would eventually arrive at Cavendish Square, with or without their large trunk.

When the train arrived at Liverpool Street station, Hadley

waited until all the passengers had left the train before he and Cooper led Lefevre off and out to a police four wheeler that had been sent by Chief Inspector Bell to await their arrival. After Lefevre was placed into custody, Hadley and Cooper went immediately to the Chief's office.

"Bad business, Hadley."

"Yes, sir."

"I want you to get to the Bank as quickly as possible and begin your investigation" said Bell in a grave tone.

"Yes, sir, what do we know so far?"

"Sir John was found dead by a senior manager first thing this morning when he opened for business" replied Bell.

"Cause of death, sir?"

"Apparently he had fallen from the first floor to the vestibule below" said Bell.

"That is suspicious, sir."

"Very, now get over there straight away and begin, the Commissioner is already demanding immediate action."

"Right, sir."

"The damned Press has already got wind of it and it will be splashed over all the evening papers" said Bell.

"A pity, sir."

"Yes, it will effect the share price no doubt, by the way, have you arrested that damned French man?"

"Yes, sir."

"Good, leave him to sweat awhile, the Simmons case is top priority now."

"Yes, sir." The detectives nodded, left the office and made their way outside where Cooper hailed a Hansom.

When Hadley and Cooper arrived, the doors to the Anglo American Investments Bank were closed with two constables on duty outside. Once inside the building they were met by Sergeant Collins, who was first on the scene, accompanied by a constable.

"We haven't moved the body, sir" said Collins.

"Good, let's have a look at it" replied Hadley. Collins led the way across the marble floor of the impressive vestibule to the body, now covered with a sheet. Hadley lifted it and looked down on the corpse of Sir John. He lay on his back, mouth open and unseeing eyes staring up to the ceiling. Hadley replaced the sheet and then looked up to the balustrade on the first floor from where it appeared that Sir John had fallen. Hadley then went to the stairway and climbed the stairs, followed by Cooper. Once on the landing above, they peered over the balustrade at the corpse below and Hadley thought for a while.

"Sergeant."

"Yes, sir."

"How tall are you?"

"Six feet and one inch in my stocking feet, sir" replied Cooper in a surprised tone.

"I'm about the same, Sergeant."

"Indeed, but you're a little heavier than me, if that helps, sir" replied Cooper.

"No, it doesn't, so don't remind me, Sergeant."

"Right, sir."

"Stand against the rail, if you would."

"Right, sir" and Cooper stood close to the top of the balustrade.

"Put your hand on the rail and turn sideways to face me" said Hadley and Cooper did as he was asked.

"The top of the rail is well above your waist, would you agree, Sergeant?"

"Yes, sir."

"How tall do you think the victim is?"

"When we followed him into lunch at Pangbourne, it struck me then that he was quite a short gentleman, probably about five feet seven or eight inches, sir."

"I agree, so, the top of this balustrade would have been at chest height on Sir John."

"Indeed, sir."

"That means if he'd stumbled against it, he would not have fallen over…"

"Then he was murdered, sir."

"Yes, Sergeant, he was thrown to his death."

"Falling to the marble floor from this height would have killed him instantly, sir."

"Indeed, now let's begin our inquiries." Cooper nodded and followed Hadley down to the ground floor.

"Sergeant Collins."

"Yes, sir?"

"Who found the body?"

"Mr John Augustus, sir."

"Where is he?"

"Through there, sir, with his assistant, Mr Wells" replied Collins, pointing through an archway to an office beyond.

"Thank you" replied Hadley.

The Inspector and Cooper entered the spacious office where Mr Augustus stood immediately on their arrival. Hadley made the introductions and then sat down opposite the distressed Bank Manager and his assistant, a well dressed young man.

"Mr Augustus, at what time did you discover the body of Sir John?"

"Just after nine o'clock, Inspector, I came in as usual through the side entrance to my office here at eight thirty exactly, then Mr Wells arrived a few minutes later, we did some paperwork, then I went through to the vestibule to open the main doors for the rest of the staff and I saw the poor man lying there..." he faltered and wiped away a tear.

"Was Sir John popular with the staff?"

"Yes indeed, Inspector, he was well liked and respected" came the reply from the pale faced manager.

"When did you last see him alive?"

"When I left the Bank last night after six o'clock, Sir John was still here with Mr Hudson."

"With Mr Hudson?"

"Yes, apparently they were having a private meeting in Sir John's office, and I just interrupted them, only for a moment you understand, to inform Mr Hudson that all was well and I was leaving" replied Augustus.

"Did you have any indication that their meeting was coming to an end?" asked Hadley.

"No, Inspector, in fact quite the opposite, they seemed to be quite relaxed and were enjoying a drink together" replied the manager.

"I see, now, have you informed Mr Hudson of the tragedy?"

"Yes, I sent a messenger to his home straight away and I'm sure he'll arrive at any moment" replied Augustus.

"Very good."

"It's a terrible accident and could not have happened at a worse time, Inspector."

"Believe me, there's no good time for a death, but explain why this is a bad moment?" said Hadley.

"There were plans for Sir John to bring his nephew into the Bank to relieve Mr Hudson of his heavy work load so he could develop the business with the Bank in Boston" replied Augustus.

"Was Mr Hudson content with that proposal?"

"Yes indeed, Inspector, he said he was looking forward to travelling over to America soon on business."

"How soon?"

"After Christmas, I understand."

"That's interesting, sir" replied Hadley as Sergeant Collins entered the office.

"Sorry to disturb you, sir, but the ambulance has arrived to collect the body" said Collins.

"Not yet, Sergeant."

"Very well, sir."

"Not until it's been photographed" said Hadley.

"Photographed, sir?" asked the Sergeant with surprise.

"Yes, will you please get to the Yard and ask Jack Curtis to come at once with all his photographic paraphernalia" said Hadley.

"Yes, sir, right away" replied the bemused Collins. After the Sergeant had left the office, Cooper leaned towards the Inspector and whispered "photographs, sir?"

"Yes, Sergeant, I've given the matter some thought and I believe that photographs of a crime scene could be invaluable when we are writing our reports and reviewing the facts before us."

"An interesting idea, sir."

It was an hour before Jack Curtis arrived and at Hadley's direction the body of Sir John was photographed from all angles as well as the landing from where the banker had fallen. Cooper was required to stand next to the balustrade as a marker for the height of the rail before it was photographed several times by the industrious Mr Curtis. The session had just been completed when

Anthony Hudson arrived and strode angrily into the vestibule.

"What the damned devil is going on here?" he demanded and his voice echoed around the large, pillared entrance hall as he looked up at Hadley and Cooper gazing down from the first floor.

"Mr Hudson I'm glad you've arrived at last" said Hadley as he pulled out his fob watch and glanced at it.

"What do mean, Inspector?"

"It is now half past three in the afternoon, sir, and Mr Augustus informed me that he sent a message to you home this morning after he discovered the body of Sir John" replied Hadley.

"And what of it?"

"I am somewhat surprised that you did not come sooner, sir."

"That's because I was not at home!" Hudson replied angrily.

"Indeed, sir."

"I was staying at my club."

"Which club would that be, sir?"

"The Dreyfus Club in Curzon Street, if you must know!" exclaimed Hudson.

"Would you like to come up to your office, sir?" asked Hadley.

"Why?"

"I have a few questions for you, sir." Hudson walked calmly to the stairway, glancing briefly at the corpse, before proceeding up to the landing. He stared hard at the Inspector and said "this way, if you please." Hadley and Cooper followed him along a corridor and then into a large office.

"Is this going to take long, Inspector?" he asked as he sat behind his desk.

"No, sir, I shall be brief, this time."

"Before you start, Inspector, I have to ask…"

"Yes, sir?"

"Have you been taking photographs of Sir John's body?"

"I have, sir."

"That's bloody well outrageous!" shouted Hudson.

"You may think so…"

"I do, Inspector, you're treating this great man like some cheap vaudeville act!"

"No, sir…"

"Yes, Inspector, a cheap, titillating spectacle for prying eyes with no conscience…"

"I had never regarded the Commissioner in that light before, it will be interesting to note his reaction when I tell him what you have said" replied Hadley. That stopped Hudson in his tracks and he sat with his mouth open in amazement.

"I'm horrified by your attitude, Inspector."

"I am horrified by murder, Mr Hudson."

"Murder?"

"Yes, Sir John was murdered."

"How do you know that, I mean, surely it was an accident?"

"The killer would like us to think that, sir."

"Good God" Hudson looked pale and glanced down at his desk.

"Now, please tell me exactly what happened last night" asked Hadley.

"What do you mean?" Hudson asked in a surprised tone.

"I understand you were in a meeting with Sir John and enjoying a drink after six o'clock, is that so, sir?"

"Yes, yes, we we're discussing future business" replied Hudson.

"What time did your meeting finish?"

"I can't be sure, Inspector…"

"Come, come, sir" Hadley interrupted.

"Probably about eight o'clock, Inspector."

"Did you leave the Bank then?"

"Yes."

"Where did you go, sir?"

"Straight to my club, I dined there with a friend and stayed the night, as I often do" replied Hudson.

"Did Sir John appear well when you left him?"

"Yes, very well, although…"

"Yes, sir?"

"I thought that he had drunk a little too much brandy" replied Hudson.

"The pathology report will confirm if that is so, sir."

"Indeed, Inspector." At that moment, Sergeant Collins entered the office.

"Sorry to disturb you, sir, but may I have permission to get the corpse away in the ambulance now?"

"Yes, Sergeant, and ensure it goes to Doctor Evans at the

Marylebone" replied Hadley.

"Yes, sir." Just as Collins turned to leave, the constable arrived and said to Hadley "sir, there's a message from Chief Inspector Bell, would you please return to the Yard, the Commissioner wants to speak to you urgently."

CHAPTER 11

Hadley stood alongside Chief Inspector Bell in the Commissioner's office watching him read the report on his desk in front of him.

"God, this is a bad business, gentlemen, I think you had better sit down for a minute" the Commissioner said wearily. They sat and waited patiently as he read on.

"This report of yours Chief Inspector doesn't tell me much, other than a prominent City Banker has been found dead in his Bank this morning, apparently from a fall" said the Commissioner shaking his head slowly.

"It is only my preliminary report, sir" replied Bell.

"Yes, I realise that, but I need some more information, the Press are waiting for a statement and I've had Sir Charles Reeder in the office demanding a thorough investigation into the matter" said the Commissioner.

"Sir Charles Reeder, sir?" queried Bell.

"He's the head of the Bank of England's security department" replied the Commissioner.

"Hadley's on the case, sir, and I'm sure we'll have…"

"I want action, Chief Inspector" interrupted the Commissioner as he looked up from his desk.

"Yes, sir" replied Bell.

"What do we know so far?" demanded the Commissioner.

"I'm sure that Sir John was murdered, sir" replied Hadley.

"Murdered?"

"Yes, sir."

"By whom?"

"Anthony Hudson is the prime suspect…"

"You can't be serious, Hadley" interrupted Bell in alarm.

"I am deadly serious, sir."

"Hudson is a prominent man, a pillar of London society, why should he do such a thing?" asked Bell.

"At the moment, I have no idea, sir, but I think somehow the murder of Sir John may be linked to the bullion case" replied Hadley.

"How can the murders of a couple of drunken French sailors be connected to a City Banker?" asked Bell.

"Never mind the French, where does Hudson fit into all this?" asked the Commissioner, as his face turned red and his side whiskers twitched.

"He's involved with Count Castellini, who I suspect is behind the bullion robbery in Istanbul, sir" replied Hadley.

"That reminds me, I've heard back from our Ambassador out there and he says that the Turkish authorities are remaining tight lipped about it all" said the Commissioner.

"Really, sir" said Hadley.

"Yes, so think again about the source of the gold that you retrieved in Liverpool" said the Commissioner.

"Yes, sir."

"Now, what am I going to say to the Press about our investigations, Chief Inspector?"

"That we're well on with the investigation to this tragic accident, preliminary inquiries proving fruitful at this stage and you will release a further bulletin tomorrow on our progress, sir" replied Bell. The Commissioner thought for a moment before he asked "no mention of suspected murder then?"

"No, sir, that would only add scandal and uncertainty to the situation" replied Bell.

"And that would cause the shares to plummet" murmured the Commissioner.

"Quite so" nodded Bell.

"What about the Hudson diamonds?" asked the Commissioner.

"Hadley believes that's a case of fraud, sir" replied Bell.

"Who by?"

"Mr Hudson, sir" replied Hadley.

"By God, Hadley, you've certainly got it in for him" said the Commissioner.

"My investigations and conclusions are guided by the facts, sir" said Hadley.

"You had better be certain of your facts, otherwise your head will be firmly on the block!"

"Yes, sir."

"Let me have detailed reports on everything by midday tomorrow, gentlemen."

"Yes, sir" replied Bell.

"You may go now" said the Commissioner as he returned his gaze to the report before him.

As soon as Hadley returned to his office he ordered a pot of tea from George and slumped down behind his desk.

"Where's Sergeant Cooper, George?"

"He's down in custody with the officer from Tilbury, sir, showing him around" replied George.

"Ah, good, that means the suspects have settled somewhere, Cavendish Square if I'm not mistaken" murmured Hadley. A short while later, Cooper arrived back in the office with the young policeman in tow and introduced him to the Inspector.

"This is Constable Barnes, sir, he's one of the surveillance officers" said Cooper.

"Pleased to meet you constable" smiled Hadley.

"Thank you, sir" replied Barnes.

"Sit down and join us in a cup of tea, and then tell us what we want to know" said Hadley.

The Inspector waited patiently, after they had finished drinking the tea, for Barnes to take out his notebook and begin his report.

"The man and woman under surveillance left the Tilbury quay in a four wheeler which took them to the train station. They boarded a first class compartment on the London train and were followed by myself and Constable Norton in plain clothes. Before the train departed a large trunk was brought from the four wheeler to the guards van and loaded therein. During the journey Sergeant Cooper of New Scotland Yard approached us and emphasised the importance for us to remain with the suspects at all times and after they had reached their final destination, I was detailed to report to Inspector Hadley whilst Constable Norton remained observing the residence until being relieved by other officers. The suspects alighted from the train at Liverpool Street station and along with the trunk, journeyed by a four wheeler to Kings Cross station where the trunk was deposited in left luggage. The suspects then continued on to number twelve, Cavendish Square, where they remain at the moment with Constable Norton in attendance."

"Thank you, Constable Barnes, a good report on duty well done" said Hadley with a smile.

"Thank you, sir" beamed the young constable.

"Now go and rescue your colleague from Cavendish Square and get off home to Tilbury, we will take it from here" said Hadley.

"Right, sir."

"Tell Inspector Gray that you have been of great assistance to me, your efforts are appreciated and I will telegraph him in due course" said Hadley.

"Yes, sir" smiled the constable and after thanking Hadley once more, he left the office

"Now, Cooper, we're off to the Marylebone to see what Doctor Evans has to say."

"I'll call a cab, sir."

It was now dark and the rain drizzled down past the gas street lamps outside the Hospital giving an eerie glow to the street as the Hansom pulled up.

"Hadley, I'm just about to go home" said Doctor Evans as the detectives entered his office.

"If only we could go with you, Doctor, do you think your dear wife could find a little supper for Cooper and me?" grinned Hadley. The Doctor shook his head and replied "Hadley, if I didn't know you so well, I'd be really angry instead of only moderately so." Cooper grinned and looked away.

"Indeed, I'm sure that's the case."

"I suppose you want to know about Sir John?"

"Yes."

"Come with me then" said the Doctor and they followed him out into the mortuary where the body of Sir John lay under a white sheet on a marble slab. The Doctor uncovered the pale corpse and said "death was instantaneous, the skull was severely fractured and the neck vertebrae snapped immediately the head hit the floor."

"The most important thing I need to know was the time of death" said Hadley quietly.

"I estimate that death occurred between twenty four and twenty six hours ago" replied the Doctor. Hadley did the calculations and said "that was no earlier than six o'clock last night and no later than eight, then."

"Yes, that's about right" replied the Doctor.

"Stomach contents?"

"Quite a lot of brandy, not much else."

"Thank you, Doctor, that's all I need to know for the moment" said Hadley.

They left the Marylebone Hospital and made their way in the rain to Kings Cross station.

"I hope you have your special little key set with you, Sergeant" said Hadley as they crossed the concourse to the left luggage office.

"Yes, sir, I find it useful for opening doors…"

"And large trunks" interrupted Hadley.

"Full of gold" added Cooper.

"Yes, Sergeant."

"Do you intend to confiscate the bullion, sir?"

"No, Sergeant, we'll check the contents of the trunk and if it contains what we think it does, we will set a trap for the Count and his wife" replied Hadley.

"Right, sir."

"We know that they are travelling to Liverpool tomorrow to board the ship for Boston and after we find out the time of the first train, we'll be here before then, waiting for them."

"Catch them red handed when they collect the trunk, sir."

"Precisely, Sergeant."

"Then get them back to the Yard and see what they have to say for themselves."

They reached the left luggage office and Hadley smiled at the young man behind the counter.

"Can I help you, gentlemen?"

"Yes, I am Inspector Hadley and this is Sergeant Cooper of Scotland Yard."

"Yes, sir."

"As part of an ongoing investigation we need to locate a large trunk that was deposited with you earlier today" said Hadley.

"Yes, sir, what was the name?"

"Castellini."

"Well bless me, sir, Mr Castellini collected the trunk not more than an hour ago" replied the young man and Hadley stood silent and totally surprised.

"It was very heavy, sir, I had to get help to lift it onto a trolley…"

"Thank you for your help" interrupted Hadley. He turned away and left the office angry with himself.

"What a mistake to make, Sergeant, letting the Tilbury lads go before we got there" said Hadley as he strode across the concourse towards the exit.

"Now what, sir?"

"To Cavendish Square, Sergeant, if we are lucky, we may catch them yet!"

As the Hansom pulled up outside number twelve, Cavendish Square, Hadley leapt out, almost before it had stopped, leaving Cooper to pay the cabbie. The Inspector rang the bell soundly and he waited impatiently for the door to open. Copper joined him just as the butler opened the door.

"Yes, gentlemen?"

"I wish to see Mr Hudson immediately" Hadley replied.

"That is not possible, sir."

"Why?"

"The master has gone to his club this evening and is not expected to return, sir" smirked the butler.

"Then I wish to see Mrs Hudson…"

"Again, an impossibility, sir, as the mistress has gone down to Pangbourne by train, she left not more than an hour ago with the Count and the Countess Castellini" smiled the butler in triumph.

"I see."

"So, as there is no one of any importance left in the house, I cannot help you further, good night, gentlemen" and with that he closed the door. The falling rain matched Hadley's state of mind but he remained deadly calm.

"Call a cab, Sergeant."

"To Paddington Station, sir?"

"No, we'll go to Pangbourne first thing in the morning but now it's to the Dreyfus Club in Curzon Street."

Hadley was glad to get out of the rain and into the select club. The detectives approached the reception desk where a tall, distinguished looking man eyed them up and down before asking "can I help you, gentlemen?"

"Yes, if you would, I am Inspector Hadley and this is Sergeant Cooper of Scotland Yard, we'd like a few words with one of your members, please."

"Who is that person, sir?"

"Mr Hudson."

"I'll see if Mr Hudson is available, please wait here, gentlemen." With that the receptionist strode away across the deep carpeted hallway and disappeared through double doors into the room beyond. Whilst they waited, several club members wandered by smoking large cigars and talking loudly as they moved from one lounge to another.

"I expect you have to be very wealthy to be a member here, sir" whispered Cooper.

"Yes, or very crooked" replied Hadley as the receptionist reappeared. He cleared his throat and announced "Mr Hudson is not receiving guests this evening, so I suggest you make your request to see him in the appointments book." Hadley remained silent for a few moments before tossing his wet, battered top hat on to the reception desk. He moved forward and glared into the eyes of the receptionist who began to look anxious.

"I am a senior police officer investigating murder, fraud and international theft, I have come here on the strict instructions of the Commissioner of the Metropolitan Police, to interview Mr Hudson, so please go and tell him that I want to see him now, otherwise, both of you will be under immediate arrest, do I make myself clear?"

"Yes, sir" stammered the receptionist and he almost ran back through the double doors.

"It's my battered hat that does the trick, Sergeant." Cooper smiled and replied "don't get a new one then, sir." Hadley nodded as Hudson appeared in the hallway followed by the anxious receptionist.

"Inspector, what's this all about?" he demanded angrily.

"Can we go somewhere more private to discuss matters, sir?" asked Hadley.

"Not until I damned well know what this is all about!"

"Very well, sir, it's about the murder of Sir John Simmons to start with…" at that Hudson went pale and the receptionist's hands began to shake.

"Where can we go for a little privacy, Smethurst?" asked Hudson as he turned to the receptionist.

"In the secretary's office, sir, Mr Bolting is out at present and not expected back until much later" replied Smethurst in an anxious tone. Hudson nodded and led the way down a corridor off the hallway to a large, comfortable office.

"You'd better sit down, gentlemen" said Hudson as he slumped into the large chair behind the paper strewn desk. The detectives sat and Hadley fixed Hudson with a steely gaze before speaking.

"To begin with, the pathology report states that Sir John died instantly when he fell to the floor and the time of his death was between six o'clock and eight last night, the very time that you were alone in the bank with Sir John..." said Hadley.

"Are you accusing me of his murder, Inspector?" interrupted Hudson.

"No, sir, I'm just hoping that you can shed some light on the events of last night before he met his tragic end" replied Hadley.

"I've told you all I know, Inspector."

"Please be kind enough to tell me again, sir, and this time, leave nothing out." Hudson glared at the Inspector as Cooper produced his notebook.

"I went to Sir John's office about six o'clock at his invitation, he poured drinks for us both and we began an informal meeting. I thought at the time that he had been drinking heavily beforehand as his movements were unsteady and his speech slurred..." Hudson paused.

"Do go on, sir."

"We discussed the new business that we were planning in America and he was very pleased at the prospects of substantial profits..."

"I understand that you were planning to go out there after Christmas, is that so, sir?"

"Yes, Inspector, Sir John wanted me to go and begin negotiations and, at his suggestion, my wife was to accompany me."

"For the social side of business, no doubt."

"Precisely, Inspector."

"Carry on, sir."

"We just talked for a while, reviewing the opportunities in

America and then, at about half past seven, I took my leave of Sir John, left the bank and came here, dined with a friend and played cards for a while, then retired for the night" said Hudson.

"How was Sir John when you left him?" asked Hadley.

"He was fine, other than a little weary from his over indulgence in brandy" replied Hudson.

"I see" mused Hadley.

"Do you really believe that he was murdered?"

"I do, sir."

"For heaven's sake, Inspector, it's obvious that the man was drunk, he stumbled and fell to his death!"

"No, sir, he was lifted over the balustrade and thrown to the floor below…"

"Inspector, your attitude is so typical of the muddle headed thinking that pervades the police force, you spend your time following up situations that simply do not exist" interrupted Hudson.

"You may believe that, sir, I couldn't comment, but I assure you the facts speak for themselves" replied Hadley.

"I think you are wasting your time and more importantly, mine also!"

"Not at all, sir, now I understand that Mrs Hudson has left London for Pangbourne with the Count and Countess…"

"Yes, what of it?" demanded Hudson angrily.

"I thought that the Count and his wife were travelling to Liverpool tomorrow to embark on a steam ship bound for America."

"They've had a last minute change of plan and will be staying at Pangbourne for a while" replied Hudson.

"Why is that, sir?"

"None of your damned business, Inspector."

"Could it be because I have Captain Lefevre in custody at the Yard on the suspicion of murder, sir?"

"I have no idea, Inspector."

"You were aware of the arrest, I take it?" asked Hadley.

"I believe something regarding that incident was telegraphed through to the bank for the Count's attention" replied Hudson.

"What was his reaction to the news?"

"Again, I've no idea, Inspector, I sent the message to

Cavendish Square and I can only presume he would discuss it with his wife."

"Will you be joining them at Pangbourne, sir?"

"Possibly."

"Thank you, sir, that will be all for the time being."

It had stopped raining when the detectives left the Dreyfus Club and hailed a cab to take them home.

"Well, Sergeant, I think we've a more complex and difficult investigation than I originally thought."

"I agree, sir."

"It's going to be very hard to prove that Hudson murdered Sir John" said Hadley thoughtfully.

"Does he know what the Castellini's have been up to, I wonder?"

"I'm confident that they are all in this together."

"Why, sir?"

"There are too many loose ends, Sergeant, for that not to be the case."

"So it is to Pangbourne tomorrow to question the Count and look for the trunk, sir."

"Yes, Sergeant, but I have a feeling that will have vanished like the Hudson diamonds."

"Indeed, sir."

"Meet me at the left luggage office at Paddington Station tomorrow morning, we'll start there in our search for the trunk."

"Yes, sir, what time should I be there?"

"Eight o'clock and don't be late, Sergeant."

"I'm never late, sir."

"That's good, keep it up, I also am never late, but I do confess that when I was your age, I was nearly late once." Cooper looked away and grinned to himself.

CHAPTER 12

Cooper was waiting for Hadley at the left luggage office when the Inspector arrived.

"Good morning, sir."

"Morning, Sergeant, what time is the next train to Reading?" asked Hadley as he glanced at his fob watch.

"It leaves at a quarter to nine, sir."

"Good, we'll be on it after we've been in here." Cooper followed Hadley into the office where Hadley introduced himself before asking the attendant "has a large trunk been deposited here last night in the name of Castellini?"

"I don't think so, sir, but I will check the paperwork" replied the young man. The check was made but to no avail.

"Perhaps they left it at Reading, sir" said Cooper as they strode from left luggage to the ticket office.

"Possibly, but I'm beginning to think that they have taken it all the way to Pangbourne" replied Hadley.

"It will be almost impossible to find it there, sir."

"I know, Sergeant, and it concerns me."

The journey to Reading was un-eventful and inquiries at the left luggage were fruitless. The detectives hired a four wheeler and set off for Pangbourne in the cold November mist. The house looked grey and forbidding when they arrived outside its pillared portico. The butler opened the door and Hadley asked to see Mrs Hudson. They were admitted and waited in the hall before they were ushered into the formidable lady's presence. The Count and his wife were seated on a sofa close to the fire and Mrs Hudson rose from her chair to greet them.

"Good morning, Inspector... Sergeant" she said in a cold tone.

"Morning, Madam, Count and Countess" Hadley nodded.

"Have you come to tell me that you've recovered my diamonds?"

"No Madam, but I'm sure that they will be with you in plenty of time for your Christmas party" replied Hadley.

"Why are you so sure may I ask?"

"Years of experience tells me so, Madam."

"We wait to see about that" she retorted.

"Your patience will be rewarded for certain" smiled Hadley.

"Well if you haven't yet recovered my diamonds, why have you come to Pangbourne?" she asked.

"I've come to interview the Count, Madam."

"Why, for heaven's sake?"

"Because investigations into certain matters have made it necessary for me to do so" replied Hadley.

"I see."

"Now, I would prefer it if we could have our discussion in private…"

"Nonsense, Inspector, we have no secrets, so carry on and we'll listen with interest" interrupted Mrs Hudson and the Count nodded his approval.

"Very well, Madam."

"Please sit down gentlemen." Hadley nodded his thanks and sat with Cooper on a sofa opposite the Count.

"Sir, you and the Countess were seen in Tilbury yesterday…"

"Si, we went there to meet the 'Arabesque' and Captain Lefevre…" interrupted the Count hastily.

"Quite so…"

"And I have been informed that you have arrested Captain Lefevre and accused him of murder!" said the Count angrily.

"That is so, sir."

"Why, Inspector? Where is your proof? You have none and I have asked Mr Hudson to stay in London to arrange Captain Lefevre's release immediately!"

"I'm sorry, sir, but that will not be possible…"

"Do not attempt to tell me what is possible, I am Count Giovani Castellini, and I tell you what is going to happen!"

"Under British law…"

"I am not interested in your law, when it imprisons an innocent man!"

"I have reason to believe that Captain Lefevre murdered Pascal Dalmas and Jacques Mornay…"

"For what reason?"

"That is not absolutely clear at the moment, sir."

"You're a stupid man, Inspector."

"Possibly, sir, now back to the matter in hand, at the time you and the Countess left Captain Lefevre, to return to London, a large trunk was loaded on to your coach and accompanied you eventually to Kings Cross station where it was deposited in the left luggage office…"

"You have been spying on us!" exclaimed the Count angrily.

"Keeping you under observation, sir."

"This is outrageous, Inspector!"

"To continue, sir, after you left the trunk it was recovered by yourself not an hour or two later, why was that?" the Count looked shocked at that.

"Mon Dieu" whispered the Countess.

"I…I did not collect the trunk…" stammered the Count and the horrified look on his face showed his great concern.

"Then some other person has your trunk, sir."

"Then I must officially report to you the theft of my trunk, get back to London immediately and find it, then arrest the thief!"

"All in good time, sir, now, what was in this trunk of yours?"

"Personal things belonging to my wife and I" replied the Count.

"What sort of things, sir?"

"Why do you ask, Inspector?"

"It was observed to be particularly heavy, sir."

"So?"

"It raises suspicions, sir."

"Why, Inspector?"

"The 'Arabesque' sailed back from Rotterdam and un-loaded one item only, your trunk, which took four of the ship's crew to lift on to your coach, then the ship was scheduled to depart for Nantes immediately, curious, I'm sure you'll agree, sir"

"There is nothing strange about that, Inspector, I would remind you that my wife is the niece of Monsieur Michel Roguefort, the owner of the 'Arabesque', and if her uncle wishes his ship to bring personal things to his niece from Rotterdam, then it is no concern whatever of the British police!"

"Indeed, sir."

"My uncle will be arriving in England on business in a few days, Inspector, then you will have the chance to ask him yourself why he was so considerate to us, if you have the impertinence to do so" smiled the Countess.

"I look forward to the meeting, Countess" replied Hadley with a smile.

"When he discovers that one of his senior captains is accused of murder by the incompetent British police, he will look forward to meeting with your Commissioner, after which, Inspector, I can guarantee that your career will be at an end!" exclaimed the Count.

"As I said, I look forward to meeting Monsieur Roguefort in due course" replied Hadley calmly.

"I think you'd be better employed searching for my diamonds than arresting innocent people" said Mrs Hudson. Hadley ignored the remark and asked "where will your uncle be staying in London, Countess?"

"He is the guest of Mr and Mrs Hudson and will be at Cavendish Square, Inspector" replied the Countess.

"How very convenient" said Hadley.

"Now if there's nothing else, Inspector, I wish you good day" said Mrs Hudson primly.

"Just one more thing, Mrs Hudson."

"Yes?"

"Is your groom, Mr Woods here by any chance?"

"No, Inspector, he is at Cavendish Square, why do you ask?"

"He is helping us with our inquiries, Madam" replied Hadley with a smile and noticed that Mrs Hudson looked anxious.

"Really?"

"Yes, Madam."

"Does my husband know?"

"Only if Mr Woods has told him, Madam" Hadley replied with a smile.

"Good day, Inspector."

The detectives left the house and walked down towards the village to find a pub and have an early lunch before returning to London. As they strode along in the chill air, the sun began to break through and Hadley felt elated by the events of the morning.

"Why did you ask Mrs Hudson if Woods was here, sir?"

"Because I think the Count and his wife were genuinely surprised when I told them that the trunk had been collected and my thoughts then turned towards Mr Hudson and his reliable groom, Eddie Woods" replied Hadley.

"You think that Hudson has the trunk, sir?"

"Possibly, Sergeant, that's why when we return to London, I want you to bring Woods in for questioning and we'll have him photographed whilst he's with us…"

"And then we'll show his photo to the chap in the left luggage office, sir" interrupted Cooper.

"Precisely, Sergeant."

"If we get a positive identification of Woods, what then, sir?"

"We arrest him and question him until he breaks, Sergeant."

"Right, sir."

"It's imperative that we find that trunk."

"Yes, sir."

"I wonder how good the ale is down here in Pangbourne" mused Hadley as they approached a small, thatched pub called 'The Partridge'. Once inside the warm, cosy bar they ordered pints of the local ale and ploughman's lunches from the elderly barman before sitting by a roaring wood fire.

It was just after five o'clock when the train pulled into Paddington Station and Hadley set off for the Yard in a Hansom whilst Cooper went to Cavendish Square to arrest Eddie Woods.

"Chief Inspector Bell wishes to see you in his office, sir" said George as Hadley slumped down behind his desk.

"Alright, George, in a minute."

"I think it's urgent, sir" said the clerk in a serious tone. Hadley, sighed, nodded and left his desk.

"Where have you been, Hadley?" demanded the Chief Inspector angrily.

"Down to Pangbourne, sir."

"In heavens name, why?"

"To interview Count Castellini, sir."

"You were supposed to be here to write a report for the Commissioner by midday!"

"It slipped my mind, sir" replied Hadley sheepishly.

"Paperwork is important, Hadley, the whole system of good policing revolves around accurate reporting!"

"Yes, sir."

"And you, Hadley, are behaving like some giddy young girl

who has just fallen in love for the first time instead of a senior police officer!"

"Yes, sir."

"The Commissioner is furious, Hadley."

"Indeed, sir."

"I can't defend your behaviour if you consistently go against the Commissioner's direct orders" said Bell as he shook his head in frustration.

"No, sir."

"You'll be out on your ear if you're not careful."

"Yes, sir."

"Or, if you're lucky, the Commissioner may spare you and move you to another department."

"Yes, sir."

"You could end up under Chief Inspector Barton, and he hasn't got my sense of humour…"

"I'd miss that, sir."

"And well you might, now, what's going on, Hadley?"

"Count Castellini and his wife deposited a trunk, which I believe contains more gold bullion, at Kings Cross Station, sir…"

"I thought you'd recovered everything in Liverpool" interrupted Bell.

"This is more, sir."

"What are they doing at Pangbourne? I thought they were sailing to America" said Bell.

"It's been put back, sir, and I think that is because Michel Roguefort is arriving in London soon."

"Remind me again, who's he?"

"The owner of the 'Arabesque', head of Maritime du Provence and uncle of the Countess Castellini, sir."

"Oh, yes, and we've had his man in custody."

"Yes, sir, Captain Lefevre."

"He's out on police bail now, Hadley."

"What, sir?" queried the Inspector with alarm.

"Mr Hudson came in to see me with a solicitor, and whilst you were wasting time in Pangbourne, made the case for his release and posted bail accordingly…"

"But the man is held on suspicion of murder, sir."

"Your case against him looks somewhat flimsy" Bell replied.

"I must protest, sir!"

"Protest all you like, Hadley, but I had no option."

"This man is dangerous, sir."

"So you say, but he is bound by surety and he will appear before magistrates in due course" said Bell with authority.

"Do you know where he has gone to, sir?"

"No idea, I'm afraid."

"Probably to his ship at Tilbury, if I'm not mistaken, sir."

"Mr Hudson has given five hundred pounds as surety, Hadley, so, I don't think that Lefevre is going anywhere" said Bell calmly.

"There's more at stake than five hundred pounds, sir."

"Hadley, you're making a mountain out of a mole hill…"

"I don't think you understand the seriousness of the situation, sir."

"Yes, I do, Hadley, and do not ever question my understanding, I am the Chief Inspector and you are forgetting who you are!" Hadley remained silent for a few moments before asking "is there anything else, sir?"

"Yes, I want a full written report on everything before you leave to-night."

"Yes, sir."

Cooper was sitting at his desk when Hadley arrived back from the Chief's office.

"Woods is waiting in the interview room, sir."

"Right, Sergeant, but before we interview him, I must send a telegraph immediately to Inspector Gray at Tilbury to arrest Lefevre if he returns to his ship."

"He's escaped, sir?"

"No, the Chief has released him on bail."

"Good heavens."

"Precisely, Sergeant, then I think we'll have a pot of tea before we speak to Woods."

"Yes, sir."

"When we've finished with him get his photograph taken and tell Jack Curtis that I want it as soon as possible."

"Right, sir."

Eddie Woods looked nervous when Hadley sat down opposite the young groom.

"Tell me, Mr Woods, where were you last night?"

"At home, sir, in Cavendish Square" he replied.

"Did you go out at all?"

"No, sir."

"Not to Kings Cross station by any chance?" at that Woods went pale and began to sweat.

"No, sir, I was at home, like I said" he replied.

"Have you ever seen a large trunk that belongs to Count Castellini?"

"No, sir."

"Are you absolutely, sure?"

"Yes, sir." Hadley remained silent for a few moments before asking "how long have you been a groom in Mr Hudson's employ?"

"Two years now, sir."

"Is he a fair master?"

"Yes, sir, he treats all the staff well."

"Would you say he was generous?"

"Yes, sir."

"And would you do anything for him?"

"Yes, sir, I would."

"Presumably then, if he was in trouble, you would help him?"

"If I could, sir."

"Well, Mr Woods, I think Mr Hudson is in a great deal of trouble, and now is your chance to help him" said Hadley firmly. The groom began to sweat profusely.

"Really, sir?"

"Yes, I think that you approached Harry Grover in the 'Blind Beggar' pub and commissioned him to force the back door of Mr Hudson's house, then paid him ten pounds for his pains…"

"No, I didn't, sir" interrupted Woods.

"Oh, yes, sir, and then last night, at the request of Mr Hudson, you went to Kings Cross and collected the trunk belonging to Count Castellini and took it to a safe place!"

"Sir…"

"I want to know where you took it!"

"Sir, you're making a mistake."

"Am I?"

"Yes, sir, I've done nothing wrong."

"Really?"

"It was the Count who asked me to collect the trunk from Kings Cross then take it to Paddington and wait for him to meet me there, sir." Hadley was stunned by what the groom had just said. He glanced at Cooper and said "a word outside, Sergeant." Cooper nodded and followed the Inspector out into the corridor.

"We've been made fools by the Count and his wife, Sergeant."

"I've never trusted Italians, sir."

"They must have taken the trunk down to Pangbourne and by acting surprised at the news that the trunk had been collected, they managed to mislead us."

"Back to Pangbourne with a search warrant, sir?"

"Not yet, Sergeant, I think we may have a little time left."

"Why is that, sir?"

"Monsieur Michel Roguefort has yet to arrive and I don't think the trunk is going anywhere until he is here, Sergeant."

"What about Woods, sir?"

"Have him photographed and then let him go."

"Right, sir."

"Then come to the office, we've to write up detailed reports for the Chief before we go home tonight."

When Hadley at last arrived home, tired and hungry, he was pleased to sit by the parlour fire while Alice warmed up his supper.

"What a day, my dear" he said as he began his meal.

"Sometimes you work too hard" she replied with concern.

"It's my duty to do so" he replied.

"I know."

"My word, this stew is good" he smiled.

"It's what you need after a hard day" she smiled. They sat in silence whilst Hadley finished his meal and then he sat back in his chair and said "a man I was interviewing today called me 'stupid', and I must admit, Alice, I began to think he was probably right…"

"James Hadley, you are not stupid and you never have been" she interrupted and he smiled.

"What would I do without you, Alice?"

"I don't know dear."

"The suspect lied to me so convincingly that his act was as professional as an Italian opera at Covent Garden" said Hadley.

"The trouble is, that you James are an honest man doing his duty and sometimes you cannot believe that someone is so devious" she said calmly.

"Possibly, my dear."

"Now, you look tired, so go up to bed while I clear away." Hadley nodded and made his way upstairs where he undressed and then fell into his comfortable bed.

CHAPTER 13

As soon as Hadley arrived in his office he telegraphed Inspector Gray again and thanked him for his support during the Tilbury operation and commended the constables who had kept the Castellini's under surveillance. He inquired if Lefevre had been seen and requested a prompt reply.

"I'm sure he'll make an attempt to escape, Sergeant." said Hadley.

"Yes, sir."

"I don't trust that man for one moment and I'm sure he's as guilty as hell."

"You think he'll try to get away, sir?"

"Yes, I think he probably will, Sergeant."

"What now, sir?"

"A visit to the Bank is in order to have words with Mr Hudson to see if he knows where Lefevre is at the moment."

"The captain could be anywhere, sir."

"Indeed, but as long as he is still in the country, we'll find him, so run down and hail a cab, Sergeant."

At the reception in the Bank, Hadley demanded to see Hudson and after a short delay the detectives were shown up to his spacious office.

"Good morning, Inspector,… Sergeant, please take a seat" smiled Mr Hudson. His geniality made Hadley instantly suspicious and he wondered what would be the next turn of events.

"Good morning, sir" replied Hadley as he sat down opposite Hudson.

"How can I help you gentlemen today?" asked the Banker.

"I understand that you have stood surety for Captain Lefevre, sir."

"That is correct, Inspector."

"Why, sir?"

"Because Count Castellini asked me to and furthermore, I believe that the Captain is an innocent man, wrongly arrested by you, Inspector."

"The Captain is the prime suspect in two murder cases, sir."

"Well, my solicitor, Mr Justin Hargreaves is not convinced of that and it would appear that your Chief Inspector Bell also has his doubts."

"Nevertheless, sir…"

"Look, Inspector, you would do well to concentrate on recovering my wife's diamonds instead of running around the country arresting innocent foreign nationals" interrupted Hudson in an angry tone.

"Where is Captain Lefevre now, sir?"

"In a safe place, Inspector, where he cannot be harassed by you!"

"I need to know, sir."

"I have assured Chief Inspector Bell that Captain Lefevre will present himself to the magistrate when he is required to do so, and that is an end of the matter."

"Mr Hudson, you are obstructing my inquiries and I warn you…"

"Warn me! You damned impertinent fellow!" interrupted Hudson angrily as just then there came a knock at the door and Mr Augustus entered the office.

"What is it, Augustus?" demanded Hudson angrily.

"I'm so sorry to interrupt you, sir, but this was just delivered to reception, marked for your immediate attention" said the anxious manager as he held out a neat brown paper parcel.

"Give it here then" said Hudson and Augustus placed the package on the desk in front of him.

As the Banker started to untie the string he said "you may go now."

"Yes, sir" replied the manager and he left the office as Hudson unwrapped the brown paper to reveal a large, blue velvet, jewellery box.

"My God" he murmured and he then opened the box to reveal the Hudson diamonds. They sparkled and gleamed in the hazy sunlight that streamed through the window from behind the surprised Banker. Hadley reacted immediately and said "Sergeant, get down to reception and see if you can catch the person who delivered this package."

"Right, sir" Cooper replied and hurried out of the office..

"You can confirm that those are your wife's diamonds, Mr

Hudson?"

"Yes, Inspector, I can."

"I'm sure that she will be overjoyed at their recovery, sir."

"Indeed, she will" said Hudson with a smile.

"All we have to do now is apprehend the thief, sir."

"Yes, Inspector."

"Then when we have him in custody, we'll learn the truth" said Hadley as he fixed Hudson with a steely gaze.

"Quite so."

"Now, to return to the other matter, where is Captain Lefevre, sir?"

"I am not prepared to divulge that information, Inspector."

"You must understand that you place yourself in a very serious situation by withholding vital information" said Hadley firmly.

"So be it, but I think that you should direct your inquiries to Monsieur Roguefort when he arrives in London" smiled Hudson.

"Be assured that I will do so, and always remember, sir, that neither he nor you are above the law and I will not hesitate to bring charges against you both if necessary" replied Hadley.

"We'll see about that, because once Monsieur Roguefort has met the Commissioner and discussed your cavalier and slip shod approach to matters, then I believe your days are numbered" replied the banker with a grin. Hadley remained silent whilst he calmed himself and was just about to try a different line of attack when Cooper burst into the office.

"I just missed him, sir, but we know who he is, sir."

"Go on, Sergeant."

"It's Eddie Woods, sir."

"My groom? How do you know it was him?" asked a pale faced Hudson.

"Your receptionist recognised him immediately from this photograph, sir" replied Cooper as he showed the sepia tint likeness to the amazed Banker.

"Good God!" exclaimed Hudson.

"Not a moment to lose, Sergeant, call a cab and let's get to Cavendish Square, hopefully, we'll catch him there and then we will finally get to the bottom of this tomfoolery!"

"Right, sir."

"So Woods was the thief…" murmured Hudson.

"I don't think so, Mr Hudson, but rest assured that I will speaking to you again very shortly sir" said Hadley and he gave a nod before he left the speechless Banker.

The door to Hudson's London home was opened by the indifferent butler, Wilkes, and when Hadley asked to see Eddie Woods the reply was "I'm afraid he is not here, sir."

"Do you know where he is?" demanded Hadley.

"No, sir."

"I wish to search his room, so please lead the way" said Hadley.

"I'm afraid I can't allow that without the master's permission, sir."

"We have just come from Mr Hudson's office and he is fully aware of our intentions, so lead on" replied Hadley firmly.

"Mr Woods has a room over the stables in the mews, so if you would care to go around and tell the head groom, Mr Edmunds, he will direct you accordingly" said the butler in a resigned tone. The head groom was duly found and he lead the way up the open wooden stairs to Eddie Woods room. It was sparse, small and empty of any sign of recent habitation.

"When did Mr Woods leave?" demanded Hadley angrily.

"Yesterday, sir, he said he was going to see a friend and stay for a few days, he told me that Mr Hudson had given him permission, which I thought at the time was a bit unusual" replied Mr Edmunds as he scratched his head.

"Thank you for your help, come Sergeant, there's nothing here for us" said Hadley.

As the Hansom conveyed the detectives back to the Yard, Hadley remained silent and Cooper knew that it was for the best that he did not interrupt the Inspector's thoughts. As they drew close to Parliament Square, Hadley said "they're running rings around us at the moment, Sergeant, but I'll be damned if we'll be beaten!"

"Quite so, sir, but what next?"

"I'm not sure, but a pot of tea and a review of the facts will help" replied Hadley with a smile.

George made the tea and shortly after the detectives began

discussing the events of the day, the affable clerk returned to the office and said "sorry to disturb you, sir, but a message by telegraph has just arrived from Inspector Gray." He handed the note to Hadley, who read it out aloud.

"Many thanks for your message, your comments greatly appreciated, surveillance by my officers and inquiries at the dock regarding the whereabouts of Lefevre prove negative. The 'Arabesque' departed yesterday on the evening tide. Mr Wright also unable to confirm whether or not Captain Lefevre was aboard the ship. Hope all goes well with the investigation, yours, Peter Gray, Inspector." Cooper remained silent then looked at Hadley, who sat, disappointed and frustrated.

"As I said, they're running rings around us."

"Yes, sir."

"I'll go and brief the Chief, whilst you write your report on the day's events, so far."

"Right, sir."

"What are you telling me, Hadley?" demanded the harassed Chief.

"That the Hudson diamonds have been recovered…"

"Thank God for that, at least we can get some respite from Mrs Hudson and her Christmas party can proceed" interrupted Bell.

"Yes, sir, but the groom, Eddie Woods, has disappeared."

"So what, the diamonds are back where they belong, all we have to do is inform the Commissioner, so he can announce it triumphantly to the Press, then we can all go home tonight and sleep soundly, for a change!"

"But, sir…"

"Never mind the groom, we'll probably never see him again…"

"Sir, I'm sure that Woods is the unwilling accomplice of Hudson and the Count" interrupted Hadley in a firm tone.

"Hadley, I do wonder about you sometimes, sufficient unto the day is the evil thereof, be thankful that the diamonds are recovered!"

"I am, sir, but my investigations show that somehow the gold bullion theft is linked to the Count and the Hudson's."

"You'll be telling me next that Captain Lefevre murdered Sir

John…"

"No, sir, Hudson committed that crime and I suspect that Lefevre has now left the country…"

"Why do you say that?" asked Bell with a worried look.

"I've just received a telegraph from Inspector Gray at Tilbury, the 'Arabesque' left yesterday on the evening tide…"

"Good God, do you think Lefevre was on the ship?" Bell asked anxiously.

"Yes, I do, sir, but unfortunately I've no proof as both the harbour master and officers who kept the ship under surveillance are unable to confirm my suspicions."

"We've let him get away again" murmured Bell.

"You released him, sir."

"Don't remind me, Hadley."

"Well, I'm afraid we're back to square one, sir."

"What do you mean, Hadley?"

"Lefevre has disappeared and I'm not certain if Hudson really knows where he is, the suspect trunk of gold bullion has also vanished along with Eddie Woods…"

"Do you think Woods has it?" interrupted Bell anxiously.

"I have no idea, sir."

"What do you plan to do now, Hadley?"

"I think a visit to Pangbourne for a frank discussion with the Count, sir."

"Oh, go steady, I don't want any further upset."

"I am the very soul of discretion, sir" smiled Hadley.

"That's your opinion, Hadley."

"By the way, sir, I must inform you that Mr Hudson has told me that Monsieur Roguefort will be arriving in London within the next few days and he will demand a meeting with the Commissioner…"

"What for?"

"To complain about me, sir."

"Oh, dear God" said Bell as he shook his head slowly.

"It was inevitable, sir, given all the facts, when he finds out that his captain was arrested by me on suspicion of two murders, his niece and her husband have been followed at my instigation and along with everything else."

"He could make things very difficult for you, Hadley."

"I know that, sir."

"Well, for one brief moment I felt elated that the Hudson diamonds had been recovered, now because of you, I've sunk down once more into a gloom of stygian darkness."

"Do not worry, sir, I'm sure that everything will end satisfactorily" Hadley smiled.

"If only I could believe that" said Bell sadly.

"I'll make sure you have up to date reports before I leave for Pangbourne tomorrow, sir."

"Thank you, Hadley."

The detectives went for a late lunch at the Crown Inn in the Strand and over pints of stout and ploughmen's lunches, discussed the plans for the visit to Pangbourne.

"I'm sure that the trunk is hidden there, Sergeant."

"Do you think Woods knows where it is, sir?"

"No, I am fairly certain that the Count only used Woods to collect the trunk from Kings Cross and take it to Paddington."

"Right, sir."

"The Count wanted it to disappear because he may have thought we were on to him."

"And he wouldn't want Eddie Woods to know where the trunk would end up, sir."

"Exactly, he knew if we got hold of Woods we would break him and all would be revealed."

"Do you think Woods had a hand in the diamond theft, sir?"

"Only as the 'go between', Hudson arranged the sham break in and took the diamonds and hid them somewhere, Sergeant."

"Is Mrs Hudson involved at all, sir?"

"Right up to her neck, Sergeant!"

"We might find out more when she comes back to London with the Count and Countess to meet Monsieur Roguefort, sir."

"Indeed, Sergeant, and I'm sure that our meeting with Roguefort will be more than routine!"

"I'm looking forward to it, sir" smiled Cooper.

"So am I, Sergeant, so, let's drink up and get back to the office, we've reports to write for the Chief Inspector before we go home."

Cooper met Hadley at Paddington Station just before eight thirty the next morning and they caught the first train to Reading. They hired a trap and in the weak, late autumn sunshine, made their way to Pangbourne. Hadley remained silent during the journey and only spoke to comment on the view from the hilltop as they entered the gates of Pangbourne House. As the trap made its way along the gravel drive up to the front portico, Hadley saw two men walking across the spacious lawn in front of the house. The men looked across at the trap as it drew near to the pillared entrance.

"My God" whispered Hadley and Cooper followed the Inspector's gaze.

"Now there's a surprise, sir" said Cooper and Hadley nodded.

"Good morning, Gentlemen" called the Inspector as the two men walked towards them.

"Good morning, Inspector" replied the Count whilst Captain Lefevre glared at Hadley.

"I'm pleased to see you both" smiled Hadley.

"Mon Dieu! Pleased to see me? You insult my intelligence, Inspector" said Lefevre angrily.

"Come, come, sir, I'm only being pleasant whilst attempting to do my duty" replied Hadley.

"Why are you here today, Inspector?" asked the Count.

"I have a few questions for you, sir, but finding Captain Lefevre here at Pangbourne, will allow me to broaden out my lines of inquiry" replied Hadley with a smile.

"You had better come in, but I warn you, Mrs Hudson will not be pleased to see you" said the Count.

"On the contrary, sir, she will be very pleased when she hears my news" said Hadley as he stepped down from the trap. Whilst Cooper paid the driver and made arrangements for the return journey, Hadley followed the Count and Lefevre up the steps to the front door. The party was admitted by the butler and whilst the detectives waited in the hall way, the Count went into the drawing room to announce their arrival. They were then summoned into the warm room, where Mrs Hudson fixed Hadley with a withering stare and asked "why are you here again, Inspector, uninvited as usual?"

"Good morning, Mrs Hudson."

"Never mind the pleasantries, my guests and I are inconvenienced yet again by your intrusion into my house!"

"I am sorry to hear that, Madam."

"I will tell my husband as soon as he arrives and I assure you that he will be making a further complaint about you to the Commissioner…"

"I don't think so, at least not this time, Madam" interrupted Hadley in a firm tone.

"Why, pray?"

"Because, your diamonds were recovered yesterday and Mr Hudson now has them safely in his possession!" That stopped her dead and with her mouth open in surprise, she looked at the Count.

"Excellent!" beamed the Count as Mrs Hudson began to cry and was immediately comforted by the Countess.

"I'm sorry that the good news has distressed you, Madam" said Hadley, with a touch of sarcasm, but Mrs Hudson made no reply and continued to weep into her handkerchief.

"Have you caught the thief?" asked the Count.

"Not yet, sir, but we know who he is" replied Hadley.

"Who is it?"

"Eddie Woods, the groom at Cavendish Square" replied Hadley. The Count went a little pale when he heard the name.

"Woods?" queried Mrs Hudson and she stopped crying immediately.

"Yes, Madam, Sergeant Cooper and myself were in your husband's office when Woods brought the diamonds into the Bank…"

"Why did you not arrest him?" demanded the Count.

"Because he left them at reception and ran off, but when Sergeant Cooper showed the clerk a photograph of Woods, he was immediately identified" replied Hadley.

"Dear God, a thief living in my house" murmured Mrs Hudson.

"We went to Cavendish Square immediately, hoping to arrest him there, but discovered that Woods had left for a few days holiday with your husband's permission, madam."

"Holiday?" she queried.

"Yes."

"What nonsense, I can assure you that servants in my house are not given holidays, Inspector" she said.

"Nevertheless, those are the facts, Madam."

"So, will you be able to find Woods?" she asked.

"Without doubt, and I think that the Count may be able to help us on that score" replied Hadley.

"Me, Inspector?" asked the surprised Italian.

"Yes, sir."

"How?"

"Woods was brought in previously for questioning over the matter regarding your missing trunk, sir."

"Go on, Inspector" said the Count with a concerned look.

"He said that he was instructed by you to collect your trunk from Kings Cross Station and take it to Paddington to wait for you, sir." The Count went very pale and glanced at his wife who looked anxious.

"That is untrue, Inspector, the boy is obviously telling lies, I mean, why should I want him to do such a thing?" said the Count with a little forced laugh.

"I have no idea, sir, but if it is true, then you may know where your trunk and the thief are at this moment" replied Hadley.

"These are foolish questions, Inspector, I suggest you go back to London, look for my trunk and plan what you will say to Monsieur Roguefort when he arrives" said the Count.

"I will do that, sir, after I have questioned both you and Captain Lefevre" said Hadley.

"Me?" asked Lefevre in surprise.

"Yes, you, sir."

"Mon Dieu! Have I not suffered enough at your hands, Monsieur Inspector?"

"I must remind you that I arrested you on suspicion of murder, Captain, and when you appear in front of the magistrate, I will oppose your bail vigorously…"

"Mon Dieu! You are mad!" interrupted Lefevre.

"And if all the money in London is paid to clever solicitors and barristers they will not save you from a trial at the Old Bailey!"

"I assure you, Monsieur Inspector, that when Monsieur Roguefort learns of all this, he will see to it that you are dismissed and never work again, you will be a beggar on the streets of London!" exclaimed Lefevre.

"He can try, Captain, but I can assure you that we are not diverted from our duties at the Yard by complaints from rich Frenchmen" said Hadley calmly.

"Mon Dieu! You are insufferable!"

"So I'm told; now, may we have somewhere more private to discuss matters?" Hadley asked.

"I think we would all be interested to hear what you have to say, Inspector" said Mrs Hudson and the Count nodded his approval.

"Very well then, first of all, I have to advise you Count Castellini that you are under suspicion of a gold bullion robbery from a Bank in Istanbul…"

"Preposterous!" interrupted the Count as Hadley observed the Countess becoming very pale.

"Nevertheless, I can reveal that three cases, labelled 'machinery', unloaded from the 'Arabesque' in London were sent by rail to Liverpool where they were opened by myself and Sergeant Cooper…"

"Mon Dieu! This is madness!" exclaimed Lefevre.

"And inside we discovered sixty bars of gold, which were destined to be shipped to Boston" said Hadley and he looked at the stunned Italians.

"You are making a big mistake, Monsieur Inspector" said Lefevre.

"I don't think so, Captain. To continue, I believe that the missing trunk contains more gold…"

"If any of this nonsense was true, why would I take the risk of keeping a trunk full of gold with me when I could send it on by train?" interrupted the Count with a smile.

"As insurance, sir, just in case the agents, Garstang and Fletcher discovered what they were transporting from the station to the dock and stole it…"

"How dare you accuse my husband in this manner, Inspector, you are a disgrace!" said the Countess, her eyes blazing with fury.

"I dare, Countess, because it is true, as are the murders of Dalmas and Mornay by Captain Lefevre to silence them forever" said Hadley and at that moment Lefevre could contain himself no longer and lunged at Hadley, attempting to grab at his throat.

"You swine, you meddling pig!" shouted Lefevre as he wrestled with Hadley. Cooper sprang to the Inspector's defence and grabbed Lefevre, putting him into a headlock and forcing the Captain to the floor. Hadley stood back for a moment and said

"Captain, if you will cease to struggle and agree to behave with decorum, I will instruct Sergeant Cooper to release you."

"Oui, oui, let me go" replied the Captain, his face buried into the thick carpet. Cooper released his neck hold and then helped the shaken Frenchman to his feet.

"You have a violent temper but I will not press charges for your assault on a police officer as I believe the two murder charges you face are sufficient for the moment, sir" said Hadley.

"Sit down here, Captain" said Mrs Hudson, pale faced at the violence.

"Give him some water" said the Countess.

Hadley waited for a few moments before saying "so, I think that is all for the time being, Captain, you and the Count now know the seriousness of your situations."

"Yes, Inspector, Captain Lefevre and I are fully aware of your ridiculous accusations" said the Count. Hadley nodded and said "Sergeant Cooper and I will leave you for the time being and return to London where we will wait with interest for the arrival of Monsieur Roguefort, good day, Mrs Hudson, Count, Countess and Captain Lefevre." They all looked at Hadley and he could see that they were completely stunned. He then added, with a smile, "by the way, I must inform you that you are all under constant surveillance, good day once again" and he left the room followed by Cooper.

Once outside the house they walked briskly down the drive towards the gated entrance.

"You certainly stirred things up in there, but why did you tell them that they were under surveillance when they're not, sir?"

"They don't know that, Sergeant, and it will keep them on their toes, possibly forcing them into making mistakes."

"True, sir."

"Now let's have a very early lunch in that village pub, 'The Partridge' I believe."

"Good idea, sir."

"I thought the ale was rather good last time, didn't you, Sergeant?"

CHAPTER 14

It was just after four o'clock when Hadley went up to see Chief Inspector Bell in his office.

"Good afternoon, sir."

"Is it, Hadley?" asked Bell as he looked up from his paper strewn desk.

"I think so, sir."

"Umm, I judge by that comment that possibly you've made some progress down at Pangbourne this morning" said Bell.

"Yes indeed, sir, I can report that Captain Lefevre is there…"

"Good news indeed, Hadley" interrupted Bell.

"I thought you'd be pleased, sir."

"Anything else?"

"Well, other than accusing Count Castellini of stealing the gold bullion from Istanbul…"

"What? Are you mad, Hadley?" interrupted Bell in a raised voice.

"I don't think so, sir."

"You haven't any evidence, he will have you crucified!"

"He's guilty as hell, sir" replied Hadley in a firm tone.

"Listen to me, Hadley, once Roguefort has arrived and learns from the Count, Hudson and Lefevre what you have been up to, I can see you in the horse traffic division before Christmas!"

"Possibly, sir."

"The Commissioner will have to act when Roguefort makes his complaints."

"I will defend my actions and hope that you will support me, sir."

"Well, I don't know about that" replied Bell with some hesitation.

"The facts speak for themselves, sir."

"Look, Hadley, I've read your reports carefully, that's what I do all day long for God's sake, and to my way of thinking your evidence against Lefevre for the murders of his men is almost nonexistent!"

"Not so, sir, we have a flake of gold from the head injury that killed Dalmas before he was dumped in the river and an eye witness to the murder of Mornay in Whitechapel…"

"A flake of gold and the word of some prostitute count for very little, Hadley, and there is no proof that Lefevre was even in Whitechapel that night."

"I'm sure he was, sir."

"If this case ever gets to court, defence lawyers will have a field day with the girl, if she has the courage to speak up, as well as you, mark my words."

"Possibly, sir."

"Then when it all gets thrown out, Roguefort will demand compensation for unlawful arrest of his Captain, the Count will demand a written apology for your intemperate accusation and Hudson, well, he and his wife will dine out for a month in London society whilst they blacken the reputation of the Metropolitan Police" said Bell as he shook his head slowly.

"I'm sure that we'll obtain convictions, sir."

"I admire your optimism, Hadley, but do not share it, furthermore, the Commissioner has grave doubts about it all."

"I'm sorry to hear that, sir."

"Things are not looking good, Hadley."

"No, sir."

"See if you can pull the chestnuts out of the fire before it's too late."

"I'll try, sir."

"That will be all, Hadley."

"Yes, sir" he replied and left the office.

Hadley asked George for a pot of tea before sitting at his desk and glancing through Cooper's notes on the visit to Pangbourne. When he had finished reading, he closed the folder and sat back in his chair, gazed at the ceiling for a while, deep in thought. George arrived with tea for two and placed one steaming cup on the Inspector's desk, the other on Cooper's.

"Thank you, George" murmured Hadley and the clerk nodded

"Was the Chief relieved to know that we discovered Captain Lefevre at Pangbourne, sir?" enquired Cooper.

"Yes, but he's concerned about the evidence that we have against him and, furthermore, he's put some doubt in my mind about the woman who saw Mornay in the Lane when he was murdered…"

"You've doubts about Molly Barnet, sir?"

"Yes, she's a nervous young woman and she may be too frightened to testify in court" replied Hadley.

"As she's our only witness, sir, that would be the end."

"Possibly, Sergeant, but I think we'll go along to the 'Kings Head' later, find Agnes and then pay a visit to Miss Molly Barnet to see if we can strengthen her resolve."

"Right, sir."

"Overall, things look bad, Sergeant, and we need some luck."

When the detectives arrived at the pub in Whitechapel it was full of early evening drinkers, wharfmen, market traders and fish wives who had stopped on their way home from work. Hadley caught sight of Agnes and Florrie seated at a table and the women smiled when they saw the policemen. As they approached the bar, Vera, all hot and bothered, smiled then asked "what can I get you, gents?"

"Two stouts and two sixpenny gins, please Vera" said Hadley. Vera nodded and Cooper asked "are the ladies here already, sir?"

"Yes, Sergeant, they're over there, so I'll take the gins and you bring the stout after you've settled up with Vera" replied Hadley as the barmaid placed the gins on the bar. Hadley winked at Cooper and the made his way through the crowded, smoke filled pub.

"You are a true gent" said Agnes as Hadley put the glasses of gin on the table.

"So I'm told" replied Hadley as he sat opposite the two women.

"You can always tell a gent" said Florrie.

"How?" asked Hadley with a smile.

"He takes his weight on his elbows!" exclaimed Agnes and Florrie laughed out loud as Cooper arrived with the stout.

"Evening, ladies" said Cooper as he placed the pints of stout on the table and sat next to Hadley.

"I bet the Sergeant does" said Florrie.

"Does what?" asked Cooper with a smile.

"I'll tell you later, Sergeant" said Hadley quickly before Florrie could reply.

"Jim, you are old fashioned" smiled Agnes.

"Possibly. Now Agnes, I want you to accompany us later, when we call on Molly Barnet…"

"Is she in trouble, Jim?" interrupted Agnes.

"No, not at all, I just want to go over what she saw when the French sailor was murdered and give her some support" replied Hadley.

"I know she's worried by it all, Jim" said Agnes.

"That concerns me, I've got to try and put her mind at ease and explain that when she gives evidence in court…"

"She won't go to court, Jim, that's for sure" interrupted Agnes before she sipped at her gin.

"The case will collapse without her evidence" said Hadley calmly, trying not to show his concern at what Agnes had said.

"Well, she'll need a lot of persuasion, Jim."

"Please help me, Agnes."

"I'll try, Jim, but no promises, mind."

"No promises."

"What about that other French man that Doris saw?" asked Florrie and Hadley's mind raced on hearing that.

"Oh, that French man, yeah, I remember now" said Agnes.

"Tell us all about this other man" said Hadley with a smile.

"He was with Doris the night that the sailor got killed outside Molly's place" said Florrie.

"What's her full name and where can I find this 'Doris'?" asked Hadley.

"Doris Spencer and she usually drinks in the Blind Beggar" replied Florrie.

"Sometimes she comes in here" said Agnes.

"But mostly she picks up customers in the Blind Beggar" added Florrie.

"Is she likely to be there tonight?" asked Hadley.

"Probably" nodded Florrie as Agnes looked up and suddenly smiled.

"Jim, you're in luck, she's just walked in here!" Hadley turned to see a tall, dark haired woman of about thirty, quite well dressed and smiling at Agnes.

"Come and join us, Doris" said Hadley as he stood.

"Do I know you, sir?" asked Doris.

"Not yet, but you will do after Agnes introduces us and my assistant goes to the bar to get you a drink" smiled Hadley.

"Thank you, a brandy if you're buying" replied Doris and she sat in Cooper's seat as he hurried off to the bar.

"This gent is my good friend Jim Hadley and his man, Cooper" said Agnes as Doris shook hands with Hadley.

"Is Jim a customer?" asked Doris with a smile.

"No, I'm afraid not, Doris, although I've promised him an experience that he'd remember for the rest of his life, I can't tempt him" replied Agnes.

"Perhaps you should let me try" smiled Doris coyly.

"You're wasting your time, Doris, he's married and even worse than that, he's a Bobby!" said Agnes.

"Oh, my Gawd" said Doris in horror.

"But despite all of that, we love him because he's good to me and Florrie" said Agnes.

"Thank you, Agnes" Hadley smiled as Cooper arrived back with the brandy.

"Are you a Bobby too?" asked Doris as Cooper placed the drink in front of her.

"I am" he smiled and sat on the bench next to Florrie who snuggled up to him.

"Now, now, Florrie, the Sergeant is on duty" said Hadley as he sipped his stout and Agnes laughed.

"Well, cheers, Jim, nice to meet a sweet Bobby" said Doris as she raised her glass.

"Cheers, Doris." They all sipped at their drinks before Doris asked "what brings you to the 'Kings Head', Jim?"

"I came here especially to meet you, Doris" replied Hadley and they all laughed.

"My word, Agnes, he's a saucy one and no mistake" said Doris.

"You don't know the half, my girl" replied Agnes.

"I'm hoping you can help me…" Hadley began.

"Anytime, Jim, just say the word!" interrupted Doris with a coy smile.

"No, Doris, not that…"

"Its half price for good looking Bobbies with blue eyes" she said still smiling.

"Doris, this is serious…"

"I am serious, Jim" she laughed.

"I hope you now understand, Sergeant, how you can be so easily led astray when on duty" said Hadley.

"I can indeed, sir."

"Well now you've met me and you don't want my personal service, what do you want, Jim?" asked Doris as she sipped her brandy.

"Agnes tells me that on the night that the French sailor was murdered in Gypsy Lane, you met another one in the 'Blind Beggar', is that so?" asked Hadley.

"Yeah, I did" replied Doris.

"Tell me all about him" said Hadley.

"He was sitting alone in a corner and I went up to him and asked if he'd like some company for the evening, he smiled, nodded and said he would, I told him like, it would cost him, and he said he'd buy me a drink first, and I wasn't going to say 'no' to that, was I?" Doris smiled.

"Of course not" said Hadley.

"He bought me a brandy and we started talking, he had a very strong French accent but spoke good English."

"Do you remember everything he said?"

"Not everything as I had my mind set on what I was going to charge him, I mean normally it's seven and six for straight, but I thought he may have money, so I hoped he might go to ten shillings" replied Doris.

"Quite so" nodded Hadley.

"I mean, I have to keep up appearances otherwise I'd only get drunks with no money or boys with pimples" said Doris with feeling.

"That's understandable, but do go on" smiled Hadley

"Well, he told me that his ship was the Arab something…"

"The 'Arabesque'?" interrupted Hadley.

"Yeah, that sounds like it, and he said he lived in Marseille with some girl, he said he wasn't married or anything like that."

"Would you recognise him again, Doris?"

"Oh, for sure I would."

"Describe him to me if you can."

"He had a swarthy, dark look about him, he was grey haired

and he had a scar on his cheek, just here" and she touched her face.

"Go on, Doris."

"He told me his name, but for the life of me I can't remember it" said Doris.

"Try, Doris."

"Leave it, I'm sure it'll come to me in a minute, especially if I have another brandy, it helps me think, Jim."

"Sergeant, if you please."

"Right, Agnes, Florrie, the same again?"

"Oh you are an angel, Sergeant" smiled Agnes and Florrie nodded.

"Carry on, Doris" said Hadley.

"Not a lot more to say, Jim, we just talked for a while and when I said I'd charge him ten shillings for personal relief, he said he didn't want it, can you believe that?"

"No."

"I thought that the price put him off, so I offered myself for eight shillings, but he said he had to meet another sailor and had an important job to do that night, so I thought that he preferred a bit of bum, if you get my meaning" she said.

"You have a way with words, Doris" Hadley smiled.

"All I got out of it was a couple of brandies, and that's not a lot of good for a working girl who's got to keep up appearances."

"Understandable" nodded Hadley

"Then he looked at his watch and said that he had to go to meet this other bloke."

"What time was that, Doris?"

"About half past ten, and I was put out, so to speak, because it didn't give me a chance to pick up another customer before we all got chucked out at closing time" she replied as Cooper arrived back with the drinks.

"Cheers" said Doris and the women sipped at their fresh drinks.

"Now, Doris, see if you can remember this man's name" said Hadley.

"No, it's gone, Jim…"

"Try, if you can."

"Hmm, something like Marcus…"

"Marcel, perhaps?"

"Could be, anyway, it was definitely something like that" she nodded.

"Marcel Lefevre?"

"No, he didn't say his other name, Jim."

"Pity."

"I'm sorry I'm not much use."

"You've been very helpful, Doris, and if you're certain that you would recognise this man, I'd like you to come along to the Yard when I next have him in for interview and identify him."

"Would I get expenses, Jim?"

"I'll send the Sergeant here to collect you in a Hansom and bring you back, then buy you a large brandy…"

"No money then?" she asked.

"Ten shillings for your trouble?" smiled Hadley.

"Make it a guinea, Jim, and I'm yours" Doris smiled.

"Keeping up appearances is obviously expensive" said Hadley.

"I know, Jim, but it works, doesn't it?" Doris replied and he laughed.

"A guinea it is then, but for that you'll have to appear in court and give evidence."

"Court? I'll want more than a guinea for that, Jim!"

"We'll haggle nearer the time, but first things first, I need you to identify this man without fail" said Hadley.

"I will, Jim."

"Thank you, give the Sergeant your address if you please."

"It's number twelve, Brick Lane, Whitechapel" she said and Cooper wrote it down in his book.

"Now, if you would like to finish your drink, Agnes, I'd like to go and see Molly" said Hadley.

"Yes, Jim" Agnes replied.

"Sergeant, you stay here if you will and entertain the ladies, I'm sure that they could manage another drink or two."

"It's my pleasure, sir."

"No, Sergeant, it's your duty."

Molly Barnet opened her door to Agnes and Hadley then welcomed them into her small room.

"I'm sure that you know why we're here, Molly" said Hadley as he sat on a rickety hard back chair.

"Yes, it's about the murder of the Frenchie" she nodded.

"Indeed, so cast your mind back, if you will, and tell me once again everything you heard and saw that night" said Hadley with a reassuring smile. Molly paused, looked up at the grubby ceiling before returning her gaze to Hadley and said "it was late, my last gent had gone and suddenly I heard loud voices outside in the Lane, I was in bed and wasn't in a mind to get up and see what the ruckus was all about, seeing that we have so many down here at night…"

"Quite so."

"But it carried on and then got much louder, something alarming it was…"

"Indeed."

"Then I got up and went to the door and…"

"At that point, did you hear what the men were saying?"

"No, sir, they were just shouting, then there was a scream and I was afraid to peep out, then it all went quiet, so I opened my door and saw the Frenchie in the gutter, he looked blimmin' awful in the gas light, white as a sheet he was, and then he held up his hand when he saw me and said something like 'feather', then he fell back and his head rolled to one side."

"Did you see the other man at all?"

"No, sir, I just heard someone running off down the Lane in the fog."

"What happened next?"

"I heard someone shout for a Bobby and then a police whistle, after that several people came and then the Bobby arrived, sir."

"I have to ask you again, Molly, when the man called out 'feather' do you think he said 'Lefevre'?"

"I couldn't say for sure, but it might have been" she replied.

"Thank you very much, now, you do understand that you are a very important witness and I'm going to have to ask you to come to court and tell the judge what you witnessed that night" said Hadley in a gentle tone.

"Yes, sir."

"Are you anxious about that?"

"If Agnes will come with me I'll be alright and you'll be there, won't you, sir?"

"Most certainly I will be and I'm sure Agnes won't mind

keeping you company" replied Hadley with relief.

"I'll go with you, Molly, don't worry" said Agnes and Hadley could have kissed them both.

Hadley arrived back at the 'Kings Head', with Agnes, just in time to stop Cooper buying another round of drinks for the two women who were by this time, a little worse for wear and making improper advances to the young, handsome Sergeant.

"Time to go, Sergeant, so say goodnight to the ladies."

"Oh, stay and have another drink before you go, Jim" said Doris.

"No thank you, Doris, we've work to do" replied Hadley.

"You're a spoil sport, Jim, d'you know that?" asked Doris.

"So Agnes tells me, but I'm afraid that duty calls" replied Hadley as he tapped Cooper on his shoulder and the two detectives said 'goodnight' before they left the pub. As they waited for a Hansom in the cobbled street, Hadley said "a very good ending to the day, Sergeant, finding Doris and then to have Molly agree so easily to come to court and give evidence."

"Yes, sir, we needed some luck and we got it, where to now?" asked Cooper as he waved down a cab.

"Home, Sergeant, we've had enough today, we'd better rest and prepare ourselves for tomorrow as I think once Roguefort arrives, things could get very difficult."

The next morning, after Hadley had finished his first cup of tea and was reading Cooper's notes, George came into the office.

"I'm sorry to disturb you, sir, but a Mr Augustus, from the Bank, has arrived downstairs, and wishes to speak to you privately." Hadley looked up at George and then at Cooper, who had a surprised look on hearing what had just been said.

"Bring him up, George, right away if you please."

"Certainly, sir."

"This will be interesting, Sergeant."

"It will indeed, sir." They waited for what seemed an age before Mr John Augustus was shown into the office by George.

"Good morning, Mr Augustus, please come in and do sit down" said Hadley as he stood and extended his hand to the Bank Manager.

"Thank you, Inspector" replied Augustus and Hadley noted the man's nervousness as he shook hands and sat down opposite the Inspector's desk. Cooper pulled up a chair next to Hadley and produced his notebook.

"How can we help, sir?" asked Hadley with a smile.

"Well, Inspector, this visit is to remain confidential…"

"Yes of course, sir, we fully understand, now why have you called to see us today?"

"Well, after the death of Sir John, we're all still very upset at the bank, I mean, he was such a gentleman and so well liked, it's a tragedy, a terrible tragedy, none of us know what to think, now there's a rumour that the dear man was murdered…"

"Yes, I think he was" interrupted Hadley and Augustus went pale.

"Oh, dear God, it's true then?"

"I'm afraid so, sir."

"I don't know what to say."

"Just explain why you're here"

"I don't know what to tell you, Inspector…"

"The truth and all the facts will do nicely" interrupted Hadley.

"I don't want anything I say to be misconstrued or held against Sir John…"

"It won't be, but in any case, let us worry about that, sir."

"I don't know where to start…"

"Would you like a cup of tea to help you gather your thoughts?" asked Hadley attempting to put the anxious manager at ease.

"Er, no thank you, Inspector."

"Well Sergeant Cooper and I are listening, so we're ready when you are, sir" said Hadley and he waited patiently for Augustus to begin.

"Some months ago, it was in September to be correct, that Mr Wells, my assistant, and I noticed some slight irregularities in an overseas account…" Augustus paused and Hadley's mind raced.

"Do go on, sir."

"Well, they were only slight anomalies, nothing to be too concerned about you understand, just normal banking fluctuations" said Augustus and Hadley nodded as if he understood the vagaries of bank fluctuations.

"Then in October, the amounts were slightly larger, and I became concerned…"

"Why, sir?"

"Because the anomalies were only present in the one account…"

"Pray tell us which one" interrupted Hadley certain that he knew the answer.

"The Boston First National Bank" replied Augustus and Hadley smiled.

"How much is involved in total?"

"I hardly like to say, Inspector, it is confidential to the Bank…"

"I'm investigating the murder of your chairman, sir, so nothing is confidential as far as I'm concerned" interrupted Hadley.

"Well, I, er, er…"

"How much?"

"Over one hundred thousand pounds…" At that Hadley fixed his steely gaze on the manager and Cooper pursed his lips.

"Make a careful note of that, Sergeant."

"I have, sir."

"Who has access to this account, Mr Augustus?"

"Only the senior staff who deal with overseas accounts" replied the Manager.

"And of course, Mr Hudson and his colleagues on the Board" Hadley smiled.

"Yes, that is so."

"Did Sir John know of these 'irregularities'?" asked Hadley.

"I don't know, I certainly did not draw them to his attention" replied Augustus.

"Why not?"

"I was unsure whether to or not."

"Did you not think that you had a duty to do so?"

"Possibly, now in hindsight" replied Augustus nervously.

"Do you know where the money went to?"

"Yes, an account at the Banque du Sumaris."

"Where are they?"

"In Paris but they have a branch in London."

"I take it that they are a French Bank?"

"Yes, they are a Merchant Bank, quite well known."

"Indeed, have you the name of the account?"

"No, Inspector, the credits have gone into a special reserve account, which only has a number."

"Very interesting, now do you think that Sir John had any suspicion that something was amiss?"

"Possibly, now I think of it."

"Go on, sir."

"On the day he died, in the morning, he sent down for the overseas accounts ledger, and did not return it until mid afternoon, which put my work back a little, Mr Wells and I could not understand why he kept it so long."

"I see" said Hadley and he then remained silent for a few moments.

"Mr Augustus, you have been very helpful."

"I'm glad that I've been of assistance" smiled the Manager.

"You have, sir, now please return to your office whilst I inform my Chief Inspector of what you have told us and a senior Fraud Squad Officer will be appointed to look into matters at the Bank."

"Very good, Inspector, I wish you good day."

"Good day."

"Sergeant" Augustus nodded to Cooper and left the office. The detectives sat in silence for a few moments before Hadley said "Sergeant, I think we have the motive for Sir John's murder."

CHAPTER 15

It was the following morning when Chief Inspector Bell sent for Hadley.

"You'll not be surprised to hear that Monsieur Roguefort has arrived with Hudson and his solicitor, Hargreaves, they're all with the Commissioner now."

"You're right, sir, I'm not surprised" replied Hadley.

"I hope that you are not treating this matter lightly, Inspector."

"No, but I'm confident in the facts that my investigations have uncovered."

"That's as maybe, but prepare yourself, because the Commissioner is under great pressure to drop the charges against Lefevre and he wants to see us in his office at midday."

"Right, sir."

"I suggest that you bring all the relevant notes on the murder case and, whatever you do, stick to that, I'll back you as long as you don't wander off the subject" said Bell firmly.

"So, we have to justify our actions to a Frenchman with money?"

"Careful, Hadley, Roguefort has powerful friends as well as money…"

"He's not above the law, sir" interrupted Hadley.

"Indeed…"

"Neither is his Captain" said Hadley firmly.

"Just be tactful, if you would, and save the Commissioner from any unwanted pressure…"

"From whom?"

"Wheels within wheels, just leave it at that" replied Bell.

"I'm not impressed by that, sir."

"Listen to me…"

"You'll be pleased to know that I have another reliable eye witness, who spent some time with Lefevre in Whitechapel the night of the murder of Jacques Mornay."

"What?"

"It's all in my report."

"I haven't read it yet…"

"I suggest you do, sir, before we see the Commissioner…"

"Hadley, you're impertinent!"

"Along with the bank embezzlement of a hundred thousand pounds, the murder of Sir John Simmons and the gold bullion seized at Liverpool, I think, with respect, that Roguefort and his nefarious friends are a bunch of criminals!"

"You're on dangerously thin ice, Inspector!"

"I don't think so."

"I suggest you go back to your office before you say anything more that might lead me to take disciplinary action against you!"

"Right."

"Be here before midday, if you please."

"Yes, sir."

Hadley looked at his fob watch as Chief Inspector Bell knocked on the Commissioner's door. It was exactly twelve noon when the officers entered the spacious office and both nodded to the Commissioner.

"Come in, gentlemen, and let me introduce you, this is Monsieur Roguefort, his assistant, Monsieur Benoir, Mr Hudson you know of course and Mr Hargreaves, his solicitor" said the Commissioner waving his hand towards the visitors. Hadley and Bell shook hands with each and nodded as the Commissioner said "this is Chief Inspector Bell and Inspector Hadley, now gentlemen, let us proceed." As they all sat down, Hadley eyed the two Frenchmen and came to the conclusion that his suspicions were correct. Roguefort was a thickset man in his fifties with a dark, swarthy complexion and black eyes. He was dressed in expensive clothes and had a silver topped cane by his side. He had a cruel look about his 'Mediterranean appearance' and Hadley thought that the man was ruthless and would act without mercy to achieve his ambitions. Benoir, his assistant, looked more like a quayside ruffian than a gentleman's aide. He was a thickset, powerfully built man in his thirties with a scarred face and stood behind Roguefort like a bodyguard rather than anything else.

"Monsieur Roguefort has made representations to me, through Mr Hargreaves, that he wishes that the case against Captain Lefevre be dropped and no further action to be taken, I have advised him that Lefevre faces serious charges of murder and he is due to appear at Bow Street Magistrates next week for a hearing" said the Commissioner.

"Yes, Commissioner" said Bell.

"I must say, however, as there is little evidence to hand that implicates Lefevre in the murders of Dalmas and Mornay, it would seem that I have to withdraw the intended prosecution before it appears before the Magistrates, what do you say Chief Inspector?" asked the Commissioner as Roguefort nodded his head slowly.

"Sir, I must advise you that Inspector Hadley has two reliable witnesses that put Lefevre at the scene of the crime the night that Mornay was murdered" said Bell and Roguefort looked surprised at that.

"Why do you pursue such a hopeless case, Inspector Hadley?" demanded Roguefort in a thick French accent, his black eyes blazing with anger.

"Because I believe that Lefevre murdered Dalmas and Mornay to keep them quiet" replied Hadley.

"Keep them quiet about what?" asked Roguefort.

"A gold bullion theft, sir" replied Hadley and there was a collective gasp and Roguefort narrowed his eyes and said "Inspector, you are making accusations that you can't possibly substantiate." Hadley knew that he had hit the mark to the fury of Roguefort.

"Let us test it in court, sir."

"Hadley, we are discussing the case against Captain Lefevre, nothing else" said the Commissioner.

"With respect, Commissioner, I have just provided the motive for the murder of the two Frenchmen, and although I admit that it will be hard to secure a conviction for the killing of Dalmas with a bar of gold, the killing of Mornay with a knife, witnessed by onlookers will ensure that Lefevre is brought to trial and when found guilty, as I believe he will be, hanged for his crime."

"You are not the judge, jury and executioner, mon ami!" exclaimed Roguefort angrily.

"Quite right, I'm just a policeman investigating a double murder and bringing the facts to my superiors who will, in due course, arrange for my accusations to be tested before a judge and jury" replied Hadley with a smile.

"Mon Dieu! Such insolence…"

"Commissioner, Monsieur Roguefort is offended by Inspector

Hadley's remarks and I suggest he apologises to my client immediately!" said Hargreaves angrily.

"Hadley!" hissed Bell.

"What have I to apologise for?"

"May we withdraw for a few moments, Commissioner?" asked Bell. The great man nodded and said "Don't be too long, Chief Inspector." Bell nodded and got up from his seat followed by Hadley into the corridor.

"Are you completely mad, Hadley?" asked Bell in a half whisper.

"I don't think so, sir."

"Well I do! I told you to keep strictly on the subject of the Lefevre case, Roguefort is furious and you are making things worse by the minute in there!"

"I am not going to be silenced."

"Listen, Hadley, you have very little evidence to show that Lefevre is a murderer and no proof that the Count is involved with the bullion theft or that Hudson embezzled the money from the Bank, everything you've presented so far is circumstantial" said Bell firmly.

"I have two witnesses..."

"Women of low moral standing, Hadley."

"They may be but that fact does not mean that they are unable to see or hear or tell the truth, sir."

"If this goes to trial, Hargreaves and Counsel will reduce those women's evidence to nothing, followed by your reputation and as I told you earlier, you'll end up in the horse traffic department!"

"Don't be too sure."

"For once I agree with you, I'm not sure of anything you do or say, that's why I can't sleep at night."

"I'm sorry to hear that."

"So let's go in and see if we can smooth things over, Hadley."

"Yes, sir."

"And for God's sake, be diplomatic!"

They returned to the Commissioner's office and resumed their seats.

"Well, Chief Inspector?" asked the Commissioner.

"Thank you for that brief moment, sir, it enabled Inspector Hadley and myself to clear up a few points regarding the Lefevre investigation" replied Bell.

"Glad to hear it and…"

"Chief Inspector, are you going to drop the charges against Captain Lefevre?" interrupted Roguefort in an angry tone.

"No, Monsieur Roguefort" replied Hadley before Bell could answer, leaving him open mouthed.

"So, the puppet answers for the master" said Roguefort with a sly grin.

"Monsieur Roguefort, I assure you…" the Chief Inspector began.

"You can assure me of nothing, Monsieur, not while you allow your subordinate here to answer for you!"

"Gentlemen, gentlemen, please" said the Commissioner with his side whiskers twitching.

"Enough of this nonsense, I will not endure it!" said Roguefort angrily.

"Monsieur Roguefort, I wish you to know…" began the Commissioner.

"Monsieur Commissioner, I wish you to know that if the charges against Lefevre are not withdrawn then I shall issue writs against the police for wrongful arrest and claim substantial compensation for the loss of my Captain and possibly my ship, the 'Arabesque' which has now sailed from Tilbury without its Captain!" interrupted Roguefort.

"Loss of your ship, sir?" queried the Commissioner with a frown.

"The 'Arabesque' is bound for Nantes then after that she has to cross the Bay of Biscay, a treacherous stretch of water, where many ships have foundered, and if I lose the 'Arabesque' I shall extract the full value of her and her cargo from you, Monsieur!" exclaimed the angry Frenchman.

"Good God" whispered the Commissioner.

"The departure of your ship without the Captain, Monsieur Roguefort, was the decision taken by your crew and nothing whatever to do with my investigation, therefore you must look to them for any loss that you might suffer" said Hadley.

"Mon Dieu! This puppet is insufferable! I will not stay another moment, good day, Monsieur Commissioner!" said Roguefort as he stood and glanced at the shocked Commissioner.

"Er, good day…"

"Monsieur Hargreaves, you stay with Monsieur Hudson, and sort this mess out with these fools!"

"Yes, Monsieur Roguefort" replied Hargreaves as he stood whilst the Frenchman, along with Benoir, swept out of the office. Everyone in the office remained in stunned silence for a few moments.

"Gentlemen, I suggest that we all calm down before we continue" said the Commissioner.

"Yes, a few minutes of tranquillity will not come amiss" said Hudson and Hargreaves nodded whilst Bell looked relieved.

"However long we wait will not change the situation, sir" said Hadley to the Commissioner and Bell groaned on hearing the remark.

"Inspector Hadley, I fear you have not been as diplomatic as you might have been, given the circumstances" said the Commissioner.

"I'm sorry, but I believe…" Hadley began.

"Chief Inspector, will you please return to your office with Inspector Hadley and remain there until I send for you" interrupted the Commissioner.

"Yes, sir" replied Bell as he stood and then left with Hadley in tow.

Back in his office, Bell paced the floor whilst Hadley sat with a glum look on his face.

"I think you've overstepped the mark this time, Hadley."

"No, sir, and I'm sure that events will prove that I'm right in my suspicions about Lefevre, Hudson, Castellini and Roguefort, they're all involved…"

"You've no proof against any of them that will stand up in court, Hadley!"

"Not yet, but I'll not be defeated by this circus of wealthy criminals" replied Hadley.

"I've heard enough from you today, Inspector, so I think you'd better return to your office, I'll send for you if I need you."

"Very good, sir."

"A pot of strong tea, George, if you please" said Hadley as he slumped down behind his desk whilst fixing his eyes on Cooper.

"Was it that bad, sir?"

"Yes, Sergeant, the Chief Inspector thinks I'll be lucky if the Commissioner transfers me to horse traffic rather than dispensing with my services."

"Oh, dear, sir."

"If only we had something really positive to go on, Sergeant."

"Well, in the Lefevre case we've got our two witnesses…"

"According to the Chief, they'll be next to useless in court" interrupted Hadley.

"Then there's the gold that we found in Liverpool…"

"Anybody could have hidden that in the crates."

"What about the murder of Sir John?"

"Perhaps he did fall after drinking too much."

"There's a hundred thousand pounds missing from the Bank, sir."

"Fluctuations due to the exchange rate between the dollar and pound" replied Hadley and Cooper shook his head. He remained silent until George appeared with the tea.

"This'll revive you, sir" said George as he placed the cup on Hadley's desk.

"Thank you, George." Cooper waited until the Inspector had finished his tea before he asked "what next, sir?"

"I'm not sure, I'll have to think carefully, Sergeant." Just then the Chief's clerk entered and said "Chief Inspector Bell would like to see you now, sir." Hadley nodded and followed the clerk upstairs.

"Sit down, Hadley" said Bell.

"Yes, sir."

"You're not going to like this."

"No, sir."

"But the Commissioner has decided to withdraw the charges against Lefevre…"

"I must protest, in the strongest possible terms!" interrupted Hadley.

"Protest as much as you like, Inspector, the decision has been made, and that's an end to it" replied Bell.

"I can't believe that the Commissioner has been persuaded to do this" said Hadley.

"I keep telling you, Hadley, you've got no evidence, the

Commissioner had no choice!"

"He could have kept the investigation open, sir."

"Do you presume to challenge the Commissioner's decisions, Hadley?"

"No, sir, but..."

"There are no 'buts', Hadley, the charges are dropped and you'll make no further inquiries concerning Captain Lefevre, is that clearly understood?"

"Yes, sir."

"Good."

"What about the gold bullion investigation?"

"You may continue with that, providing that you keep me full informed and you proceed in a discreet and diplomatic way, is that understood?"

"Yes, sir."

"At last we're getting somewhere, Hadley."

"Indeed."

"Now I suggest you take some time to re-think your strategy before you go off on some wild goose chase again."

"Right, sir."

"I think that's all for the moment."

"What about the murder of Sir John Simmons?"

"The Commissioner has read your reports and seen the photographs, they were useful and he was impressed."

"I'm pleased."

"He has, however, come to the conclusion that Sir John accidentally fell to his death and no further investigations are necessary" replied Bell with a smile.

"Very good, but I must say, with respect, the Commissioner is wrong!"

"Enough, Hadley, that'll be all now."

"Yes, sir."

When Hadley arrived back in his office he told Cooper what Bell had said and the Sergeant was as deflated as the Inspector at the news.

"Never mind, Sergeant, we'll find a way to crack this case and when we do the Chief, as well as the Commissioner, will be heaping praise on us from a great height."

"I'm glad you see it that way, sir."

"I do, Sergeant, I'm an optimist, something will turn up, just you wait and see."

"I hope so."

"Now, it is a pleasant afternoon, the sun is shining and it's not too cold, so I suggest we take a stroll along the Embankment."

"Good idea."

"We can review our strategy and make some plans at the same time, Sergeant."

"Right, sir."

The detectives walked in the November sunshine, alongside the Thames, and discussed the way forward, occasionally drifting away from the subject and talking about Christmas. Much to Cooper's surprise and delight, the Inspector invited him and his wife to join the Hadley family for lunch on Boxing Day.

"That's very kind, sir, my wife and I would be honoured to be your guests."

"Good, that's settled then" smiled Hadley and he made a mental note to tell Alice.

They eventually returned to the office and after another pot of tea, left for an early night at home.

It was a day later that Hadley and Cooper went to see Anthony Hudson at the Anglo American Investment Bank.

"Mr Hudson is not here at present, Inspector" said Mr Augustus.

"Do you know where he is, sir?"

"Yes, he's gone down to his house in the country."

"When do you expect him to return?"

"Well, to be honest, Inspector, I really don't know."

"Didn't he say?"

"No, not really, can I help you at all?" asked the Manager.

"We came to just go over some formalities regarding the death of Sir John…"

"Have you caught the murderer?" interrupted Augustus.

"No, sir, the case is closed as the Commissioner has decided, after careful consideration of all the evidence, that Sir John's death was an accident."

"Surely you don't believe that, Inspector?"

"No, Mr Augustus, I think he was murdered, but the investigation has been closed I'm afraid."

"What a disgrace!"

"I agree with you, but that is the decision from the highest authority" smiled Hadley.

"I am outraged that such a good man as Sir John should be murdered and the killer is allowed to escape justice by the decision of some detached person in authority, sitting in an office!"

"I understand your feelings, sir, and can only sympathise" said Hadley calmly.

"Well I promise you, Inspector, that if I manage to find out anything that may lead to the case being re-opened, no matter how insignificant it may be, I will be sure to let you know whatever it is."

"Thank you, your help would be much appreciated" replied Hadley.

The detectives then made their way to the 'Kings Head' for lunch, where Hadley planned to see Agnes and tell her that the case against Lefevre had been dropped. The bar was busy as usual and after ordering lunch they awaited the arrival of the women. It was some time before they wandered into the smoke filled bar and spotted Hadley and Cooper sitting in the corner. After the pleasantries and a round of drinks, Hadley told Agnes that the investigations into the murders would go no further and he asked Agnes to let Molly and Doris know. He said that he would see the ladies in due course and inform them officially of the decision.

"You're really disappointed aren't you?" asked Agnes.

"I am."

"You poor old thing, Jim."

"That's life, Agnes."

"You look a bit peeky, you need a holiday somewhere in the country" said Agnes and Hadley thought for a moment, smiled, nodded before he replied "that's a very good idea, Agnes."

"All my ideas are good where you're concerned, Jim" she said with a smile.

It was late in the afternoon when the detectives returned to the

Yard and Hadley went straight to the Chief's office.

"Why do you want to go to Pangbourne for a few days, Hadley?"

"To keep Hudson and his entourage under surveillance, sir."

"Surely a day would be sufficient?"

"Not really."

"I think the cost of you and Cooper staying down there for any period of time would be prohibitive, I mean, there would be lodgings and meals, plus whatever else you always seem to find to spend money on, I…" Bell shook his head, momentarily lost for words.

"I believe that Castellini has hidden gold bullion at Pangbourne, the Hudson's know about it and somehow Roguefort is implicated…"

"Whatever you do, don't involve that man Roguefort…" interrupted Bell.

"I'm sure that he's…"

"Hadley, you're always sure about everything but can never prove anything, if I agree to this Pangbourne jaunt then you must assure me that you will take no action that could cause more embarrassment to the Commissioner."

"Very good, sir."

"Alright then, you can go, but keep the expenses down."

"I will" nodded Hadley.

"And for God's sake, stay out of trouble, Hadley!"

"Yes, sir."

"Have you any idea where will you stay, in case I need to get hold of you?"

"Yes, we'll be at 'The Partridge', in the village" smiled Hadley.

"Umm, a pub that you have frequented before no doubt" mumbled Bell.

"Yes, sir."

Hadley returned to his office and made detailed plans with Cooper for the surveillance of Pangbourne House and its occupants. When they had finished and were enjoying a cup of tea, Cooper asked "do you think Roguefort is there, sir?"

"I'm not sure, but tomorrow we'll find out after we've booked into 'The Partridge' and called upon Mr Hudson and his guests."

"Right, sir."

"So meet me at Paddington at nine o'clock and bring enough clean shirts to last you a week" said Hadley.

"A week?"

"Yes, I fancy that our investigations could be somewhat lengthy, Castellini has that trunk somewhere down there and I'm determined to find it before he and the Countess disappear to America."

"You think it will take a week to find it, sir?"

"Who knows, Sergeant, who knows?"

CHAPTER 16

It was almost lunchtime when the detectives arrived at 'The Partridge', which Hadley thought was fortuitous, so they ordered pints of the local ale with two fresh cheese salads for lunch. When they had finished, Hadley went to the bar and asked the young woman who was serving "I take it you have rooms here?"

"Yes, sir" she replied with a smile.

"In that case, may I book two rooms for myself and my assistant?"

"I'm sorry, sir, we've only got three rooms and two are already taken, so as long as you don't mind sharing, then you can have the double that's left" she replied.

"That will be acceptable, thank you."

"Very well, sir, I'll just get the book for you to sign in and then I'll show you the room."

"Thank you." The young woman disappeared and Hadley glanced around the bar at some of the occupants who were eyeing him up and down. When Hadley signed the book, the girl asked "Is it for just the one night, sir?"

"No, we need to stay for up to a week, we're from the Thames River Board in London, surveying the river up as far as Wallingford" replied Hadley in a loud voice so everybody could hear.

"Very good, sir, we charge ten shillings a night and that includes breakfast in the morning."

"Thank you."

"Would you be requiring dinner in the evenings?"

"Yes please."

"Very well, I'll make a note" she smiled.

"Thank you."

"This way then, sir" and the young woman led the way through a short corridor and up stairs to the double room, which was large and comfortable with two single beds.

"This will do admirably" said Hadley as Cooper arrived with their cases. When the detectives were alone Hadley said "I hope you don't snore, Sergeant."

"Just a little, according to my wife."

"Oh, dear."

"Sorry, about that, sir."

"Well if you must snore, do it quietly as I wish to have my much needed sleep undisturbed."

"I'll do my best" grinned Cooper.

"Now that we are comfortably settled in here, I think it's time we visited Pangbourne House to have words with Mr Hudson and make a note of his guests."

"Right, sir."

The detectives hired a pony and trap from the village and as they journeyed towards the house Hadley noted the cross roads at the end of the main street. The road to the right led to Oxford in the north and to his left, Newbury in the south.

"When Hudson or any of his guests return to London they will have to come back past 'The Partridge' to go to Reading, but I'm concerned if anyone decides to go elsewhere, Cooper."

"Who do you have in mind, sir?"

"The Castellini's" replied Hadley.

"To America via Newbury and then Southampton?"

"Precisely." They remained silent, each deep in thought regarding the implications of the Count and his wife disappearing with the trunk before they could intervene. As they approached the house along the sweeping, gravel drive, Hadley saw three men climbing the front steps to the portico. He recognised them instantly.

"Ah, Lefevre, Castellini and Benoir, if I'm not mistaken" said Hadley and as he spoke, Cooper caught sight of them.

"Benoir! That means his master is here."

"This is true, Cooper, and it will be interesting to note his re-action to our presence" replied Hadley.

"Indeed."

"But take a careful note of all their re-actions as I play my little game of facts laced with misinformation."

"I will, sir" replied Cooper as the trap stopped outside the imposing residence. The driver was paid off and the detectives climbed the steps before Cooper rang the door bell. They were admitted to the hallway before being announced by the butler and proceeding into the drawing room. Hadley glanced at the guests before he fixed his gaze on Mr Hudson, standing with his back to the fire.

"My God, Inspector, I thought after your recent humiliation at the hands of the Commissioner you would have thought it prudent to stay away from my guests and me!" exclaimed Hudson.

"It is my duty to pursue other matters, sir, unconnected with the investigations into the murders of Captain Lefevre's crew" replied Hadley.

"He is like an old dog with a bone" said Roguefort slowly with menace.

"We call it 'persistence' at the Yard, Monsieur Roguefort, and we find that we usually get positive results in the end." Roguefort did not attempt to hide his anger.

"If we were in France, Monsieur, I assure you that you would have been dismissed from your post by now and would find yourself begging in the streets…"

"I am pleased to advise you, Monsieur Roguefort, that you are in Queen Victoria's England and therefore your threats against my livelihood are not valid here, nor would they be in any civilised country where a servant of the Crown was carrying out his duties!"

"Mon Dieu! This is insufferable, Anthony, I insist you throw this man and his accomplice out of this house!"

"Michel, I really think…" began Hudson, nervously.

"If you don't, I'll have Benoir do it!" interrupted Roguefort.

"If you order Benoir to assault us, Monsieur Roguefort, I will overpower him and arrest you both, do you understand, sir?" There was a stony silence and Cooper hoped that it would not end in violence as Benoir looked like a man who could take good care of himself.

"Very well, Monsieur Inspector, if you will not leave, then I will!" said Roguefort and he stood up before striding towards the door, followed closely by Benoir. The Frenchman then hesitated, turned to face Hudson and said "I shall go to my room, Anthony, please inform me when this meddling 'servant of the Crown' has left the house!"

"Of course, Michel" stammered Hudson as Roguefort swept out of the room.

"Now, Mr Hudson, the purpose of our visit today is…" began

Hadley.

"Inspector, once again you have over stepped the mark and insulted my guest" interrupted Hudson.

"I apologise for any offence, sir, but I'm conducting an investigation into murder…"

"The case against me is dropped, Monsieur Inspector, your Commissioner told you that, are you deaf as well as stupid?" asked Lefevre with a grin.

"You are quite correct, Captain, the investigation into your involvement of the murders of your crew is at an end, I'm talking about the murder of Sir John Simmons." Hudson went pale at that and Mrs Hudson blurted out "I thought that Sir John's death was an accident, Inspector."

"I'm afraid not, Madam, new information has come to light from inside the Bank that ensures that the case is re-opened" replied Hadley and he thought that Mr Hudson wobbled a little on hearing his reply.

"Well, how can I help, Inspector?" asked Hudson anxiously.

"I need to talk to you about the murder of Sir John as well as other matters concerning the Bank" replied Hadley.

"Yes, of course, shall we discuss things in private?" asked Hudson.

"That would be sensible, sir."

"Please excuse us" said Hudson to his guests as he led the way out of the room and across the hallway into his study. When they were all seated, Hudson mopped his brow with his handkerchief and tried to smile bravely. Hadley was sure that the Banker was deeply implicated in the murder, the embezzlement as well as the bullion theft.

"Now, sir, first of all, I wish officially to bring to your attention that over one hundred thousand pounds has been removed from an overseas account at your Bank and deposited with a French Merchant Bank in London…"

"Oh, God" murmured Hudson.

"Are you aware of this, sir?"

"Well, I er, er, I think that it may have been brought to my attention, Inspector" stammered Hudson.

"Who by?"

"Mr Augustus, if I remember correctly."

"Not Sir John on the afternoon before his murder?" Hudson's face then became ashen.

"I can't remember, Inspector."

"Come, come, sir, a hundred thousand pounds goes missing and you can't remember who told you?"

"Look, Inspector, I've been under a lot of pressure lately and quite honestly, I have to confess that I've not been paying much attention to business at the moment."

"Hmm" mused Hadley, giving the impression that he was not impressed by Hudson's reply.

"I'd like to help but I'm not sure that I can add much more to what I have already told you about the evening that Sir John died" said Hudson plaintively. Hadley decided on another tack.

"What are your plans for the immediate future, Mr Hudson?"

"What do you mean, Inspector?"

"Are you still going to go to Boston after Christmas?" Hudson looked surprised at that.

"Possibly, Inspector, but that is now under review after the death of Sir John" replied Hudson.

"But you don't rule it out?"

"No, not at the moment." Hadley changed tack once again.

"I've been informed that you gave your groom, Mr Woods, permission to take a holiday to 'see friends', is that true, sir?" Hudson looked startled for a moment.

"Well, I may have, I'm not sure, Inspector…"

"Your wife tells me that she was surprised as your good lady insists that servants at your London home 'do not get holidays', sir."

"My wife runs the household very efficiently, and it is very rare for me to be involved, Inspector."

"In that case you would recall giving Woods a holiday."

"I might have done, look, where is all this leading to, Inspector?" asked Hudson sharply.

"It is leading to the facts…"

"What facts?"

"That you are implicated in murder, fraud, embezzlement and bullion theft, sir."

"You're completely mad, Inspector!"

"Am I? Let's look at what we know so far, you are the last

person to see Sir John alive and you had a motive for killing him…"

"That's nonsense!" interrupted Hudson.

"Woods delivered to the Bank the diamonds that you had stolen before attempting to defraud Lloyds…"

"I can't believe what I'm hearing!"

"Woods admitted that he collected the Count's trunk, full of gold bullion, from Kings Cross and took it to Paddington, where he waited for the Count to collect it before it came here…"

"Inspector, I promise you that…"

"Woods has now vanished, with your connivance…"

"Not true!"

"Lastly, a vast sum of money has been taken from your Bank and placed in a numbered account in a French Bank, so, Mr Hudson, you are now under suspicion of committing a number of serious crimes."

"I can see another meeting with the Commissioner looming, after which, you will no longer be a police officer, Inspector" said Hudson with malice.

"I doubt that very much, sir."

"I had nothing to do with the tragic death of Sir John, or a gold bullion theft or the theft of my wife's diamonds and I do not know where Woods has disappeared to, or who transferred the money from the overseas account to a French bank, all senior staff have access to those accounts, it could have been anyone" replied Hudson.

"We will find out, I assure you, as we have our best fraud officers looking into it" replied Hadley as he watched Hudson mop his brow once again.

"Good, then I will be exonerated, Inspector."

"Time will tell, sir."

"So, what now, Inspector, are you going to arrest me?"

"Not yet."

"I'm pleased to hear it."

"Sergeant Cooper and I will return to London this afternoon and begin preparing our reports for the Crown Prosecution, they will decide how and when to proceed against you."

"Then I shall instruct Mr Hargreaves to begin my vigorous and robust defence, Inspector."

"So be it, sir, before we leave, I'd like to have a quick word in private with the Count if I may?"

"I'll let him know, Inspector."

"Thank you." Hudson left the room and returned a few minutes later with the Count.

"You wish to see me, Inspector?" asked the Italian with a look of disdain.

"Yes, sir, I have a few questions for you."

"Very well, but I must warn you that I am not prepared to be humiliated by you and I have asked Mr Hudson to remain here as my witness" said the Count as he sat down opposite Hadley whilst Hudson resumed his seat.

"Quite understandable, now, first of all, where is the trunk that you collected from Woods at Paddington Station?"

"I know not what you speak of" replied the Count.

"Come, come, we have a confession from Woods and several eye witnesses to support his story" said Hadley.

"You, Mr Woods and all your witnesses are mistaken, Inspector."

"I don't think so, sir."

"Prove it in court then!"

"I will, sir."

"You said Woods was a thief who returned the diamonds to Mr Hudson and now has run away, so, Inspector, I do not know how things work in an English court, but in Italy, if the accused is missing then the case collapses."

"He will be found, never fear, sir."

"I will believe that when I see him, but I expect the Countess and I will be on our way to America before you find him" smiled the Count.

"Ah, yes, sir, when are you leaving?"

"I haven't decided yet."

"Will you be taking your trunk with you?"

"Only if you find it in London, after arresting the thief, Inspector!"

"What is in the trunk, Count?"

"Personal things."

"Gold, for instance?"

"No, Inspector, personal things" replied the Count firmly with a smile.

"I shall not hesitate to obtain a search warrant."

"Please go ahead, but you have to find my trunk first before you can open it" the Count grinned.

"Once we have Mr Woods in custody, I'm sure that he will be able to give us the information we require, sir" replied Hadley.

"But, Inspector, like the trunk, he is missing and you also have to find him first!"

"We will, sir, I'm confident of that."

"I grow tired of this, Inspector, so, have you any more silly questions?" asked the Count. Hadley realised that it was pointless to continue and he shook his head and replied "no, sir, that will be all for the time being."

"Then I shall join the ladies, are you coming, Anthony?"

"Yes, Giovani, like you, I've had enough of all of this nonsense" replied Hudson as he stood.

"You may call my inquiries 'nonsense', gentlemen, but I would remind you both that at the moment there are three unsolved murders being investigated" said Hadley firmly.

"Nothing to do with us, Inspector, good day to you" replied Hudson as he left the room followed by the Count, who smiled at Hadley for a moment.

The detectives walked back to the village in the crisp November air.

"Do you think any of them will make a run for it, sir?"

"Possibly, Sergeant, I don't know for sure but I expect that Hudson will return to London soon."

"To find out what's been going on at the Bank?"

"Exactly."

"Do you think he's bluffing, sir?"

"Yes, Sergeant." They walked on in silence, both deep in thought.

"We need somewhere under cover from where we can watch these cross roads" said Hadley as they approached the crossing.

"How about the church tower over there, sir?" said Cooper, pointing at the grey stone building.

"Very good, Sergeant, it's not too far away and provided we can find a suitable vantage point, it will serve well."

They went to the vicarage, next to the church and Cooper knocked at the door which was eventually opened by a diminutive woman with grey hair drawn back into a bun.

"Yes, gentlemen?"

"May we have a few words with the Reverend, please?" asked Hadley with a smile.

"Who shall I say is calling?"

"My name is Hadley and this is Mr Cooper."

"Please wait there whilst I go and see" she said and disappeared into the dark hallway. It was some minutes before an elderly clergyman appeared and asked with a quizzical look "how can I help you, gentlemen?"

"I wonder if we might come in for a moment, sir?"

"By all means, by all means" he replied and led the way down the hallway to a warm, comfortable parlour.

"Please sit down" the Reverend waved them to a sofa.

"Thank you, sir."

"Now, if you've come about the wood worm in the pulpit..."

"No, sir, we're police officers from London" interrupted Hadley.

"Good heavens, this must be serious" said the Reverend.

"Indeed, Reverend, I'm Inspector Hadley and this is Sergeant Cooper, we're from Scotland Yard..."

"Bless my soul, this is exciting, wait until I tell the ladies sewing circle about this!"

"I'd rather you didn't, sir."

"Oh, what a great shame, they do need some stimulation at the moment, so, am I helping you with your inquiries?" asked the Reverend, wide eyed with excitement.

"In manner of speaking, Reverend" Hadley smiled.

"I can see it in the Parish magazine, Reverend Thomas Crabtree assists Scotland Yard detectives in their hunt for..." the Reverend paused for a moment before continuing "oh, what is it your hunting for, Inspector?"

"We just want to observe the movements of some guests who are at present staying at Pangbourne House..."

"That's the Hudson's place."

"Indeed it is, Reverend."

"He's a very important man in the City, you know, he's a

Banker, I believe" said the Reverend.

"He is, sir, now we wondered if we might take up a position in the church tower?"

"By all means, Inspector, there's a small window that looks out over the cross roads and one that overlooks the river, but it will be cold up there" replied the Reverend.

"Not to worry, sir, we'll be alright."

"Very well, I'll just get my coat and will show you the way and then you can come back and have a pot of tea before you set up your position, if that's agreeable?"

"Very agreeable, sir" replied Hadley and Cooper smiled.

They followed the Reverend Crabtree up the winding stone steps in the bell tower to a small landing where the lead cross latticed window overlooked the crossroads.

"This will do admirably well, Reverend" said Hadley.

"Good, I am pleased that it will serve your purpose, now tell me, confidentially, what are they up to at Pangbourne House?" Hadley smiled and decided to take the man into his confidence.

"Please, whatever you do, Reverend, keep this information to yourself until after our investigations are completed."

"Oh, you have my undying word, Inspector" replied the Reverend with excitement.

"There are three Frenchmen…"

"I've never trusted the French" interrupted the Reverend.

"Quite so, sir, and an Italian Count and his wife…"

"All Catholics without doubt" interrupted the Reverend.

"Yes, I'm sure, sir."

"Are they involved in some plot to overthrow our beloved Queen and declare a Republic?"

"No, sir."

"I wouldn't put it passed them you know."

"They are engaged in grand theft and are under suspicion of murder" said Hadley.

"Oh, dear God, I don't think I want to hear anymore, Inspector."

"Very good, sir."

"I'm in need of a cup of tea to calm my nerves, Inspector" said the Reverend Crabtree anxiously.

An hour later, after tea and biscuits, the detectives were stationed in the tower and watching the crossroads.

"Do you think Mr Hudson will leave for London today?"

"Yes, Sergeant, he believes that we have already returned and I expect that he will go to Reading station this afternoon."

"What are your thoughts about the others, sir?"

"I'm not sure, we'll just have to wait and see."

They did not have to wait long. Hudson in an open four wheeler drawn by two horses, suddenly appeared at the bottom of the hill. Then the coach made its way at speed along the High Street towards Reading and Hadley smiled saying "true to form, Sergeant."

"Yes, sir, shall we remain here just in case anyone else leaves the house?"

"Yes, until it gets dark, Sergeant."

"Right, sir."

"Then we'll enjoy a hot meal in the pub with a few pints of ale."

After a good dinner followed by a restful night the detectives enjoyed a breakfast of porridge followed by kippers the next morning. When they were ready they walked across to the church tower and resumed their look out position. Nothing happened and nobody came down the hill from Pangbourne House all morning.

"It is nearly lunch time, Sergeant" said Hadley as he glanced at his fob watch.

"Right, sir, do you want to go first while I stay here?"

"No, you get across to the pub for a bite and I'll wait here."

"Yes, sir."

"Don't be too long though" said Hadley with a smile.

"No, sir" Cooper smiled before making his way down and out of the tower across to the pub. He had just arrived in the bar when a young policeman followed him in. The constable went up to the bar maid and said "I've an urgent message for Inspector Hadley, do you know where he is?"

"We've got a Mr Hadley from the Thames Water Board staying here…"

"I'm Sergeant Cooper, constable, you can give me the message" interrupted Cooper to the bar maid's surprise.

"I'm afraid not, sir, I've been given strict instructions…"

"Right, follow me then!" said Cooper. The two officers made their way across the street to the church tower and up the stairs to Hadley.

"Urgent telegraph message from London for you, sir" said Cooper and he nodded to the young constable who handed the Inspector a buff envelope. Hadley tore it open and read out aloud "Hadley, return to London immediately, Hudson found dead this morning in Cavendish Square, Bell."

CHAPTER 17

Cooper could hardly keep up with Hadley as he raced up the stairs to Chief Inspector Bell's office.

"Glad you're back, Hadley, this is a bad and unexpected turn of events" said Bell in a serious tone as he waved the Inspector to a seat.

"Indeed."

"I've sent Carstairs over to Cavendish Square for the moment, just to keep an eye on things and make a few preliminary inquiries, before you take over."

"Right, sir."

"I've also sent Curtis, with his photographic equipment, to record the scene."

"That's very helpful, sir."

"Yes, the Commissioner is quite taken with the idea of photographic records."

"I am pleased. Tell me, how was Hudson killed?"

"Apparently, a single shot to the head, the body has been removed and taken to the Marylebone" replied Bell.

"Any suspects?"

"Not at this stage, Hadley, but that's for you to find out."

"Yes, sir."

"The servants are in a state, so get over there, calm everything down and tell Carstairs to come back and see me immediately as I must have a preliminary report on the Commissioner's desk by five o'clock to-night, the Press are going mad, un-explained deaths of two executives from the same Bank in the City, even they couldn't make it up!"

An ashen faced Wilkes opened the door of number twelve, Cavendish Square to the detectives.

"Please come in, gentlemen" said the butler in a hushed tone. From the hallway they were then shown into the library where Inspector Richard Carstairs stood surveying the room and Jack Curtis was adjusting his camera on its tripod. Carstairs glanced towards Hadley and smiled.

"Afternoon, Jim."

"Afternoon, Dickie."

"Well, you'll be pleased to know that this is an open and shut case for once" said Carstairs as Curtis fired off his flash illuminator.

"Really?"

"Yes, Hudson committed suicide with that revolver" and Carstairs pointed at the weapon on the blood spattered desk. Hadley approached and peered down at the Colt six shot revolver as it lay on the right hand side of the ornate desk. The blood was lying in a pool to the left and un-opened letters in a tray were covered in droplets of Hudson's blood. Hadley stood for a while deep in thought and the silence was interrupted by Curtis saying "I've finished now, Inspector, unless there's anything else that you want photographed."

"No, thank you Mr Curtis, I think that's enough for today" replied Carstairs and Curtis nodded before beginning to dismantle his equipment.

"I've taken statements from Wilkes and the housekeeper, they both say that they heard a shot at about half past six this morning and Wilkes came in here to find Hudson dead, slumped at the desk" said Carstairs.

"Curious" mused Hadley.

"What's curious, Jim?"

"That he should kill himself at that time of the morning" replied Hadley.

"There's an empty bottle of brandy on the side there, Jim, perhaps he spent all night drinking to pluck up enough courage" said Carstairs.

"Possibly, Dickie" Hadley mused before asking "have you found a suicide note?"

"No, but it might be in that pile of letters in the tray." Hadley nodded and went through them until he found a blue envelope with just the word 'Rowena' written in an unsteady hand.

"This might be it" he said before placing it on the desk.

"Well, I leave it all for you to sort out, I'll let you have a copy of my report in due course, Jim" said Carstairs.

"Thanks, Dickie, and you'd better hurry back to the Yard, Bell's last words to me were that he had to have your report on the Commissioner's desk for a Press statement this evening."

"I'm on my way, good afternoon gentlemen" said Carstairs with a smile as he left the library.

"Well, Sergeant, what do you make of all this?"

"It does look like a case of suicide, the weapon is lying where it fell and the bloodstains are consistent with the shot being fired from the gun held in the right hand, sir. I'm sure that Doctor Evans will be able to confirm that the shot was fired at very close range, sir."

"Yes, I think we had better get over to the Marylebone and find out what the Doctor has to say, before he goes home for the night."

"Right, sir."

"Call a cab while I have a quick word with the butler." Cooper nodded and left the room. Hadley stood for a moment, deep in thought, before he rang for Wilkes.

"You rang, sir?" asked the butler as he appeared in the room.

"Yes, Mr Wilkes, I know that this tragedy must have shocked you all…"

"Oh, it has, sir, it really has, all of the servants, even Woods, when he called this morning to see the master…"

"Woods was here?"

"Yes, sir, about nine o'clock and when he was told what had happened he quickly left…"

"Do you know where he went to?"

"No, sir, I can only assume that he returned to his 'so called' friends" replied Wilkes.

"I see" said Hadley slowly, his mind racing.

"Was there anything else, sir?"

"Yes, has Mrs Hudson been informed of the tragedy?"

"Yes sir, Inspector Carstairs arranged for a message to be sent by telegraph to the police at Reading from where it would be sent on with a constable to Pangbourne, advising Madam to return to London."

"Very good, Mr Wilkes, I shall leave you now but I will return later and I do not wish anything to be disturbed in here, is that clear?"

"Perfectly, sir."

As Hadley climbed into the Hansom alongside Cooper it began to rain, bringing a dreary end to the late afternoon. As the cab made its way towards the Marylebone Hospital amongst the heavy traffic, Hadley remained deep in thought but Cooper decide to ask a few questions.

"What do you think the reaction will be at Pangbourne when they find out what has happened, sir?"

"Your guess is as good as mine."

"I doubt that."

"Carstairs has sent a message to Mrs Hudson advising her to return to London, so when she receives that, our foreign friends will wonder what's up and either depart in fear or remain calm until they know what it is all about, Sergeant."

"And we're here and can't watch what they're up to."

"Exactly, but once I've spoken to Mrs Hudson and found out if they're still at Pangbourne, we're back there as soon as possible."

"Yes, sir."

"That gold is somewhere and I'm determined to find it."

Doctor Evans looked up from his desk as the detectives entered his office.

"I thought that you'd be here soon, Hadley" said the Doctor.

"Good afternoon, Doctor" smiled the Inspector as Evans looked over his glasses and inclined his head slightly before he asked "why is it that every corpse that ends up on my marble slab recently is connected with you, Hadley?"

"I have no idea, please tell me..."

"Well either, you are the only detective employed by the Metropolitan Police or you're mixing with the wrong class of people!" replied the Doctor and Hadley laughed whilst Cooper grinned.

"The latter, I expect."

"Come on through then and examine the latest exhibit" said the Doctor and they followed him out into the morgue where the body of Anthony Hudson lay under a white sheet. The head was uncovered to reveal the wound and Hadley peered down as the Doctor pointed to the right side of the pale face.

"The bullet entered here, just behind the right temple and the exit wound is further back on the left side of the head, which shows that the gun was at an angle when it was fired, death was instantaneous" said the Doctor.

"Could the shot been fired at a distance?" asked Hadley.

"No, the barrel of the gun was placed right against the head, look at the hair, it is all burnt away around the entry wound" replied the Doctor.

"So, Mr Hudson did commit suicide then" mused Hadley.

"Yes, I'm certain of that."

"What about the stomach contents?"

"Very little food but a lot of alcohol" replied Evans.

"I see."

"I expect the wife will want to see her husband so I'll cover the wounds up, which will make the ordeal a little easier" said the Doctor.

"That will be appreciated."

"I'll send my report through in due course, Hadley."

"Thank you, Doctor."

Hadley and Cooper returned to the Yard and sat drinking tea whilst discussing the latest turn of events and writing reports. It was seven o'clock when they left the office and journeyed to Cavendish Square in the expectation of interviewing Mrs Hudson. Wilkes opened the door and informed them that Madam had arrived back from Pangbourne alone but was now being comforted by Mr Hargreaves.

"I know that this is a very difficult time, but ask Mrs Hudson if she will see us" said Hadley and Wilkes nodded before disappearing into the drawing room. Some minutes later the butler joined them in the hallway.

"Madam will see you now, please come this way." They followed him in to the room where the red eyed and tearful widow sat on the sofa with the solicitor standing with his back to the fire.

"I think your visit at this time is a little insensitive, Inspector" said Hargreaves.

"I appreciate that, sir, but I just want to ask Mrs Hudson a few questions then I will leave immediately" replied Hadley and Mrs Hudson turned to face the Inspector and asked angrily "what is it now, Inspector?"

"I am truly sorry for your loss, Madam, but I have my duty…"

"Oh, damn your duty, my husband is dead, for God's sake!"

"I know…"

"What do you know, Inspector?"

"Mrs Hudson…"

"The answer is 'nothing' but I'll tell you what I know, my husband killed himself because he had many worries and being harassed by you was the final straw!"

"I can understand that you are distressed, Madam…"

"Distressed? You are the master of understatement, Inspector, I loved my husband very much and I am distraught at my loss, can you possibly understand that?"

"I can…"

"Good, so please ask your irrelevant questions and then leave me to grieve in this house of deep sorrow" she interrupted.

"Did your husband leave a suicide note, Madam?"

"Yes, he did."

"May I see it?"

"Certainly not, it is private and for my eyes only" she replied.

"Madam, I know that this is difficult, but there may be a clue in the letter that would be helpful to my inquiries…"

"I said 'no'!"

"Mrs Hudson, I realise that…"

"Let him see it, Rowena, it's for the best and I'm sure the Inspector will keep it confidential" interrupted Hargreaves and Hadley nodded.

"Very well" she replied and took the blue envelope from her handbag and gave it to Hargreaves who handed it to the Inspector. Hadley took out the letter and read it in silence.

'My dearest, forgive me, forgive me, forgive me for what I have done. I have been a weak and foolish man who has been led into dark, devious ways by others and circumstances beyond my control. I have not deserved your love and understanding for all these years of our marriage, but you have given those things that I hold most dear without a second thought and I am truly grateful to you. You must know that my creditors will strip me of everything including our lovely house at Pangbourne and as I must end my life to avoid the ignominy, I can only pray that you leave England and find a better life for yourself away from the sad disaster of my demise. I want you to know that I have always been faithful to you and the only wicked mistress I ever had was an unlucky pack of cards. All my love, dearest one, Anthony'. Hadley remained silent for a few moments before handing the letter back to Mrs Hudson.

"Are you satisfied now, Inspector?" she asked angrily.

"Yes, thank you, Madam."

"Good."

"Do you know the extent of your husband's gambling debts?" asked Hadley.

"No, but I will be made aware of them in due course by the creditors" she replied.

"Indeed" nodded Hadley.

"Mrs Hudson has had a dreadful shock today, so if there's nothing else, Inspector, I think you should leave now" said Hargreaves.

"Yes, of course, but just one more thing, Mrs Hudson, are all your house guests still down at Pangbourne?"

"They are."

"Do any of them plan to leave in the immediate future?"

"No, not that I'm aware of" she replied.

"Thank you, Mrs Hudson, and once again I offer you my condolences" Hadley smiled and left the room. Once the detectives were outside in the rain, Hadley told Cooper to hail a cab.

"Where to, sir?"

"The Dreyfus Club in Curzon Street, Sergeant."

The detectives entered the club and were seen from the reception desk by Mr Smethurst, who recognised Hadley immediately and asked in an anxious tone "good evening, sir, how may I help you?"

"Good evening, I'd like to have a few words with the club secretary, Mr Bolting, if you please."

"Certainly, sir, I'll inform him immediately" replied Smethurst as he gave a little bow before hurrying away down the adjacent corridor.

"A prompt response this time, Sergeant."

"It's the hat that does the trick, sir" grinned Cooper.

"Why is that, Sergeant?"

"It's so battered, it looks as if it belongs to a bare knuckle prize fighter!"

"Everyone is scared of me then?"

"Yes, they are, sir."

"Now I'm in two minds whether to buy a new one or not" smiled Hadley as Smethurst re- appeared.

"Please come this way, gentlemen, Mr Bolting will see you now." Hadley nodded and they followed the receptionist into the office of Mr James Bolting, secretary of the club. Smethurst announced them and Bolting waved the detectives to seats in front of his imposing desk.

"How can I assist you, Inspector?" asked the secretary with a nervous smile. Hadley eyed the man carefully and noted that he had the appearance of a moderate person in his mid forties with little sign of excessive drinking.

"You may know already that Mr Anthony Hudson has been found dead this morning…"

"Good God, Inspector, this is the first I've heard of it!" interrupted Bolting.

"I'm sorry to be the person bringing the sad news…"

"What happened?"

"We believe from our initial inquiries that the gentleman committed suicide, sir."

"Oh, dear God, what a tragedy."

"Indeed, sir, now we are making further inquiries…"

"His poor wife must be devastated" interrupted Bolting.

"Yes, indeed, sir, now, if you don't mind, I need to ask you a few questions."

"Yes, of course, Inspector, I'll do anything to help."

"That's appreciated, sir, so tell me, to your knowledge, was Mr Hudson a heavy gambler?" On hearing that, Bolting's face went quite pale.

"Er, yes, he was, but he was a very wealthy gentleman who obviously could withstand his losses without difficulty" stammered the secretary.

"I see, and what would those losses have amounted to, Mr Bolting?"

"I couldn't possible say even if I knew, Inspector" replied the secretary.

"Indeed, sir, but as a responsible officer of the club, you must have had an inkling of what was going on at the card tables?"

"Well, yes, it's not out of order for me to tell you that Mr

Hudson belonged to a group of select members, used to playing for very high stakes, but of course you must understand that these gentlemen are very wealthy and…"

"Quite so, Mr Bolting, I'd be obliged if you would give me their names please" interrupted Hadley.

"I'm not sure that I am at liberty to do that, Inspector."

"Let me advise you of this fact, the Commissioner has given a statement earlier this evening to the Press regarding Mr Hudson's suicide and I can assure you that they will be here in due course, demanding answers to questions that may be embarrassing to the Dreyfus Club and all its members!"

"Oh, dear God!"

"Now if I have the opportunity to interview these gentlemen before that unpleasant Press intrusion occurs, then I may be able to diffuse the situation somewhat" smiled Hadley as he watched the secretary's face become flushed.

"I would be very grateful if you could do that, Inspector."

"The names, if you please, sir" said Hadley in a firm tone.

"Yes, right, er, well, there's Mr Lawrence Burgoyne, he's a very respectable member, and there's Mr Harvey DeVere, he's in tobacco I believe, then Mr Oscar Johnstone, he's a great friend of Mr Burgoyne and then there's Mr Phillip Brackley, the textile magnate, I'm sure you've heard of him, Inspector" stammered the secretary.

"Can't say I have, sir, now are any of these gentlemen in the club this evening?"

"I would think that possibly Mr Burgoyne and Mr DeVere might be" nodded Bolting.

"Perhaps you would find out and if they are here, inform them that I wish to see them privately" said Hadley.

"Yes, Inspector, I'll see to it right away" replied the secretary and he arose from his chair and left the office.

"Well, Sergeant, wealthy men gambling for high stakes is always a backdrop to someone's personal tragedy, I do believe."

"Yes, sir, I agree, and it will be interesting to find out if Mr Hudson's losses are anything like a hundred thousand pounds" replied Cooper.

"Indeed it will." The detectives waited for a while in silence before the secretary arrived, accompanied by a tall, distinguished looking man with grey hair, side whiskers to match and sporting a large gold rimmed monocle.

"Gentlemen, may I introduce Mr Burgoyne, one of our most prominent members" said Bolting.

"Good evening, sir, I'm Inspector Hadley and this is Sergeant Cooper."

"I hear that Hudson is dead, is that so?" asked Burgoyne abruptly.

"Yes, sir, it is true" replied Hadley.

"When did this happen?" asked Burgoyne.

"This morning, sir. Now would you please sit for a moment and help me with my inquiries" asked Hadley.

"Inquiries? What inquiries for God's sake?"

"Just routine ones, sir."

"Damn your routine inquiries, Inspector, I didn't kill the man!"

"I know that, sir."

"How do you know?"

"Because we are certain that Anthony Hudson committed suicide, sir." On hearing that Burgoyne looked pale and sat down on an adjacent chair.

"Good God, poor Anthony" whispered Burgoyne.

"If I may continue, sir" said Hadley in a firm tone and Burgoyne nodded.

"Was the late Mr Hudson a regular card player with you here, sir?"

"Yes, he was."

"Would you say that he was a member of your inner circle of gentlemen who played for high stakes?"

"Yes he was, and what of it, Inspector?" Hadley ignored the question and continued.

"Would you say that he lost more times than he won, sir?"

"Yes, I suppose so, but overall…"

"How much did he lose, sir?" interrupted Hadley.

"I do not intend to reveal that confidence, Inspector" replied Burgoyne firmly.

"Very well, sir, then I must ask if you intend to make a claim against Mr Hudson's estate to settle any outstanding debt to you?"

"Yes, I will do so, it's a point of honour amongst gentlemen of a certain class, Inspector."

"Quite so, sir, but if you tell me now it will save time as I shall find out in due course" smiled Hadley and Burgoyne fixed him with an icy stare.

"So, if you please, sir, how much?" persisted Hadley. Burgoyne wrestled for a while before murmuring "about a hundred and twenty thousand pounds."

"A tidy sum, if I may say so, sir" replied Hadley.

"We are all gentlemen of substance, Inspector."

"Indeed you are, sir."

"Have you finished or is there more of this?" asked Burgoyne angrily.

"That will be all for the time being, sir, thank you for your assistance" Hadley smiled as Burgoyne stood up and with a nod of his head, left the room.

Harvey DeVere was a short, plump man in his forties with a bald head and heavy side whiskers which made him look a little absurd. He answered all of Hadley's questions in an offhand and perfunctory manner but the Inspector managed to discover the amount that Hudson owed him. It was over eighty thousand pounds.

"Why did you allow such an amount to accrue, sir?" asked Hadley.

"Because Anthony was always good for his debts up 'til recently and he told us that he was expecting a considerable amount of money from an overseas investment in the very near future."

"I see, sir."

"When a Merchant Banker in the City talks of 'considerable amounts' then I assure you his credit is good at the table" smiled DeVere.

"I'm sure it is, sir." Hadley sat in silence for a few minutes pondering the desperate situation that Hudson must have experienced. Trapped on a merry-go-round of debt, travelling ever faster towards financial destruction and being unable to stop. On learning that the gold, which might have saved him, had been recovered in Liverpool, may well have been the final straw that brought about his suicide.

"Is there anything else, Inspector?" asked DeVere.

"No, sir, not for the moment."

"In that case, I bid you goodnight, Inspector" said DeVere and he left the room. Hadley then thanked Mr Bolting for all his assistance and the detectives left the Dreyfus Club and headed home in the rain.

After supper, Hadley sat in front of the fire, gazing into the glowing embers, deep in thought.
Alice looked at her tired husband and became concerned for him.

"Are you alright, my dear?" she asked. Hadley turned to his wife and smiled "yes, thank you, Alice, it's just that I've had a difficult day and I'm tired."

"Well you shouldn't work so hard, you're not getting any younger, dear."

"That's true." They remained silent for a while.

"Something is bothering you, what is it, Jim?" Hadley thought for a few moments before he replied "a woman, whose husband committed suicide this morning, blames me for his desperate actions."

"In her distress, that may be what she thinks, but I know that if a man takes his own life it's not because a policeman is making inquiries, Jim, it's because the man can't face the reality of whatever he has done, that's for sure!" Hadley smiled and said "Alice, you are very good for me."

"I know that, Jim, and I think it's time for bed" she smiled.

CHAPTER 18

The first thing Hadley did when he arrived in his office the next morning was to prepare an application for a warrant to search Pangbourne House. Hopeful that the permission would be granted, he telegraphed Reading Police for a number of officers to accompany him and Cooper in the search and planned to catch the one o'clock train from Paddington.

He was just about to enjoy a mid morning pot of tea when George came into the office and announced "there's a Mr Woods downstairs, sir, and he insists he speaks to you privately." Hadley looked up at Cooper and said "well, this is a turn up for the book, Sergeant."

"Indeed it is, sir."

"Please show Mr Woods up right away, George."

"Yes, sir." A few minutes later a very pale and nervous looking groom arrived in the office and after wishing the young man a good morning, Hadley waved him to a chair.

"I'm glad you've come to see me, Mr Woods, it saves me the bother of having to search for you" smiled Hadley.

"Yes, sir."

"So, now tell me everything, take your time and leave nothing out, if you please."

"Yes, sir, I've come to see you because I went to Cavendish Square yesterday and Mr Wilkes told me that the master was dead, he said he shot his self, well, I was shocked I can tell you."

"I'm sure you were, tell me, why did you go there?"

"I needed some more money…"

"More money?" queried Hadley.

"Yes, Mr Hudson only gave me enough for lodgings in Clapham for a few days and by the time I had dinner and a few pints each night, well, I had nothing left…"

"Why did he pay for your holiday?"

"It wasn't supposed to be a holiday, sir, he just wanted me out of the way for a bit, whilst things cooled down, as you might say."

"Tell me about the 'things' that needed to cool down" smiled Hadley.

"I've done nothing wrong, I only did what Mr Hudson told me

to do…" Woods said anxiously.

"Go on."

"I thought that he was up to something, he said it was for a bet, but I didn't believe him, sir."

"Continue."

"He told me to find someone who'd break into the house by the back door and then leave it open when everyone was out for the night, he said he'd pay ten pounds to the fella and five pounds to me for my trouble and not to tell anyone, no matter what."

"And you found that someone in the 'Blind Beggar' pub."

"Yes, sir."

"Harry Grover, if I'm not mistaken" said Hadley.

"Yes, sir."

"Go on, Mr Woods."

"Well, the job was done and only after did I learn that Madam's diamonds were stolen that night, but I knew Grover didn't steal them and I certainly didn't."

"What did Mr Hudson say to you afterwards?"

"Nothing, sir, until he decided that I should take a leave of absence."

"That's when you went to Clapham?"

"Yes, sir."

"Then what?"

"He sent a message for me to meet him outside the Mansion House and when I got there he gave me a parcel which was addressed to himself and told me to deliver it to the Bank and leave it at the reception desk then scarper back to Clapham."

"If Mr Hudson had not been a Banker I think he would have made a very fine actor, don't you agree, Sergeant?"

"I certainly do, sir." Hadley remained silent for a few moments before he looked hard at Woods and said "now tell me about the Count and his trunk."

"Not much to tell, really, sir, Mr Hudson said that I was to help the Count and do anything he asked, so when he told me to collect his trunk from Kings Cross Station and take it to Paddington and wait for him and the Countess, that's what I did."

"Do you know what was in the trunk?"

"No, sir, but it wasn't half heavy though."

"What happened at Paddington Station?"

"Nothing, sir, the Count arrived and he arranged for porters to lift it off my carriage and load it onto the guards van on the train, he gave me a guinea tip for my troubles."

"I see" mused Hadley.

"So, I've done nothing wrong, have I, sir?"

"You've aided and abetted a fraudulent act, Mr Woods" replied Hadley.

"But, honest, sir, I didn't know what it was all about 'til after…"

"Precisely, and that's when you should have come to me, Mr Woods, I'm afraid I may have to bring about a prosecution against you…"

"Oh, Gawd!"

"But in the circumstances, I may just relent and give you a formal warning…"

"Oh, God bless you, sir."

"You must promise me that you will 'go straight' from now on…"

"Oh, I will, sir, on my Mother's life…"

"Very well then, if you will just write out a full statement of all the facts, you may go, and make sure that you give an address where you can be reached if needed."

"I will, sir, I'm going back to my Mother's place in Shoreditch and I'll get a local job there" Woods replied and Hadley nodded his approval.

The detectives were just about to set off for Paddington Station with the approved search warrant when Mr Augustus arrived unexpectedly.

"Show him up, George" said Hadley and he looked at Cooper and mused "something else falling into place, Sergeant?"

"It seems so, sir."

Mr Augustus sat down opposite Hadley and said calmly "I'm sure you are a busy man, Inspector, so I'll be brief."

"I'd appreciate that today, sir."

"As I promised you when we last met, I've been making confidential inquiries at the Bank and have discovered that Mr Hudson and Sir John were having a very heated exchange on the afternoon of Sir John's death."

"What about, Mr Augustus?"

"It appears that after Sir John had examined the overseas ledger, he sent for Mr Hudson, and Mr Morris, he's Sir John's assistant, heard them arguing behind closed doors" replied Augustus.

"But did Mr Morris actually overhear the conversation?"

"Well, yes, but he doesn't want it to become common knowledge and gossip, out of respect for Sir John, you understand."

"You can tell me, sir, as I am not bound by tittle tattle, only by the facts and the law" replied Hadley. The Bank manager looked anxious for a moment and then said "Mr Morris said that Sir John was furious about funds that had been transferred by Mr Hudson to a reserve account at the Banque du Sumaris."

"So Mr Hudson's underhand actions had been discovered?"

"Yes, Inspector."

"What else did Mr Morris have to say?"

"He said that Sir John called Mr Hudson a blackguard, a thief and told him that there would be a full internal inquiry before he would be dismissed from the Bank."

"I hear what you say, sir, but you witnessed that evening, the two men having an amiable discussion over a drink, how do you explain that?"

"According to Mr Morris, when their argument was over, Mr Hudson left Sir John's office but came back later and said something to the effect that all the money would be recovered from the Banque du Sumaris and an offshore deal that he had arranged would bring substantial profits to the Bank in the very near future."

"Go on, sir."

"Apparently, Sir John's mood changed completely and he kept saying that the shareholders would be pleased and that the earlier argument was little more than a storm in a tea cup."

"The deceit went on and on" mused Hadley.

"So, I do not know if that has been of any help to you, Inspector" said Augustus.

"It has, sir, your information has convinced me that Mr Hudson murdered Sir John because he knew that his offshore deal had fallen through and there was no hope of any profits" replied

Hadley.

"I thought as much, Inspector."

"Now, if you will excuse me, sir, I have to leave to catch a train from Paddington, and I mustn't miss it."

"I understand, Inspector."

"Thank you for coming in, Mr Augustus." The Bank Manager nodded and left the office. Hadley looked at Cooper and said "let's be on our way to Pangbourne, Sergeant."

"Yes, sir."

At Reading police station, Hadley briefed Sergeant Gibson and the five constables who had been allocated to him for the search of Pangbourne House. They fully understood what they were looking for and Hadley felt pleased with the day as they set off towards Pangbourne in a four wheeler followed by a police wagon. When they arrived at the house, Hadley and Cooper went in whilst Gibson and his men waited outside for their signal to begin the search.

"Mon Dieu! I cannot believe that you dare to show your face here once again!" exclaimed Roguefort as he stood when the detectives were shown into the drawing room.

"Monsieur Roguefort, for my purposes here, I will regard you as the principal person in the household, as Mrs Hudson is not present" said Hadley.

"She has been called back to London on urgent business, Inspector, but I'm sure that she will return soon" said the Countess.

"Yes, indeed, Madam, I am sorry to have to inform you all that the reason for Mrs Hudson's return was because Mr Hudson has been found dead…"

"Dead?" queried Roguefort in astonishment as the Countess murmured "oh, no" and began to weep. The Count placed a comforting arm around his wife and asked "what has happened, Inspector?"

"We have reason to believe that Mr Hudson committed suicide, sir."

"Oh, dear God" whispered the Count.

"I am here today to search this house for your trunk, sir, and I have a warrant here that gives me the legal right to do so…" and

Hadley held it up.

"Mon Dieu! This is an outrage, I will not allow it!" exclaimed Roguefort.

"You have no choice in the matter, sir" replied Hadley. Then Roguefort turned to Benoir and said "throw these fools out of this house now!"

"I would not advise that, sir" said Hadley firmly.

"Help him, Lefevre, help him!" shouted Roguefort and the two Frenchmen made their way menacingly towards the detectives.

"I warn you if you assault us in the course of our duty you both will be arrested along with Monsieur Roquefort" said Hadley as calmly as he could. Benoir then leapt at Hadley and grabbed the Inspector by his shoulders and attempted to push him backwards. Cooper then came to Hadley's aid by administering a hefty punch to the side of Benoir's head which caused him to shout out before twisting away from the Inspector and falling to the floor. Lefevre hesitated and drew back as Hadley said "Benoir, you're under arrest!"

"I'll call Gibson in now, sir" said Cooper as he nursed his fist.

"If you please, Sergeant." They all remained in stunned silence as Gibson and his men arrived.

"Sergeant, arrest this man for assault and handcuff him to your police wagon for the time being." Benoir was pulled to his feet by two constables, handcuffed and led away to the utter amazement of Roguefort.

"You can't do this!" he shouted.

"I just did, Monsieur, and I now advise you to remain calm, otherwise you will join Benoir out in the wagon, I do hope that is clear, sir." Roguefort slumped back down onto his seat, pale faced and seething with anger.

"Now if you will all remain here, we will now search the premises for the missing trunk" smiled Hadley.

"You're wasting your time as usual, Inspector, the trunk was stolen in London and remains somewhere there" said the Count.

"We shall see, sir, we shall see" nodded Hadley.

"I'll begin now, sir" said Gibson.

"Yes, please, Sergeant."

The constables dispersed throughout the house and searched

diligently for the trunk. An hour later, Hadley directed two officers to the stables and they returned in due course, reporting that they had found nothing. From the attic to the cellar, the house was methodically searched but there was no trace of the missing trunk and Hadley became more angry with the situation as well as himself.

"They've made fools of us once again, Sergeant" he said to Cooper as they stood in the hallway. The sergeant nodded sympathetically and asked "shall I stop the search now, sir?"

"Yes, please."

"Right, sir."

"Get Gibson and the constables assembled outside by the wagon, I just want to say a few words to them."

"Yes, sir" replied Cooper with a nod. Hadley returned to the drawing room and announced to the guests that the search had proved fruitless and he was returning to London. He informed Roguefort that Benoir would not be arrested for assault this time, but advised that he should be more careful in the future before he incited his man to violence. The smug looks on the faces of both Roguefort and Castellini made Hadley smoulder with anger but he managed a smile as he left the room. Outside, he spoke briefly to Gibson and his men, thanking them for their assistance before they released the sour faced Benoir and made their way back towards Reading. As the four wheeler reached Pangbourne village, Hadley asked the driver to stop outside 'The Partridge'.

"We're getting off here, Sergeant."

"We're not going back to London, sir?"

"Definitely not, Sergeant, now you go and see the young woman in the pub and tell her that we'll be staying for a few days, while I go and see the Reverend Crabtree to let him know that we're back in the church tower."

"Right, sir." Hadley then asked Gibson to send a telegraph message to Chief Inspector Bell advising him that they would be staying at Pangbourne, before saying goodbye to Gibson and leaving the coach.

Twenty minutes later, Cooper joined Hadley at the latticed window in the tower, overlooking the cross roads.

"How long are we going to stay here, sir?"

"I've no idea, Sergeant."

"I've not brought any change of clothes, sir."

"Neither have I, Sergeant."

"Oh, dear."

"So we'll both smell unpleasant together, Sergeant" said Hadley and Cooper laughed.

"We will, sir." They remained silent for a while before Hadley said "now that our foreign friends know of Hudson's death and believe we've returned to London with our tails between our legs, I'm sure that they'll make a move."

"Have you an idea when, sir?"

"No, Sergeant, but I'm certain that the Count and his wife are the ones to follow if they leave without the others."

"Roguefort and his man are not the prime suspects, sir?"

"I don't think so, but they are implicated, along with Lefevre." They remained in the tower until it became dark and then left for the warmth of the pub. After a good dinner and a few ales they retired to their room to make notes and discuss the events of the day.

It was just eleven o'clock the next day and they were feeling the cold as they watched from their lookout, when the Reverend Crabtree appeared with sandwiches and a pot of tea.

"Oh, thank you so much, Reverend" said Hadley.

"You're most welcome, Inspector, I thought you and Sergeant Cooper could do with a little sustenance on a cold morning" he smiled.

"Indeed, it is most welcome."

"Now, tell me, what's going on up at the house?" asked the Reverend with eyes shining with anticipation.

"Our foreign guests are still there and yesterday we searched the premises…"

"What did you find, Inspector?" interrupted the Reverend.

"Nothing, I'm afraid, sir."

"Oh, dear."

"Yes, we were disappointed."

"What were you looking for?"

"A large trunk…"

"With a body in it, no doubt" said the Reverend.

"No, sir, we suspect contraband."

"Goodness gracious me."

"Yes, I'm afraid that I was mistaken" said Hadley.

"I'm sure you had good reasons for your suspicions, Inspector."

"Yes, sir."

"Well, if you couldn't find the contraband…" he paused "by the way, what is the contraband, Inspector?"

"I can't say at the moment, sir."

"Oh, I understand, well I can tell you that if it was gold in the trunk, to avoid discovery those Catholics up at the house, would hide it in a church" said the Reverend and his words struck Hadley like a hammer.

"What is the name of the Catholic church in Reading?"

"Saint Mary's in the Oxford Road, near the railway station" replied the Reverend.

"Thank you so much, sir, you've been an inspiration" said Hadley.

"So it is gold then?" asked the excited Reverend and Hadley smiled.

"These sandwiches are delicious, sir" said Cooper, hoping to distract the Reverend from his questioning.

"Oh, good, Sergeant, I'm pleased that you're enjoying them."

"Reverend Crabtree" said Hadley firmly.

"Yes, Inspector."

"You must absolutely promise that you will keep our discussion confidential until after the case is closed" said Hadley.

"I promise to do that, Inspector, but please let me know when the culprits have been arrested so that I may be free to tell all of my congregation!"

"I will let you know in writing, sir, you have my word."

"Splendid, what a sermon that will make, my, I could run it on for a number of Sundays" said the Reverend.

"I have no doubt, sir."

"Well, I best leave you now, please let me know if you need anything" he smiled.

"We will and thank you, Reverend."

Cooper went to lunch first and when he returned from the pub, Hadley strode across the high street just as a four wheeler appeared from the direction of Reading. Hadley stood in the doorway of 'The Partridge' and watched the coach pass by with Mrs Hudson and Hargreaves sitting in the back. The Inspector gazed after it as it raced up the hill towards Pangbourne House. As he sat down to a ploughman's lunch he felt confident that things would now begin to move.

They kept a careful watch until nightfall and then retired to the pub, cold and a little impatient with the day's lack of events.
"I think they'll make a move tomorrow, Sergeant" said Hadley as they sat by the wood fire and sipped at pints of ale.
"Well, here's hoping, sir."
"I expect Mrs Hudson and her solicitor came back today to tell her guests the sad news and to get them to leave."
"Indeed, sir."
"If Hudson's gambling friends press for payment of his debts, then I should think that the house will be offered up for sale as soon as possible."
"Yes, sir."
"That means the place will be closed up and the servants dismissed" said Hadley and Cooper nodded. They sat in silence for a while, both contemplating the next probable moves.
"What about the trunk, sir?"
"We'll follow the Count and his wife to Saint Mary's in Reading and catch them red handed, Sergeant."
"Suppose Roguefort and his man get there first, sir?"
"No, I don't think so, it's the Count who's behind all this, although I must admit, I don't quite know where the unpleasant Frenchman and his thug fit in to the scheme of things" replied Hadley. They enjoyed a dinner of roast beef with all the trimmings and then after another pint of ale, retired to bed.

It was just before lunchtime on the following day when a four wheeler came down the hill from Pangbourne House, swept over the cross roads and rattled past the church tower with Mrs Hudson, Mr Hargreaves, Monsieur Roguefort and Benoir on board. Hadley and Cooper looked carefully at the passing coach, just in case the trunk was strapped somewhere on to the swaying four wheeler. Other than a selection of small travelling cases on the platform at the back, there was no sign of the trunk and Hadley felt relieved, sure that the missing item was indeed at Saint Mary's church.

"All we have to do is wait for the Count, his wife and Captain Lefevre to appear, Sergeant."

"Yes, sir, so shall I alert the driver with the trap?"

"Not yet, I think we'll wait for them to pass first, we know where they are going, so, we shall follow at a discreet distance to Reading" Hadley smiled and Cooper nodded. They remained silent for a while before Cooper said "we'd better forgo lunch today, sir, just in case they make a dash for Reading soon."

"Quite so, Sergeant."

About an hour later, Hadley looked up the hill in the direction of Pangbourne House and noticed a plume of brown smoke rising from behind the trees.

"Sergeant, look there" he pointed and as he did so, the smoke became darker and began to billow.

"It must be a fire at the house, sir!"

"Quick, there's not a moment to lose, get the trap!" They rushed down from the tower and whilst Cooper ran along the high street for the horse and trap, Hadley hammered on the door of the vicarage to tell the Reverend Crabtree that men were needed to fight a fire at Pangbourne House. Cooper arrived back in the trap within moments and Hadley swung himself up telling the driver to make haste and not spare the horse. The driver nodded, slapped the reins and the chestnut mare accelerated away as if she had been poked with a red hot branding iron. They galloped up the hill, in through the open ornate gates and along the curved gravel drive. They saw the smoke billowing from the stables behind the house and heard the cracking of burning wood as the fire raged. Suddenly, from the front door of the house, the Countess appeared and ran down the steps towards them. She was screaming and waving her arms in distress, then she collapsed down onto the gravel drive. As the detectives approached the spot where she had fallen, she raised herself up onto her knees and screamed out "he has killed my Giovani! He has killed my Giovani!" The detectives leapt down from the trap before it had stopped and rushed to the distressed woman. Hadley noticed blood on her dress as he helped her to her feet.

"Who, Madam, who has killed your husband?" demanded Hadley.

"Lefevre, with a knife, he's taken my poor Giovani to the stables, he's mad, lunatic!" she sobbed and Hadley held her close.

"Quickly, Sergeant!"

"Yes, sir" and Cooper rushed off in the direction of the burning stables.

"Countess, I must ask you to compose yourself for a few moments whilst I help my Sergeant, will you sit up in the trap until I return?" She nodded as she sobbed and Hadley, assisted by the driver, helped the Countess into the trap.

"Leave the lady with me, sir, I'll take care of her" said the driver with a smile.

"Good man" replied Hadley before he raced away towards the fire. When he turned the corner of the house he saw that the conflagration was out of control and the flames were reaching ever skyward with dark smoke billowing above them. The cracking of the burning timbers coupled with the sound of horses in panic were the back drop to the horrific scene that confronted him. The bloodstained body of Count Giovani Castellini lay on the cobbles in front of the burning building, Lefevre stood in front of the Count, clutching a large knife and glaring at Cooper who was leaning forward, his arms slightly outstretched towards the Frenchman, who looked wild and deranged.

"Lefevre! Put down that weapon!" shouted Hadley as he arrived alongside Cooper.

"Go to hell, you meddling English pig!" replied Lefevre.

"Give up now, man, can't you see your position is hopeless!"

"Never, mon ami, never!"

"This time we've caught you red handed and there's no escape!" shouted Hadley.

"You've got to catch me yet, you miserable dog!"

"Then if you intend to resist arrest, I shall not hesitate to use all the force necessary to overpower you!"

"Mon Dieu! You think that you and your puppy here can take me, you under estimate me, Monsieur Inspector!"

"On the contrary, Lefevre, as you are about to find out!"

"I shall delight in killing you both before I leave this place and return to Marseille!"

"Really?"

"Your burnt bodies will be found in the stables and that will be the end" said Lefevre.

"And what about the Countess?"

"She can either come with me back to France and hold her tongue or die here with her stupid husband!"

"Enough, Lefevre, you're under arrest for the murder of Count Castellini…"

"No one arrests me, Monsieur Inspector, no one!"

"Sergeant, keep well apart from me and that way we'll get him!"

"Right, sir." The detectives moved apart and then slowly approached Lefevre, waiting for him to lash out with his knife. The Frenchman began to look anxious as they moved closer, then suddenly he slashed at Cooper and caught the Sergeant's arm as he raised it to protect himself. Hadley leapt forward but Lefevre danced backwards and moved out of the range of the Inspector's grasp. Then a horse, crazed with fear broke loose from the burning stable, bolting out into the cobbled yard and its sudden appearance distracted Lefevre for an instant. Hadley and Cooper then both lunged at the Frenchman but with a wild slash of his knife he caught Cooper once again, the Sergeant crying out in pain as the blade cut into his shoulder. Hadley managed to grab at Lefevre's hand holding the knife and force it upwards but the Frenchman dropped the blade into his other hand before attempting to reach around Hadley's back to stab him.

Hadley swung himself round, causing Lefevre to lose his balance and stagger back, falling over the body of the Count. Hadley, still holding his wrist followed him down to the cobbles as the knife went clattering across the yard. The two men struggled for a while and Cooper, blood pouring from his wounds, joined the fray and help overpower the crazed Frenchman. The Sergeant handcuffed Lefevre and help drag him up on his feet just as Hadley grabbed his hair and pulled his head back before he hissed "I'll see you with a noose around your neck for all this you bloody murderer!" Then a number of men, lead by the Reverend Crabtree, suddenly appeared in the yard. Hadley smiled when he saw them and said "thank you for coming, gentlemen, but I fear that the building is lost!"

"Are you alright, Inspector?" asked the Reverend with concern.

"Yes, I am, but Sergeant Cooper here is wounded, can you summon a doctor?"

"He's already here, I thought that Doctor Burton might be needed so I took the liberty of asking him to accompany us" smiled the Reverend.

"God bless you, Reverend" said Hadley.

"He frequently does, Inspector." The Doctor immediately started to attend to Cooper's wounds whilst Hadley directed several men to pick up the corpse of Count Castellini and take it into the house. Three others took charge of Lefevre and were told in no uncertain terms to keep him closely guarded.

"Reverend" said Hadley in a moment of relative calm..

"Yes, Inspector."

"As you came up the drive you would have seen the Countess sitting in the trap…"

"Is that who the lady is?"

"Yes, and I'd be obliged if you would kindly take her back to the vicarage and keep her safe until I have settled matters here."

"Of course, Inspector, and may I suggest that when Doctor Burton has finished with your Sergeant, he calls to see the Countess?"

"As always, Reverend, sound advice." The clergyman smiled and the two men went off to see the distressed Countess. Hadley invited her to go with the Reverend before telling the driver of the trap to go at speed to Reading police station and summon help from Sergeant Gibson and his men. Hadley then went into the house where the servants were assisting the Doctor as he finished bandaging Cooper.

"How do you feel, Sergeant?" asked Hadley.

"Quite alright thank you, sir" replied Cooper with a faint smile.

"Good, well help is on its way, so you may rest for a while."

CHAPTER 19

An hour and a half later, Sergeant Gibson and his constables arrived in a police van. Hadley was relieved to see them and immediately briefed them on what had taken place. Lefevre was removed from the house and chained with leg irons to the interior of the van where a constable kept him company. Doctor Burton had preliminary examined the body of the Count and told Hadley that several deep stab wounds to the chest were the cause of death. It was decided to take the body of the Count to Reading Hospital in the police van and Lefevre was to be held at the police station before Hadley took charge of him. The Inspector requested Gibson to telegraph Chief Inspector Bell with all the relevant information of the day's events and after Gibson and his men had departed from Pangbourne House, Hadley and Cooper walked slowly back to the vicarage.

The Countess had recovered her senses and appeared composed when Hadley met her in the drawing room of the vicarage. He felt that the Reverend Crabtree had played an important role in ensuring that the lovely French woman was able to face the ordeal ahead of her.

"Let me arrange tea for us all" said the Reverend as he invited Hadley and Cooper to sit on a large sofa opposite the Countess.

"Thank you, Reverend" said Hadley as he looked into the tear stained eyes of the Countess.

"Tell me, Madam, do you feel well enough to talk to us?" Hadley asked and then waited for some moments for her reply.

"I want him to hang for what he's done!" she exclaimed with passion.

"I'm sure that he will, Madam, with your help" replied Hadley.

"I will tell you everything, Inspector."

"Thank you, Madam."

"I will be brief, for the moment" she said.

"Thank you."

"I met my husband at a ball in Marseille…" she said and then faltered as her tears welled up.

"Take your time, Madam" said Hadley gently and she nodded

her thanks.

"And we fell in love, but my family did not approve of Giovani as he came from a noble but very poor Italian family."

"It must have been very difficult for you, Countess."

"It was, but I insisted and we were married, my family were furious, especially my uncle, Michel Roguefort…"

"I can imagine" interrupted Hadley in a whisper.

"He wanted me to marry a friend of his who lived in Monaco, but he was an old man with plenty of money and little else to attract me" she paused and shook her head at the thought of it.

"Go on, Madam."

"So, my family, influenced by my uncle, virtually disowned me and stopped all the financial support that I had enjoyed, as a result Giovani and I were frozen out of society and desperately poor." Hadley shook his head at that just as the Reverend returned, followed by his house keeper with a tray of tea and biscuits.

"Here we are, sustenance for all" he smiled and cups of tea were distributed by the house keeper. Once they had refreshed themselves, the Countess continued.

"Then as things became worse for us, I decided to take revenge on my family, especially my uncle, who had been so cruel to me…" she faltered again and Hadley waited patiently for her to continue.

"I knew that he had great wealth from his shipping business as well as his Istanbul company, and I found out by accident that he had gold bullion deposited in a Bank…"

"Please go on, Madam" said Hadley, his eyes wide open with interest.

"I knew Pascal Dalmas, one of the captains, before I met Giovani, and we planned to remove some of the bullion from the Bank and share it between us…"

"Why should Dalmas agree to steal from the man who employed him?" asked Hadley.

"Because Pascal hated my uncle with a passion!"

"Why, Madam?"

"My uncle ruined Pascal's family business by lending them money to buy two ships and then immediately calling in the loan before they had a chance to repay even one Franc!"

"I see."

"My uncle then took over their ships and all the customers."

"What an underhand trick" said Hadley.

"Pascal's poor father committed suicide after that."

"I now understand why he would agree to the theft."

"So, then my uncle offered Pascal a position as a captain…"

"On the 'Arabesque'" interrupted Hadley.

"Oui, how did you know, Inspector?"

"We have many ways and means, Madam" Hadley smiled.

"Pascal accepted and planned for the day when he could have his revenge."

"Your idea to steal the bullion was the very opportunity" nodded Hadley.

"Yes, and it was very easy, I managed to obtain official paperwork from my uncle's office giving authority for Pascal to remove two cases from the vault at the Bank and transport them back to Marseille."

"May I ask, did the Bank in Istanbul know what was in the cases?"

"No, not officially, but I'm sure that they had some idea" she replied.

"Go on, Madam."

"The cases were off-loaded in Genoa and then Giovani arranged for them to be transported round to Marseille by road, so that they should not be discovered when the 'Arabesque' docked there."

"Then what happened, Madam?"

"My uncle became suspicious after we told him we were going to America, he did not know what had happened, but he replaced Pascal with that wretch, Lefevre, who spied on everybody and everything…"

"Dalmas stayed on board the 'Arabesque' because he wanted to keep close to the gold" said Hadley.

"Oui, indeed he did, Inspector, then Giovani and I travelled from Marseille to Paris by train and then on to Calais eventually arriving in London to stay with the Hudson's."

"What about America?"

"Mr Hudson had arranged our passage to Boston, where we planned to start a new life."

"Did Mr Hudson know about the gold?"

"Oui, Inspector, Giovani promised Anthony a big share of the gold if he would help us."

"How did your husband meet Mr Hudson?"

"Giovani came to London some years ago to try and raise money to start a business to rival my uncle's" she replied.

"Presumably, he was unable to fund his venture?"

"Oui, but they became great friends and Anthony used to take Giovani to his club, where they would play cards" she smiled.

"I see, do go on, Madam."

"Then when the 'Arabesque' arrived in London, the gold was unloaded, but before that, somehow, and I don't how, Lefevre found out about the gold and I think he murdered Pascal and then Jacques Mornay…"

"May the saints preserve us!" exclaimed the Reverend.

"Tell me about the trunk, Madam" said Hadley.

"Giovani sent it to Rotterdam by rail for collection."

"Why?"

"Because he reasoned that if my uncle found the gold in the machinery crates, he would think that all of it had been recovered, so the trunk is our insurance, just in case" she smiled.

"Where is it now, Madam?"

"We left it at Saint Mary's church in Reading" she replied quietly.

"I knew it, I knew it!" exclaimed the Reverend.

"Did Lefevre know what was in the trunk?"

"I think he suspected and he must have telegraphed a message to my uncle from Rotterdam, that's why he came to London, Giovani and I were very frightened when he arrived."

"I'm sure."

"Then, when you kept calling, we were anxious that you should discover what was going on before we could escape to America."

"Indeed, Madam."

"We just had to keep up the pretence and I'm sorry that we lied to you, but Giovani and I were desperate to get away."

"I can understand that, Madam."

"Now my uncle has gone to the church to collect the trunk and he will take it back to Marseille."

"Did you tell him where it was, Madam?"

"Giovani did, after my uncle promised that he would give us

ten thousand US dollars to start our new life in America as long as we stayed there and never returned to France."

"And you agreed?"

"But of course" she nodded.

"Why did Lefevre kill your husband?"

"I think that my uncle told that pig to do it after he had left with the others" she replied.

"May God have mercy upon his soul" whispered the Reverend.

"Continue, Madam."

"We were supposed to follow on with Lefevre to London, then collect the money before going up to Liverpool to board the next available ship to Boston, but the 'pig' made some excuse to go to the stables and when he returned he asked Giovani to go outside with him, I was suspicious and followed, then, by the back door, Lefevre turned on Giovani with a knife and stabbed him…" at that she broke down and sobbed and sobbed. The Reverend went immediately to her side and placed a comforting arm around the distressed woman. Hadley looked at Cooper, pale faced and bandaged, then shook his head slowly.

"I think a small brandy might help, Reverend" said Hadley and the clergyman nodded. After the Countess had drunk the golden reviver and had rested, she appeared composed.

"I think that you have been through enough today, Countess and I would suggest that you remain here with the Reverend before we can make arrangements for you to return to London with us tomorrow" said Hadley and the Countess nodded her approval.

The detectives left the distraught Countess with the Reverend and his housekeeper, knowing that Doctor Burton would attend her soon, and hopefully prescribe a sleeping draught that would give her a peaceful night. By the fire in the bar of 'The Partridge', Hadley tried to relax with a pint of ale before discussing the events with his wounded Sergeant. Fortunately the knife wounds were not as severe as had been first thought due to the thick over coat that Cooper was wearing and Doctor Burton told him that he would be alright but should see a doctor as soon as he returned to London.

"Well, Sergeant, what a pretty kettle of fish we have here."

"Indeed, sir."

"The Chief will find it all hard to believe."

"He will, sir" replied Cooper.

"By the way, I would like to commend your bravery in arresting Lefevre."

"Thank you, sir, I was only doing my duty."

"Nevertheless, it was very brave of you and I am proud to have you as my assistant."

"Thank you, sir" smiled Cooper and he blushed.

"Now, I think we'll have a good dinner and retire early, we've a busy day tomorrow" said Hadley.

"Back to London and the arrest of Monsieur Roguefort if I'm not mistaken, sir."

"Quite right, Sergeant, and we'll find out for certain what's in the trunk."

The next morning they collected the Countess from the vicarage in a four wheeler, and after thanking the Reverend Crabtree for all his help, Hadley gave him permission to use the events at Pangbourne House in his next sermon. The Reverend was overjoyed and stood with his housekeeper waving 'goodbye' until the coach was totally out of sight on its way to Reading.

Hadley stopped at the church of Saint Mary's where the priest confirmed that Monsieur Roguefort and his party had collected the trunk left by Castellini. The Countess asked if she could remain there, praying for a while, before returning to London and the Inspector readily agreed. At the police station, Hadley thanked Gibson and his superior, Inspector Balcombe, for all their help and requested that two constable's journey with them to London as prisoner escort. That was readily agreed and further arrangements were made for the transporting of the body of the Count to the Marylebone Hospital. Hadley telegraphed Chief Inspector Bell requesting a police van and constables to be at Paddington to meet them when they arrived on the mid-day train. The detectives then collected the Countess from Saint Mary's and proceeded to the station where Lefevre was waiting in the custody of two constables. When the party arrived at Paddington they went straight to the Yard where the detectives made the Countess comfortable in the office and left Lefevre in a maximum security cell under the watchful eye of the custody Sergeant. After a pot of tea, Hadley went upstairs to advise the Chief of his plans to bring the investigations to a conclusion.

"You're going to arrest Roguefort?" asked Bell, wide eyed at the very thought.

"Yes, sir."

"On what charge?"

"Incitement to murder and incitement to assault police officers carrying out their duties, sir."

"Well, explain yourself, Hadley."

"The Countess believes that her uncle ordered Lefevre to murder her husband, sir."

"She believes, Hadley? That won't stand up in court, an accusation by a poor woman who is demented by the death of her husband…"

"I appreciate that, sir."

"Worst still, she witnessed the foul act."

"That ensures that we'll get a conviction and the Frenchman will hang" said Hadley.

"Indeed, but I think that it will be impossible to bring a successful case against Roguefort, Hadley."

"Let me try, sir."

"Alright, but on your head be it" replied Bell in a resigned tone.

"It always is, sir" smiled Hadley.

"What about the Countess?"

"I intend to charge her with conspiracy, sir."

"Well, be careful with her, the woman has suffered enough for the moment."

"Yes, sir, and I'd like your permission to keep her in a safe house as I believe she may be in danger from Roguefort." The Chief Inspector looked anxious when he heard that but nodded and replied "make the necessary arrangements, and I'll sanction them."

"Thank you, sir."

"Hadley…"

"Yes, sir?"

"Watch your step with Roguefort."

"I will, sir."

Hadley decided to leave Captain Lefevre in his cell for the time being whilst he arranged for the Countess to be housed in convenient rooms adjacent to the Savoy Hotel in the Strand. When she was settled in, Hadley and Cooper set off to Cavendish Square with an arrest warrant for Michel Roguefort.

"He's not here, Inspector" said Wilkes.

"Do you know where he's gone to?"

"Back to France, I imagine, sir."

"I'd like to see Mrs Hudson in that case."

"Certainly, sir, please come in and I'll advise madam that you are here." Wilkes gave a little bow and left the detectives in the hallway. A few moments later they were shown into the drawing room where Mrs Hudson was relaxing on the sofa and Mr Hargreaves was standing with his back to the fire.

"Back again, Inspector?" asked Hargreaves.

"It appears so, sir."

"What is it now?" demanded Mrs Hudson.

"I regret to inform you, Madam, that yesterday, Captain Lefevre murdered Count Castellini at Pangbourne House after setting fire to the stables…"

"Oh my God!" she shrieked and began to sob.

"What are you saying, Inspector?" demanded Hargreaves anxiously.

"Do I have to repeat myself, sir?"

"Well, er, no, I…"

"I'm sure that you are both shocked at the news…"

"Yes, yes, we are…" stammered Hargreaves.

"The dreadful deed was witnessed by the Countess and we have arrested Lefevre, he is secure at Scotland Yard."

"And where is the Countess now?"

"In a safe place with us, sir."

"Where?"

"As I believe that the Countess is in danger, I'm not prepared to tell you, sir."

"In danger, from whom, Inspector?"

"Her uncle, Monsieur Roguefort" replied Hadley to the stunned couple before him.

"I can't believe what you are saying" said Mrs Hudson as she dabbed at her eyes with a handkerchief.

"Surely you've made a mistake in thinking that Monsieur Roguefort would wish to harm his niece…"

"I must advise you both to be very careful what you say…" Hadley began.

"Are you threatening us, Inspector?" asked Hargreaves angrily.

"I was about to say before you interrupted me, that yesterday, the Countess made a full confession in front of the Reverend Crabtree, Sergeant Cooper and myself at the vicarage in Pangbourne, so, we are fully aware of what has taken place."

"Good grief" murmured Mrs Hudson.

"I have come here with an arrest warrant for Michel Roguefort, if he is not somewhere on these premises then I wish to know where he is" said Hadley in a firm tone. Hargreaves and Mrs Hudson remained silent, both pale faced with shock.

"What is the charge, Inspector?" asked Hargreaves timidly.

"Incitement to murder, sir."

"Dear God" murmured Mrs Hudson.

"Do either of you know where he is?" asked Hadley.

"No, no, we don't, Inspector" replied Hargreaves.

"Sergeant Cooper and myself observed you both leaving Pangbourne in the company of Roguefort and his assistant, Benoir, further to that, inquiries at the church of Saint Mary's, confirmed that Roguefort collected the trunk that had been left there previously by the Count, now, after you travelled to Paddington by train together, I find it hard to accept that you have no idea where Roguefort has disappeared to." They both looked surprised by what Hadley had said to them and Hargreaves shifted with discomfort.

"I can only assume that he has returned to France, Inspector."

"When did you last see him?"

"Yesterday, when we arrived here, we had dinner together then he told us that he would stay in an hotel for the night before going to Dover to catch the ferry to Calais" replied Hargreaves.

"Do you know which hotel?"

"No, Inspector, he didn't say" said Mrs Hudson.

"I presume he took the trunk with him?"

"Yes, Inspector."

"Did he say what was in it?"

"He just said it belonged to him" replied Hargreaves.

"Very well, as I have no more questions for the moment, I will take my leave" said Hadley.

"Thank you, Inspector" said Hargreaves and with a nod the detectives left the room. Once outside in the Square, Cooper hailed a cab and they set off at speed back to the Yard.

The first thing Hadley did when he arrived back in his office was to send a telegraph message to the Police at Dover requesting immediate assistance in apprehending Roguefort and Benoir. The Inspector hoped that he was not too late and determined to make every effort to arrest the Frenchman.

The detectives made their arrangements to take the train to Dover in the afternoon and then, after lunch in the Strand, they returned to the office to be greeted by an anxious looking Mr Hargreaves.

"Inspector, I am very worried about the Countess after what you told us this morning" he said as Hadley sat behind his desk and waved the solicitor to a chair.

"Tell me why, sir?"

"Not long after you left Cavendish Square, the Countess arrived unexpectedly…"

"Oh, dear" interrupted Hadley.

"She said that she was very frightened and didn't know what to do next…"

"Go on, sir."

"Mrs Hudson and I tried to advise her and put her mind at rest, but she remained very anxious, the murder of the Count is still affecting her badly."

"I'm sure."

"I advised her to return to the safe lodgings that you had arranged in the Strand…"

"Did she tell you where she was staying or did you press her?" interrupted Hadley in an angry tone.

"Well, she confided in Mrs Hudson, who told me" replied Hargreaves and Hadley sighed.

"Continue, if you please, sir."

"The Countess stayed for lunch before returning to the Strand, and as it was a pleasant afternoon, she decided to walk…"

"What has happened, sir?" asked Hadley fearing the worst.

"Wilkes opened the front door for her to leave and stayed for a moment watching the Countess as she made her way across the Square, then out of nowhere a closed coach appeared and the Frenchman, Benoir got out and grabbed the Countess, forcing her into the coach, which drove off at speed…"

"It's as I feared, she's been kidnapped by Roguefort!" interrupted Hadley.

"It appears so, Inspector."

"Thank you for coming in, sir, I would ask you to remain vigilant from now on and inform me instantly if you have any further information that can assist my inquiries."

"Of course, Inspector."

"Right, Sergeant, we have work to do as I believe the Countess is now in grave danger!"

CHAPTER 20

The detectives hurried down to custody and with the sergeant in attendance the door into Lefevre's cell was opened. The Frenchman was sitting on his bed and glanced up at Hadley who towered above him.

"Where were you going to meet Roguefort after you had finished your deadly work at Pangbourne?"

"I have decided not to answer any of your questions, Monsieur Inspector" Lefevre replied with a grin.

"Listen to me carefully, the Countess has been kidnapped by Benoir in broad daylight and he has obviously taken her to meet Roguefort, I want to know where that is, Lefevre" said Hadley firmly.

"It is no interest to me, Monsieur, where Benoir has taken the silly woman" replied Lefevre.

"Well, it is to me, so, I repeat the question, where is Roguefort?"

"I have no idea, Monsieur Inspector."

"I fear that the Countess is in mortal danger, and you might be able to save her life!"

"I do not care whether she lives or dies, Monsieur…"

"Well I bloody well do!" and with that Hadley smashed his fist into the Frenchman's face with such force that his head jerked back against the wall before his nose began to pour with blood and his lips became swollen.

"Mon Dieu! You are a violent pig!"

"So I've been told, now, where is Roguefort?"

"Get out of here!"

"For the last time, where is he?"

"Go to hell!"

"Now you leave me with no alternative but to get really unpleasant…"

"Alright, alright" interrupted Lefevre. Hadley waited while the injured man composed himself.

"I'm waiting, Lefevre."

"I was to meet Monsieur Roguefort at Dover" said Lefevre.

"At the ferry terminal?"

"Non, aboard my ship."

"The 'Arabesque' is at Dover?" asked Hadley with surprise.

"Oui, Monsieur."

"I thought she was bound for Nantes and then Marseille" said Hadley.

"Non, I gave orders for the mate, LeValet, to sail out into the Channel for a few days and then return to Dover to wait for Monsieur Roguefort, Benoir and me."

"Dear God, what liars you all are!"

"That's what you think, Monsieur Inspector." Hadley nodded and then said "Sergeant, let's get off to Dover and hope that we are not too late!"

Hadley briefed Chief Inspector Bell, who looked more concerned than usual, on the events so far, before he and Cooper hurried to catch the train to Dover. It was getting dark when they arrived at the port and Hadley was anxious as Cooper hired a trap to take them to the harbour master's office.

"Good afternoon, I'm Inspector Hadley and this is Sergeant Cooper of Scotland Yard" said the Inspector to the surprised Harbour Master.

"Good afternoon, gentlemen, I'm Jack Wilson, how can I help you?" he replied as he stood up from his desk.

"I have reason to believe that a French brig, the 'Arabesque' is moored up in the harbour" said Hadley.

"Yes, Inspector, she arrived two days ago and is stationed out at the end of the breakwater, you can see her clearly from here" replied Wilson pointing out of the window. Hadley looked and saw the brig, feeling relieved that the 'Arabesque' was still there.

"We have to detain two men that we believe are aboard her, Mr Wilson."

"Right, sir."

"As speed is of the essence, we will leave you now, but I would ask you to contact officers who are at present watching the ferry terminal for these men, advise them where we are and tell them to support us as quickly as possible."

"Right away, Inspector" replied Wilson. Hadley nodded, smiled and left the office with Cooper. The detectives hurried around the dock and out towards the breakwater, which was a considerable distance from the Harbour Master's office. They walked quickly past all the ships moored and Hadley was anxious to know if Benoir had arrived with the Countess and was aboard the 'Arabesque'.

"I hope I haven't jumped to the wrong conclusion, Sergeant" said Hadley as they hurried along.

"About what, sir?"

"Benoir and the Countess."

"We'll soon know, sir" replied Cooper and Hadley nodded. It seemed an age before they reached the breakwater and began the final long walk to the French brig moored at the end. As they approached the vessel, they could see some activity on board and as Hadley stepped onto the boarding gangway he realised that the 'Arabesque' was about to set sail.

"Just in time, I do believe, Sergeant" said the Inspector as he raced up and onto the deck of the brig.

"Monsieur?" asked a nearby crewman.

"Take me to your captain, if you please" said Hadley firmly. The man recognised the detectives and nodded before gesturing for them to follow him. The crewman knocked on the door of the captain's cabin and entered followed by the detectives. Roguefort stood immediately from his chair as did Pierre LeValet, the first mate who Lefevre put in command of the ship. Benoir was standing behind the pale faced Countess, who remained seated and smiled with relief when she saw Hadley and Cooper.

"Mon Dieu! The meddling English pig and his puppy!" exclaimed Roguefort.

"Indeed, Monsieur, once again we have arrived to thwart your plans and bring you to justice this time" replied Hadley.

"I do not think so, Monsieur Inspector" grinned Roguefort.

"Really, sir? We already have Lefevre in custody charged with murder and you're next."

"You may have noticed that my ship is about to set sail for France, so you can either leave immediately or come with us, the choice is yours" said Roguefort.

"I arrest you Michel Roguefort for conspiracy to murder Count Castellini and you, Pierre Benoir for the kidnap of the Countess Castellini, please come quietly…"

"You English are so quaint! Or is it blind foolishness that

makes you say stupid things, Inspector?"

"I must warn you…"

"You do not warn me of anything, Inspector!" exclaimed Roguefort angrily and before Hadley could reply, the Frenchman turned to LeValet and said "get to your duties, Captain, I want to be underway immediately!" LeValet nodded and replied "oui, Monsieur" before he hurried out of the cabin.

"A party of armed police officers will board this ship and…" began Hadley.

"Non, Inspector, they will not, because any moment now we will cast off and be sailing out into the Channel" grinned Roguefort.

"You will both be arrested and taken to Dover police station, I assure you…"

"Too late, Monsieur Inspector, the ship is free from the moorings, did you not feel that gentle movement?" said Roguefort. Hadley did but would not admit it, although he realised that he and Cooper were now at the mercy of this evil man.

"Monsieur Roguefort, I would advise you not to add the charge of kidnapping police officers to the serious charges that you already face" said Hadley. Roguefort laughed out loud and resumed his seat.

"Now, what shall I do with you two stupid men?"

"I warn you…"

"What do you think, Pierre? Should I take them to Marseille and let them find their own way back, or throw them overboard when we cross the Bay of Biscay?"

"Whatever pleases you, Monsieur" replied Benoir with a grin.

"Very well, Pierre, if you won't make a decision, in due course I will have to, but I must admit, at the moment, I quite favour the idea of burying them at sea" said Roguefort with an evil grin.

"I advise you Monsieur Roguefort to accompany me on deck and order the Captain to moor this ship so that you, Benoir and the Countess…"

"Monsieur Inspector, you are now aboard my ship bound for Marseille, you are the prisoner, not me!"

"You behave very foolishly for an astute business man, Monsieur Roguefort" said Hadley.

"You may think so, Inspector."

"It must have occurred to you that the whereabouts of Sergeant Cooper and myself are known by not only the Dover police but also Chief Inspector Bell at the Yard…"

"So what? I care nothing for the police or your Chief, they can do nothing to help you now" replied Roguefort.

"In a short space of time a cutter with armed police will be in pursuit of the 'Arabesque'…"

"Wishful thinking on your part, Monsieur Inspector, I assure you" interrupted the Frenchman.

"When this ship is boarded, you, Benoir and the Countess will be removed and taken back to Dover, where you will be formerly charged with conspiracy to murder, Benoir with kidnapping and the Countess with conspiracy…"

"My niece is to be charged with conspiracy?" interrupted Roguefort.

"Yes."

"What conspiracy?"

"To steal gold bullion from a bank in Istanbul" replied Hadley and Roguefort remained quiet and deep in thought for a few moments.

"Will she go to prison?" asked the Frenchman.

"She will. If convicted."

"For how long, Monsieur Inspector?"

"I can't say, the sentence will be at the judge's discretion."

"For many years, no doubt?"

"Possibly."

"This changes things" murmured Roguefort as the ship began to roll gently in the swell of the Channel. Hadley glanced out of the cabin window at the white topped waves and the slowly receding breakwater of Dover harbour. He felt a chill run down his spine and he looked at Cooper before giving him a comforting smile.

"A sea voyage is always so invigorating, don't you agree, Sergeant?"

"Yes, sir."

Roguefort looked hard at the Inspector and slowly nodded his head before turning to Benoir.

"Come, Pierre, I think we'll leave these Englishmen here whilst we get a breath of sea air on deck." Benoir nodded and followed

Roguefort out of the cabin.

"Are you alright, Countess?" asked Hadley and she nodded and smiled.

"Oui, Monsieur, I am so pleased to see you both and I am very sorry that my uncle is behaving this way" she said.

"No matter" smiled Hadley.

"Will a little ship with policemen come to rescue us?" she asked.

"Without doubt, Madam" nodded Hadley.

"I do hope so" she whispered and began to cry.

"Compose yourself, Madam, we will be saved, have no fear."

"I can't believe that my Giovani is dead and I'm on a ship going back to Marseille instead of a new life in America with him" she cried and dabbed at her eyes with a handkerchief. Hadley felt sorry for the lovely woman caught up in a world of unkindness, deceit and murder. Cooper went to the cabin window and watched the breakwater now disappearing in the gathering darkness, hoping to see a vessel leaving the harbour in pursuit of the 'Arabesque'.

"I think it may be a little while before we're rescued, sir" he said and Hadley joined him, gazing back at the harbour.

"I fear you may be right, Sergeant." Some twenty minutes later, Roguefort returned to the cabin with Benoir.

"Monsieur Inspector, after careful thought, I have decided to put you, along with your boy and my niece in a small boat and allow you to return to Dover."

"Indeed, sir, but I'll only agree to that if you and Benoir accompany us."

"That is not possible I'm afraid, so if you would like to follow Pierre, he will escort you to the boat" replied Roguefort. Hadley thought for a moment and decided that the journey back to Dover in a small boat was their best option.

"Very well, Monsieur Roguefort."

"A sensible decision, and I will come to wave you farewell" grinned Roguefort.

"Sergeant, please escort the Countess."

"Yes, sir."

They were taken to a place on the deck where a small boat, equipped with two oars, swung on ropes suspended from davits. The Countess was helped aboard followed by Hadley and just as

Cooper was about to step onto the swaying boat he suddenly turned and grabbed Benoir around the waist, driving him towards the ships rail. In an instant the two men, locked together, disappeared over the side and fell into the sea below.

"Mon Dieu!" shouted Roguefort.

"Lower the boat quickly!" shouted Hadley and two crewmen released the ropes holding the boat, the Countess screamed as it plunged downwards to the sea, arriving in the water with a resounding splash. They drifted back along the side of the 'Arabesque' as Hadley searched for the two men. Suddenly Cooper's head appeared followed by a spluttering Benoir. They struggled in the sea and Hadley attempted to row towards them.

"Grab the rope, Sergeant!" he shouted as he stopped rowing and flung one of the ropes that had fallen into the boat when it had been released. Cooper splashed towards it and caught hold before grabbing Benoir around his neck. Hadley pulled the men towards the boat and then helped them on board. They both began to shiver and Hadley took off his coat and wrapped it around Cooper.

"Thank you, sir."

"That was brave thing to do, Sergeant."

"Well, at least we've got one of them, sir!"

"Indeed we have, and Benoir, I suggest you sit still and hope we can get back to Dover before you die of cold" said Hadley. Benoir nodded and turned to gaze at the fast disappearing ship with Roguefort looking back from the rail and waving to them all.

"Mon Dieu! He has deserted me" said Benoir.

"I'm afraid he has Monsieur" said Hadley.

"I have been loyal to him, always" murmured Benoir and Hadley nodded before he said "Sergeant, grab that oar and help me row with your good arm, otherwise we'll be out here all night!"

"Yes, sir." Cooper joined Hadley on the wet seat and they then pulled together towards the distant lights of Dover harbour. They had rowed for about twenty minutes and were making progress when Cooper heard the sound of a steam engine above the noise of the wind. He turned and saw the lights of a cutter moving through the sea towards them.

"Look, sir, help is on its way!" Hadley turned and when he saw the fast approaching steam boat he whispered "thank God for that." In a short while the Customs cutter pulled alongside and many hands plucked the occupants of the small boat on board and hurried them down to a warm cabin. After changing out of wet clothes and enjoying a hot drink, Hadley thanked the Captain and asked him to pursue the 'Arabesque'.

"I'm afraid she's now past the three mile limit, Inspector, and beyond our jurisdiction" said Captain Smallwood.

"That means Roguefort has escaped justice" said Hadley.

"That may be so, Inspector, but at least you and your party are safe, much longer out in the Channel on a cold night would have put pay to you all."

"Quite right, Captain, without your quick intervention the outcome might have been very different for us."

Soon they arrived in Dover harbour and were met by Inspector Bagley, a Sergeant and two constables.

"Mr Wilson, the harbour master alerted us to your predicament, Inspector" said Bagley.

"Good man, he, along with you and Captain Smallwood, undoubtedly saved us from an uncertain fate" replied Hadley.

"Let's get you all back to the station where we can sort things out then" said Bagley and Hadley nodded. Chief Inspector Bell was telegraphed with full details of the events and Hadley promised to return to the Yard with a full report in the morning.

Benoir was placed in a cell for the night and Hadley, Cooper and the Countess were taken to the Victoria Hotel where they enjoyed dinner followed by an evening in front of a roaring fire with several brandy's to drive out the cold.

The next morning they were taken to the railway station and along with two escorting constables, caught the eleven o'clock train to London. They went straight to the Yard where Benoir was placed in custody and the Countess joined the detectives in their office, where George made tea for them all.

"What is to become of me now, Monsieur Inspector?" asked the Countess.

"You will be charged with conspiracy to rob, Madam…"

"But I did not steal the gold from my uncle, it was my husband who planned it" she interrupted with a plaintive voice.

"You knew his plans and were instrumental in the robbery as

well as being complicit in the act, Madam" Hadley replied.

"Have you no mercy?"

"It is not up to me, Madam, I can only bring a prosecution on the facts before me, it could well be the case that a higher authority takes a different view" said Hadley.

"So there is hope for me?"

"I will put in a good report on your behalf, so there is always hope" replied Hadley with a smile.

"Bon, I will pray for my deliverance, Monsieur Inspector."

"By all means, now, I must ask you to write a full statement of what has transpired, including the terrible events at Pangbourne House, then your kidnap ordeal at the hands of Benoir."

"Oui, I will do that."

"Then Sergeant Cooper will escort you to the rooms in the Strand, where I insist you remain until you are called for."

"Now that you have Benoir and Lefevre in custody, am I not safe to visit Mrs Hudson?" she asked with pleading eyes. Hadley melted and replied "if you must, Madam, but I will only allow you to go to Cavendish Square."

"Merci, Monsieur Inspector, you are very kind to a poor defenceless woman, who is all alone" she smiled and Hadley blushed a little whilst Cooper grinned.

While Cooper escorted the Countess back to her accommodation in the Strand, Hadley went up to report to Chief Inspector Bell.

"My God, Hadley, is this really the end of murder and mayhem for the time being?"

"I believe so, sir."

"A full report on everything before you leave your office tonight, if you please."

"Yes, sir."

"The Commissioner has asked for all the relevant details to be on his desk by ten o'clock tomorrow, Hadley."

"Of course, sir."

"That means a late night for me as well, you know."

"Yes, sir."

"Now, has the Countess admitted everything?"

"She has given a very full account, sir, and I will put in my report that she gave great assistance to my investigations."

"That's good, Hadley, and of course, she witnessed the murder of her husband."

"She did, sir."

"That will mean certain conviction of Lefevre in court, followed by the hangman's noose, I'll be bound."

"Yes, sir, and as I am convinced he murdered his crewmen, but could not provide proof, it is fitting that he faces justice."

"Couldn't agree more, Hadley, unfortunately you can only hang a man once, but as long as he hangs, justice is content."

"Quite so, sir."

"You have this fellow, Benoir, in custody, I presume you're going to charge him with the kidnap of the Countess?"

"Yes, sir."

"Good, it's a pity that Monsieur Roguefort escaped to France, I'd like to see him charged with something, Hadley."

"I agree, sir, but it always seems to be the case that wealthy men manage to elude justice"

"Well, get it all down in your report and include the statement from the Countess."

"Yes, sir, and may I ask, what do you think will happen to her?"

"I don't know, Hadley, it is a decision that the Commissioner will make after he has read our reports."

"I'm sure you'll be lenient with her after you've read what I have to say, sir."

"I will reflect your obvious anxiety about the Countess, Hadley."

"Thank you, sir."

"Now, hold yourself ready to attend the daily meeting that I have with the Commissioner tomorrow afternoon at three, as I'm sure he'll want to question you."

"Yes, sir."

"Now get writing your report, Hadley."

Hadley and Cooper spent the rest of the day interviewing the two Frenchmen in custody and compiling their reports. It was almost eight o'clock when the Inspector arrived home to a warm house and a late supper.

"I'm glad it's all over, bar the shouting, Alice."

"I am too, dearest, you look worn out by it all" she replied.

"God knows what I would have done without Cooper, he really is an exceptional young man" said Hadley.

"Well, I'm sure that you are his inspiration, dear."

"Possibly."

"And I look forward to meeting his wife when they come for lunch on Boxing Day" she smiled.

"Yes, she's a sweet young woman."

"I hope that she realises that a policeman's wife leads an uncertain life of late meals and interrupted weekends, not to speak of the worry of danger to her husband" said Alice.

"I'm sure she does, as you know Cooper has been shot and stabbed whilst arresting suspects and the poor fellow has only been with me for a few months" sighed Hadley.

"It's the violent times we live in, dearest, and I know that you both do your best, now, I think it's time for bed."

It was exactly three o'clock the next day when Hadley and Bell entered the Commissioner's grand office. They sat quietly whilst he finished reading a report in front of him before he looked up.

"Well, gentlemen, other than the unfortunate escape of Roguefort, you seem to have brought the investigations to a satisfactory conclusion."

"Thank you, sir" Bell smiled.

"You have Lefevre, Benoir and the Countess Castellini, all in custody and charged with their nefarious misdeeds" smiled the Commissioner, his side whiskers twitching.

"Yes, sir."

"The Hudson diamonds have been recovered and that desperate man committed suicide whilst Sir John accidentally fell to his death, tragedy upon tragedy, I'm sure you'll agree" said the Commissioner. Hadley wanted to disagree and inform him that he was sure that Hudson committed fraud to pay off his gambling debts and then murdered Sir John when his deceit was discovered. He thought better of it and decided that to remain quiet as natural justice had taken its course and nothing could be gained by blackening the name of a dead man.

"Any further news regarding the gold stolen from Istanbul, sir?" enquired Bell.

"None, Chief Inspector, our Ambassador reports that the authorities have no knowledge of any bullion theft, so, that is an end to the matter" replied the Commissioner.

"But what about the gold that I recovered in Liverpool, sir?" asked Hadley.

"All I can presume, Inspector, that it was indeed the property of Roguefort, stolen by his niece and her husband, but from where, I really don't know, fortunately the Bank of England has it stored safely and there it will remain" replied the Commissioner.

"Indeed, sir, and may I ask, what will happen to the Countess?" asked Hadley.

"I've given this some thought and have decided, that as she has confessed to everything and no formal complaint has been made against her by Roguefort, I will suggest to Prosecuting Counsel that she be recognised as Queen's evidence, and other than giving her testimony in court to convict Lefevre and Benoir, all charges will be dropped against her" replied the Commissioner with a smile.

"Thank you, sir, I'm pleased to hear it" said a relieved Hadley.

"Good, well gentlemen, I'll study your reports once again before preparing my Press announcements that will undoubtedly place the Metropolitan Police in a most favourable light" smiled the Commissioner, ever politically aware.

"Yes, sir" said Bell and then they left the office. On the way down the stairs Bell asked "how is Cooper?"

"He's recovered well from the stabbing incident, sir."

"That's good news, take care of him, Hadley, he's a very fine officer."

"I know that, sir."

Hadley decided to tell the Countess the good news and along with Cooper went to the rooms in the Strand. The maid there informed them that the Countess had gone to see Mrs Hudson just an hour ago and so the detectives hurried to Cavendish Square.

Wilkes admitted them to the house and they were shown into the drawing room, where Mrs Hudson, Mr Hargreaves and the Countess were sitting.

"Good afternoon, Inspector" said Mrs Hudson and Hadley

acknowledged them all and smiled.

"Inspector, I wish you to know that I will be representing the Countess as well as Mrs Hudson" said Hargreaves.

"I'm pleased to hear it, sir, and as I bring good news from the Commissioner's office, I hope that the Countess will require the very minimum of legal advice" replied Hadley.

"Tell us the news, Inspector" said Mrs Hudson.

"All charges against you, Countess, are to be dropped…"

"Mon Dieu! Does that mean I'm a free woman?" she interrupted, her eyes bright with anticipation.

"Yes, Madam, to all intents and purposes" smiled Hadley.

"Oh, bon, bon!" she said and stood up, came to Hadley and kissed him on both cheeks whilst whispering "merci, merci." Hadley blushed and then the Countess kissed Cooper who went bright red with embarrassment.

"Thank you, Madam" spluttered Hadley.

"Non, thank you, Monsieur Inspector and you Sergeant Cooper, you are very brave and true men, you have saved my life…"

"Thank you, Madam" smiled Hadley as he blushed again.

"Now we have some news for you, Inspector" said Mrs Hudson.

"Yes, Madam?"

"Mr Hargreaves has been a tower of strength through these difficult times and on his advice, when all the court proceedings are complete and everything my late husband owned has been sold to meet his debts, my diamonds, which are legally mine, will be sold at auction, and the money raised will allow the Countess and I to start a new life together in America" said Mrs Hudson.

"That is good news indeed, Madam" smiled Hadley.

"There is nothing left for either of us in Europe, so a brave new beginning is the answer to all the sadness and loss that we have both suffered" said Mrs Hudson.

"I'm sure that is so, Madam, and I wish you the very best of good fortune."

The detectives left the house in Cavendish Square, buoyed up by their success and the good news regarding the Countess and Mrs Hudson. The days that followed were routine and uneventful, only early lunches at the 'Kings Head' with Agnes and Florrie added a little brightness to the hum drum. Then Christmas Day was celebrated in full seasonally glory at the Inspector's home in Camden and he welcomed Sergeant Cooper and his wife, Doris, to a festive lunch on Boxing Day. After a splendid meal, Hadley turned to Cooper and said "I wonder what fate has in store for us next year, Sergeant?"

"More of the same, I'm sure, sir" he smiled.

Follow Hadley and Cooper in
THE TOWER OF LONDON MURDERS

Printed in the United Kingdom
by Lightning Source UK Ltd.
120816UK00001B/13-39